JUDGMENT

HEARTLAND ALIENS
BOOK 3

JOSHUA JAMES

Cover Artwork by J Caleb Design
Edited by Scarlett R. Algee

GET FREE BOOKS!

Building a relationship with readers is my favorite thing about writing.

My regular newsletter, *The Reader Crew,* is the best way to stay up-to-date on new releases, special offers, and all kinds of cool stuff about science fiction past and present.

Just for joining the fun, I'll send you 3 free books.

Join The Reader Crew (it's free) today!

—*Joshua James*

HEARTLAND ALIENS SERIES

All books available in Kindle Unlimited

Invasion

Uprising

Judgment

PROLOGUE

Limpid Hydraxa Evacuation Vessel
Some years ago, unknown distance from Earth

PRI-NELL WOKE IN THE DARKNESS, and in those first moments—as the dreams from the prior night faded—he told himself that everything was all right. He'd been having nightmares, but he was safe now.

Then he rolled onto his side, placed one hand on the thin padding of the bed beside him, and remembered that he most definitely wasn't.

He rolled to his feet, causing the lights in his room to turn on when they sensed his motion. *"Good morning, Pri-Nell,"* Bildrax's voice purred. Pri-Nell bit the inside of his cheek to keep from saying something rude. It wasn't the AI's fault that it had been programmed to be polite.

"Good morning, Bildrax," he said instead.

"Are you ready for some refreshment?" the AI asked.

Pri-Nell pressed his three-fingered hand to his forehead and closed all three of his eyes. "Yes, thank you, Bildrax."

The chute on the far side of the room hummed, and Pri-Nell got to his feet just as the door of the chute opened to reveal a circular pouch made of silver-lined plastic.

"How long was I out?" he asked. He left his boots beside the bed, partly because they chafed and partly because there was nobody around to tell him that going barefoot was uncouth. Everyone that would have cared about such things was dead.

"Approximately one and a half solar cycles."

That certainly explained his headache. He opened his mouth and stuck out his long, hollow tongue, driving it into the seal of the refreshment pack. The cool liquid filled his tonguetip, and Pri-Nell took a long pull. He could *feel* the liquid fanning out from his digestive tract into his dehydrated tissue. After his escape from Planetoid Q42, he'd fallen onto the bed, lulled by the comforting hum of the engines. The rest of his team hadn't been so lucky.

The memory of the horrors he'd witnessed on P-Q42 gave him pause, and he glanced down at his tongue, which was still punched into the silvery packaging of the refreshment pouch. The invaders had done that, too. Their evolutionary tree had followed a very different path from the apex species of the Hydraxa Nebula, but certain overlapping biological features left Pri-Nell disturbed.

He sucked the last of the fluid from the refreshment pack and shoved it into the next chute he passed, trying not to think about the screams of his fellow chemists as the invaders descended upon them, split them in two, and gorged themselves in much the same manner as he had drained the pouch. "Thank you, Bildrax."

"*You are welcome. Would you like another?*"

"Not now."

"*Your vitals suggest that further nutrition is warranted. Please consider consuming a second—*"

Pri-Nell's middle eye twitched. "Thank you, Bildrax, I'll be sure to have one later. For now, I would prefer an update."

The ship hummed. Pri-Nell had never been sure whether that hum signified the AI's response to an answer it didn't approve of, or if he simply read too far into the silence.

After a pause, Bildrax said, "*I will brief you on my most contemporary dataset once you reach the command core.*"

The door to the core lay at the far end of the corridor, but Pri-Nell found himself walking slowly. He was tired, of course, and he'd sustained minor injuries when one of the invaders had snagged his foot, but that wasn't the real reason he wanted to put this off. The simple truth was that he was afraid to see what Bildrax had to show him.

The door hissed open well before he arrived, and Pri-Nell limped into the command core. He dropped into what would ordinarily have been the captain's seat. Technically, as the only organic lifeform aboard the vessel, he *was* the captain now. He swiveled to face the holoscreen. "Please proceed."

The screen flared to life, and Pri-Nell shuddered. Bildrax

had managed to secure live footage of the Material Acquisitions Synthesizing Station on P-Q42. From what he could see, the machines were still up and running, but the lifeless corpses of the technicians lay scattered throughout the building. They had been split open and fed upon, and many of their mouths were still agape in silent screams. Pri-Nell pressed his fingers to his mouth as his eyes darted in every direction, trying to take it all in at once. He knew those techs. He'd worked beside them. His supervisor, Agg-Garr, was sprawled next to the sodium condenser, his eyes milky and unseeing, his protective lenses splattered with gore.

"No," Pri-Nell moaned. "No, no, no... Bildrax, please tell me that someone else managed to get away. Anyone. They can't all—"

"*My records show that at least two other vessels were launched from the MASS, both in the direction of Planetoid Q7. I have been unable to make contact, but systems indicate that the inhabitants are alive, so their AI may simply have decided to let them sleep for the time being.*"

"We have to warn everyone else what's coming." The chaos had begun so suddenly that by the time Pri-Nell realized what was happening, the MASS was already overrun. "If we warn the other planetoids, they might have a chance to prepare—"

"*I have already sent out a message to the network. Every unit running a Bildrax system has received an alert, and the defense contractors on P-A and P-A1 are already engaging security protocols.*"

"I hope that's enough." Pri-Nell couldn't stop staring at the wreckage of the MASS.

"*If I may keep the system engaged for a moment, I do require directive input on another matter.*" The holoscreen changed to show a map of the galaxy, then zoomed in on the Hydraxa Nebula. "*Outside of Hydraxa, there are other solar systems populated with species that may also be in danger. Of the hundred closest bodies supporting higher-intelligence life forms, we have only ascertained how to communicate with four of them, including Beteon-86, the Jacc-Dodsin Object, Galatea Prime, and Earth.*"

"We should warn them, too," Pri-Nell said at once.

"*I agree with your assertion, but it is more complicated than that. Take Earth, for example.*" The screen shifted again, this time to depict a crude series of blocked-out images. "*We have surveyed their world extensively, but our written contact with them has been limited. This is the only communication format we know that they are able both to send and to receive.*"

Pri-Nell stared at the inelegant diagram. He recognized several of the symbols at the top on sight, due to his years of experience at the MASS, but the rest looked as though it had been drawn by a juvenile.

"*If we can draft a reply using their prime-number grid system, then I will translate it into an audio-wave format that they can understand,*" Bildrax added.

"Are all alien species this complicated to communicate with?" Pri-Nell asked in dismay.

"*Hence my need for directive input. I can make rational decisions, but I cannot always predict the ways in which an irrational mind might interpret certain images.*"

Pri-Nell only half resented the implication that he was

required to speak for the irrational minds of the galaxy. He closed his eyes, letting himself dwell for a moment on the image of Agg-Garr's remains. Agg-Garr deserved better than that.

"Bildrax, are you capable of remotely operating analytical equipment on the MASS?" he asked.

"*Of course. My ability to synthesize has been locked to avoid potentially hazardous tampering, but I can run samples at any range, so long as the connection is stable and the equipment remains operational.*"

Pri-Nell opened his eyes again to stare at the strange, clunky message from Earth. "In that case, I'm hoping that you can help gather some information about the invaders."

"*To what end?*"

He could already see how to help not only the rest of his home nebula, but the worlds beyond as well. The attack had been too carefully coordinated to be a one-time incident. This must have happened elsewhere, perhaps several times. Perhaps *dozens* of times.

Perhaps more times than Pri-Nell could imagine.

"I don't simply want to warn the worlds of what's coming," Pri-Nell said. He pressed his hands to the table, finding new strength in his conviction. "We're going to tell them how to fight back. And hopefully, we'll be able to tell them how to *win*."

JUDGMENT

PART 1

EXPEDITION

1
LEN

CLOSE ONE EYE *and find the target in your scope. As you become more comfortable with handling the gun, teach yourself to keep both eyes open. The added depth perception will make you more effective against a moving target.*

Len Bonaparte exhaled and kept his eye focused on the place where he'd last seen the creature. When he'd first taught himself to shoot, he'd had to learn from scratch. He'd had five years of backwoods self-education to become a natural.

Now he'd lost an eye, and he was forced to start learning all over again.

Beside him, Private Joe Estes checked his posture. "Shoulder still bothering you, huh?"

Len sniffed and kept his right eye pressed to the scope. "I can work with it." His left eye had been his dominant one, and now that it was gone, he'd had to adjust how he held the rifle, too. Which meant using his injured arm to support the barrel, even though it still hadn't recovered from the injury he'd sustained in Little Creek roughly three weeks prior.

Sweat trailed down his spine as he kept his scope fixed between the trees. They'd spotted their target earlier, moving broadside through the shrubbery. He'd been tempted to take a shot before, but ammo was precious, and they were going to need everything they had for their trip across the border and down into D.C. Len had felt guilty enough about wasting a handful of bullets on stationary target practice. If he was going to fire on something moving, it had better damn well be alive.

"You'll wear yourself out if you—" Estes began.

"*Ssh.*" The breath hissed between Len's teeth, sharper than he'd intended. "I see her."

At first, the figure moving through the bracken and burdock was nothing but a shadow, a flicker of movement on the fringes of his peripheral vision. Len resented how little he could see at any given time, but he'd done his best to make up for it by being twice as alert. It was exhausting, especially in this heat, when his mind's natural inclination was to wander to a cool glass of water or an afternoon nap. So far, however, he'd managed to stay sharp.

The shadow moved again, finally coming into view. Now he could make out the smooth slope of a shoulder, the cup of an ear, the slender nose and graceful legs of the doe as she bent to nibble at a nearby clump of ragweed. Len drew a long breath in, then out, forcing his trigger finger still. He'd wait until he had the perfect shot. Anything less would amount to a waste of both ammunition *and* life. A gut shot could taint the meat, and a sloppy chest wound might leave the deer alive long enough to flee. She might run two miles before she dropped, and they'd have no hope of finding her again in the dense woodlands surrounding the ghost town of Keystone.

Another step. *No rush,* Len assured himself. *She can't smell you from here. She hasn't seen you. Let her take one more step, so that she's right out in the open and you can't possibly miss.*

The doe's leg shifted, and another shadow moved beside her.

Len's eye fluttered shut for a moment. He hadn't noticed the fawn before. Either it had been hiding, or it had simply been too short to see from this distance. It was frail and delicate, so spindly that it hardly looked real. Small, soft creatures like that didn't fare well in the world these days, not when they relied on speed for survival.

Predators were faster these days, and food was growing scarce.

The doe was in the open now. It would have been an easy shot, even for a man who was relearning survival from the ground up. All the same, he couldn't bring himself to fire. On its own, that fawn wouldn't survive long.

It'll have to grow up fast, he figured. *It's so small, I doubt it remembers a time before the sky collapsed.* His hand slackened, and he caught Estes' eye, shaking his head once. If he was annoyed, he didn't show it.

They'd show mercy today. Lord knew that there was little enough of that in the world anymore.

Len had just begun to lower the rifle when the doe lifted her head in alarm. The fawn followed suit, imitating its mother as it listened for whatever had shifted around them. The leaves above them rustled, offering only the smallest warning before a sleek black shape dropped from the trees.

The doe didn't have time to run; the Clanker's front leg drove between her shoulder blades, spearing her to the ground. She bleated once and kicked her legs in a desperate attempt to free herself. The fawn darted away into the undergrowth with its tail raised high, and the Clanker that had attacked its mother rattled. An answering rattle sounded from above, and a second alien dropped to the ground only feet away from where the fawn had disappeared. There was a wet *thwipp!* and then silence.

Len clutched the gun tight and held his breath. He *wanted* to cry out, but held his tongue. Until the Clankers had appeared, he hadn't noticed anything to indicate their presence. Not a sound, not a movement, not a single sign that death waited in the branches overhead. Beside him, Estes' hand crept toward his pistol.

Were these two from Pammy's hive?

They were far enough away from the base that Len couldn't be sure that these Clankers were under the girl's thrall. Even if they were, he didn't trust them to obey the rules this far from the nest. There was no telling how much they understood, and if the aliens ever decided to return to their earlier pecking order, Pammy Mae wouldn't be able to do a thing about it, not even with all the firepower of Camp Keystone behind her.

The Clanker that had speared the doe lifted its leg free of the earth and tilted it, swinging back, then thrusting forward so that the deer slipped free. It landed in a broken heap, perhaps twenty feet from the far side of the fallen log where Estes and

Len were crouched. The alien made a strange sound, different from any he had heard them make before, low and grating and soon over. He wouldn't call that Clanker-song.

Unless he was very much mistaken, the monster was trying to talk to them.

It stood there, waiting, and sank down until its chitinous underbelly brushed the soil.

After a moment, Len pressed his gun into Estes' hands.

"What are you doing?"

"It clearly knows we're here. I'm going out." Len pushed himself upright against the log. It was rotten, and the punky wood gave beneath his palm.

"What if it attacks you?" Estes demanded.

He met the Clanker's myriad glittering eyes and spoke to it rather than his partner. "Either we're going to be fine, or I'm going to get pissed. You wouldn't like me when I'm mad."

The Clanker didn't budge, and Len decided to take that as a sign. He swung one leg over the log, trying to ignore the hive of termites that had made their nest within. Back in the day, he'd hated creepy-crawlies as much as the next person. Lately, he couldn't bother to get worked up over anything small enough to eat in a single sitting. Humanity had bigger problems.

The Clanker didn't move as his other foot hit the ground. He kept his eye on it as he approached the doe. Only when the toes of his borrowed military boots thumped against the deer's ribcage did he finally avert his gaze.

The deer wasn't dead. Her chest was still heaving, and those graceful legs stirred helplessly, scraping shallow furrows on the loam beneath.

Len had already decided on mercy. Now it simply took another form.

The Ka-Bar he'd taken from Supply hung at his waist, and he drew it free of its sheath and plunged it into the doe's neck in a single sharp movement. He didn't wait to start field dressing the carcass. Len was painfully aware of the Clanker watching him, but he made quick work of it with a steady hand. At least field dressing was second nature, rather than something he'd had to relearn. He'd gotten permits every deer season in Little Creek in preparation for the time when hunting would become a matter of survival rather than a hobby.

He split the deer open, unfazed by the warm stink of offal that hit him a second later.

At that instant, the Clanker moved.

Len flipped his grip on the handle of the knife and braced for impact, scowling up at the alien as it extended its folding proboscis overhead. He had been stupid to trust it. It went against every instinct. He'd put too much faith in Pammy Mae and her absurd plan to work together with the very monsters who had almost killed them all...

The Clanker's mouth plunged into the deer to root between its organs. Its abdomen expanded and contracted as it found some delectable morsel among the innards and began to feed. Len stared down in disgust as the deer's organs disappeared into that implacable feeding tube. It reminded him of his childhood after his mother had moved to America, sitting with his uncle to watch *Lady and the Tramp*. Two dogs kissing over spaghetti had never made much sense to him, and certainly didn't reflect anything from his native Nigeria, but that was all he allowed himself to think of as the Clanker gorged itself on the entrails of the unfortunate beast.

Only when the body cavity was empty did the Clanker step back, retract its mouth, and fix Len in its refracted gaze once more.

He swallowed past the lump in his throat. "Are we good?"

The Clanker didn't budge.

"Oh, hell no," he snapped. "I'm not eating a bite of *raw venison* just to seal this little deal."

Some lines don't get crossed. He wiped the Ka-Bar on his pants, sheathed it, and hoisted the deer over his shoulders so that its legs draped down on either side of his neck.

Still, the Clanker didn't move.

The deer was a skinny thing, and Len was strong, but he still had to move slowly as he turned his back on the Clanker and began his walk back to the log. With every step, he pictured its mouth driving into his back, or its long tongue snagging his ankle. His heart was pounding from both exertion and adrenaline when he finally reached Estes' hiding place.

"Goddamn, Bonaparte, I hope to have balls as big as yours someday," Estes said. "What was that about?"

Len twisted around to where the Clanker had stood, but it was gone. There was nothing but a rust-colored stain on last fall's leaves to indicate that it had ever been there.

"Guess I made a friend," he murmured. "Or at least not an enemy. Come on, help me with this. You owe me one."

They shuffled their load around, so that Estes was stuck with the deer and Len held the rifle. His hands were slick with sweat and blood, and his stomach churned.

"How did you know that thing wasn't gonna eat you?" Estes asked.

Len shrugged. "Didn't, but you gotta take risks sometimes, don't you?"

"Calculated risks," Estes agreed.

Len snorted and led him back toward the wall. "How do we calculate anything these days? If you'd told me a month ago that I'd be playing nice with the invaders, I'd have had a few choice words about that notion." He raised his fingers to his left cheekbone, where the scar began. He was still wearing bandages that hid much of the damage his face had sustained during and after the raid on the high school back home.

Home. He wasn't sure how to calculate that anymore, either. When he thought of *home,* he rarely thought of houses. What Len usually remembered first was the people.

That being the case, Camp Keystone was home now. And soon enough, their home would be on the move.

He belonged wherever his family was, and the Little Creek Five were his family now.

2

VERA

"MA'AM?" Klarie's face peered around the doorframe. "Mind if I come in?"

Vera looked up from the maps in front of her. She wasn't sure how long she'd been staring at them, plotting their course overland to D.C. "You don't have to be formal, Klarie. I'm not *Johnson.*"

Klarie winced at the name of the camp's former captain and stepped the rest of the way through the door. "I didn't want to bother you. I know you've been..." She trailed off.

Bitchy? Irritable? So depressed I can barely move? Vera managed a weak smile at the slew of potential adjectives that sprang to mind. In a single day, she'd transformed from someone who thought of herself as a kind person and a healer into a murderer. A spree killer, technically. She'd been standing only inches away from Private Thomas when she died, before running across the camp to put a bullet in the captain's chest.

And sure, there was no way to know whether Vera's shot had been the one to seal Kevin Johnson's fate, but that didn't make him any less dead.

"...Busy," Klarie said at last. "But we've finished scouring everything in town. If we're going to find any more supplies, we'll have to expand to the next county."

Vera sat back in her chair and rapped one knuckle against the desk, causing the map to crinkle. "I don't think that will be necessary. From what Cooper's told me, we're on track for a departure. At this point, he's just getting in as much extra work as he can before we set out."

Klarie's posture relaxed at the mention of Cooper's name. "That seems like a pretty accurate assessment. We've got a few surprises up our sleeves, for sure."

"And our rations are packed?" Vera asked.

"We're waiting for orders." Klarie cut her eyes away. "And I should tell you, not everyone's on board."

That wrung a smile out of Vera. "What? You mean there are some people who don't feel great about our plan to march side-by-side with the same aliens that have decimated the planet? I can't imagine why."

Klarie snorted and rested one hip against the desk. "Fair enough. I don't like the idea of dividing our forces, but I don't see any other way around it at this point. And Cooper said that he might have a plan for how to protect the people who end up staying behind."

"That boy's really come into his own since we took the camp." Back in Little Creek, Vera and Cooper had been two of the group's weakest links, the ones with the least training and thereby the greatest liabilities. They'd had to learn fast, but they'd both landed on their feet, although it had cost Vera more than she was initially prepared to pay.

"He's been working non-stop, ever since Maddox—" Klarie swallowed the rest of her sentence.

Vera let a moment of silence linger in the room out of respect for the dead. Then she rose to her feet, rolled up the map, and turned to the door. "I guess there's only one other major player we need to address, then."

Klarie shuddered. "Do I have to come with you? She gives me the creeps."

"No," Vera said. "Check in with Peachey and make sure that he has everything he needs, and take the rest of the night for yourself. I'll call a campwide meeting first thing tomorrow to announce our departure and let people know their options."

Klarie nodded and then, to Vera's surprise, darted in for a hug. "You're doing a great job, boss," she mumbled against Vera's shoulder. Before Vera could figure out how to respond, Klarie broke away and slipped out through the door of the camp headquarters.

When did everyday affection become so foreign to me? she wondered. *After the last phone call with Mummy?* No, she'd held out at least until they'd abandoned the bunker, and she'd helped cure Len, even if it meant causing a little pain along the way.

In fact, she'd felt like herself right up until the moment she got blood on her hands. It had taken the betrayal of the soldiers at Camp Keystone to break her.

Under the weight of that revelation, Vera made her way out

into the streets and toward the inner defensive wall, in search of the girl who had more blood on her hands than all the rest of them combined.

PAMMY MAE JOHNSON had barely shifted from her position on the walls of Camp Keystone since the day her uncle had been killed. The only thing that ever seemed to change was which tower she occupied.

When Vera found her, she was seated on the ledge of Tower 9 with a rifle resting in her lap, facing the woods. In addition to her Clanker armor, she'd taken an assortment of protective gear from Supply. Bulletproof armor overlapped with Clanker scales. She'd replaced the tymbal at her side as well. This one had been taken from the remains of the former Queen, the one Pammy had defeated in order to take her place as the Hive Mother of the local nest.

Pammy heard her coming and twisted at the waist to greet her. "Hey, Vera," she said. "I thought you were my mom."

"Where is she?" Vera asked, trying to take stock of Pammy's health without making it too obvious that she was sizing the girl up. Weeks in the sun had tanned her skin, but there was still an ashen pallor beneath that ruddy glow that made Vera think of all the wasting diseases listed in her textbooks back in med school. Dark smudges beneath her eyes made her whole face appear sunken and starved.

"Sleeping, probably." Pammy lifted her fist to her mouth and coughed twice. This was the other thing that worried Vera: the wet rattle in the young woman's lungs, reminiscent of

Clanker-song in its timbre. "Seems like she sleeps all the time these days. It's like Uncle Kevin's death shoved her back into reality, but she still can't bring herself to live here. So she sleeps." Pammy shook her head and coughed again.

"Will she be coming with us to D.C.?" Vera asked.

"Don't know if she can keep up." Pammy shrugged. "But if she wants to come, I won't stop her, and I can't see her wanting to stay. I'm all she has left."

So stay here with her, Vera almost said. *You've earned a bit of rest.* There was truth to it, but she knew better than to voice the suggestion aloud. For one thing, it was impossible. Without Pammy Mae, the people of Keystone had no way to control the Clankers. Without the Clankers, they were just a group of poorly-armed humans with no sense of where they were going or what to do when they got there. In order to give Pammy Mae an out, one of them would have had to eat Clanker-flesh and peer into the hivemind that controlled them all.

Vera couldn't bring herself to do it. Not only was she afraid of what she would see, she was no longer sure that she could stand against it as Pammy Mae had done. She'd already compromised her core beliefs in order to survive the uprising. Who was to say that the hivemind wouldn't break her? That she wouldn't become its puppet?

No, Pammy Mae had made her choice the moment she took that first bite, and Vera's job was to make the human half of their mismatched army fall in line.

"If we leave tomorrow, can you be sure the Clankers will follow?" she asked instead.

"I've been telling them to prepare." Pammy stared out at the woods, barely blinking. "The last of the eggs have hatched, and they haven't laid a new batch. They've been... restless. Impatient. I think they got the message. What I don't know is how to set the pace." She closed her eyes and pressed her fingers to her forehead. Her features pinched together, as if she was in pain, or struggling to remember some unpleasant and long-buried memory. "I think the hivemind has changed their natural patterns. There's a... how can I explain this? A *species-memory* of wandering from place to place, but the hivemind has altered it. It's pushed them to swarm between the stars. None of the ones that are alive now remember the old ways, but it's there."

Vera pressed her lips together and rubbed her sweaty palms on the thighs of her camo pants.

Pammy's eyes popped open, and she smiled wryly at Vera, still cradling her head in one hand. "You think I'm losing it."

"I certainly don't understand what's happening to you," Vera admitted. "Whatever it is, it's confusing."

"Is that really the word you'd choose?"

Recalling her exchange with Klarie earlier, and all the words that she'd have used against herself, Vera nodded. "Yes. It's hard to quantify, and I don't understand the science behind it, but that's not going to stop me from believing that you can tap into some connection with those things."

"I share my uncle's DNA and the Clankers' headspace." Pammy snorted and dropped her hands back into her lap, where they rested against her rifle. "Comforting. Really makes me feel good about my future."

"You're more than the sum of your parts." Vera reached out to rub Pammy's shoulder. "All of us are. Now, will you do me a favor and come down for a few hours? You're going to get skin cancer from sitting out here in the sun all the time."

Pammy's answering laugh turned into a hacking cough. "With all that's going on, you really think I'm losing sleep over a little melanoma?"

Vera got to her feet. "You're going to feel like an idiot if you survive this war only to end up with a skin condition."

"Yeah." Pammy thumped her palm against her chest. "Something tells me I'm not going to be around long enough for that to be an issue."

"Fine, be morbid," Vera told her, regaining a little of her old spark. "Just make sure you're ready bright and early tomorrow. We're going to rally the troops, and then we're off."

Pammy nodded. "You'd better believe that I'm more than ready to end this thing," she said, and a little of her old fire returned, too.

Vera left her there, under the late July sun, and took the stairs two at a time. The two of them had never discussed the details of the day Johnson died, or what had happened to his cronies. They hadn't needed to. Vera finally understood what people meant when they said that war changed them.

We can never go back, she thought, gripping the rolled map tightly in her hand. *We can only move on to the next thing, and do our best to make the sacrifices worthwhile.* If they managed to destroy the hivemind and disrupt the Clankers' relentless destruction of Earth's inhabitants, it would all even out in the end.

3

GUPPIE

GUPPIE HAD ALWAYS HELD a huge amount of respect for
the men and women whose service left them shy a limb or
partially immobile, yet it had never occurred to him just how
complicated the human body could be. Some parts were obviously necessary for it to function: the brain, the heart, the lungs.
But others could be damaged or lost entirely, while leaving the
person inhabiting that body fully intact.

None of which meant that he was thrilled to be stuck in a
wheelchair of his own.

"Stupid *door*," he muttered, trying to pull it open. The
hinges swung *toward* him, and some ignoramus of an architect
hadn't taken into account that if a fellow on wheels happened to
want to go *this* way through the entrance, he'd end up smacking
the damn door on his chair three or, shit, now *four* times with no
success. Guppie's muttered curses grew more vivid with each
attempt. The dogs at his side watched his efforts with interest.

"One of your lazybones wanna get the door for me?" he grumbled at them.

"Oh, sorry, Mr. Martin!" A young man on the far side hurried over and pushed the door wide for him.

Heat rose in Guppie's face. "I wasn't yelling at you, Travis. I was giving the dogs a hard time."

The young man grinned at him and flattened his back toward the door. "I know, but if I'd realized that you were having trouble, I'd have gotten here sooner."

It was nice to have help, but what Guppie *really* wanted was to be able to do things on his own. If the grid was still up, he wouldn't have struggled quite so much. He could have made use of elevators, stair lifts, automatic doors, and ramps. The fact that so little of that was available now was turning him into the type of old codger that waved his cane in the air and hollered at the kids to get off his lawn.

Guppie hated every damn minute of it.

He bit back his annoyance as he wheeled through the door. The dogs followed, and Deimos dragged his tongue across Travis' elbow.

"Good boy," Travis chuckled, scratching the crown of the bloodhound's head. Deimos wagged his tail until Travis straightened up. "Bye, Mr. Martin! Just give me a shout the next time you need a hand."

Guppie waved, but inside he was cringing. When had he become *Mr. Martin* and not just *Guppie?* That was what Vera used to call him, back when she couldn't stand him. Now he thought of the honorific almost as an insult. People who liked him didn't call him *Mr. Martin.* They called him that because they saw him as a frail old man.

The whole scenario really made him want to put his fist through something.

He wheeled out of the barracks and into the street. After the Clankers had swarmed Camp Keystone, they'd hauled debris off the streets, including not only the bodies of the dead, but the barricades and broken glass and splintered wood. Some of the refugee tents had been unsalvageable, but the rest had been restored. The dividing line between the civilians and the soldiers had begun to blur, with some of the former taking up residence in the barracks alongside their military-trained allies. A few of the soldiers had been running daily training exercises, which anyone was welcome to attend. Guppie had gone to one of them, determined to flex whatever muscles he could, but the humiliation of being so hampered in public, among the young soldiers and their strong bodies, had been too much. He'd confined himself to a solo training regimen.

It had been going well. His arms were as strong as they'd ever been, and hopefully Cooper's promise to build him an alternative to the wheelchair had been more than a platitude.

He was about to find out.

Cooper had taken over the old DARPA garage, the one Johnson had used as his own private torture chamber. As he approached the bay doors, Guppie's hands stilled on the wheels of his chair. He hated going in there. Most of the time, he was fine, but the slightly mildewed smell of the garage turned his stomach. Every time he blinked in there, he thought of Johnson, and the pleasure Johnson had taken in wringing him for information that he ultimately didn't have.

Still, no point in sitting around in the heat when there was shade just up ahead. Deimos trotted forward, and Phobos sniffed him quizzically.

"Yeah, yeah, we're going," he muttered.

At least the space had been transformed since when Johnson had used it. Cooper was intent on building, not just storing machinery.

In one end of the bay was Walk's old Cessna. They'd dragged it back into the camp and Cooper'd refueled it — Guppie was surprised to learn it would run just fine on regular automotive gasoline in a pinch.

The bay also held an upgraded transport truck, and what Guppie first mistook for a handful of Clankers. He flinched, wondering if he should have brought his gun, but when Deimos approached to sniff them, Guppie followed.

They weren't Clankers. They were *mechs.*

"Holy smokes." He bent forward to run one hand over the construct in awe. "Look at this thing. I've never seen anything like it." The mechanical DARPA robots had been retooled with Clanker exoskeletons. He could still see hoses and electronics through the joints. But like Pammy, they now bore a passing resemblance to a Clanker, although they wouldn't fool anyone who saw them up close.

"Hey, Guppie!" Cooper slid out from beneath the transport truck. He was wearing a pair of goggles, and his face was smudged with oil and grease. When the invasion began, he'd been on the pudgy side—not that Guppie could fault him for it, given how he'd let his own health go back then. Now, he was lean and strong, a mixed result of rationing their supplies and his own hard work in recent weeks. His hair had grown out long enough for him to pull it back, and when he rolled to his feet, the grin he offered Guppie was genuine. "How's it going, man? Ready to see what I've got for you?"

"Anything that'll get me out of this chair."

"Sure thing, gramps." Cooper winked at him and slung his protective goggles onto the table. He reached for a rag and wiped his hands down.

"I'm not old enough to be your grandfather," Guppie snapped. After a pause, he added, "Am I?"

"You're too *salty* to be my grandpa, that's for sure." Cooper dropped the rag and ambled over to the robot Clankers. "You like these? I call 'em MechaniClankers."

Guppie snorted. "You kids always have to have a dumbass name for your toys, don't you?"

"*Now* who's making you sound old?" The kid punched his shoulder gently as he passed. "Besides, a cool invention needs to have a cool name, don't you think?"

"Were there any other contenders?"

"Well, Boston Dynamic was DARPA's private contractor and they called them *Jackals*, but that's not very—"

"Jackal," Guppie interrupted, "is perfect."

Cooper wrinkled his nose. "It doesn't sound very awesome to me."

"Awesome enough," Guppie said. "And awesome is the right word to describe them."

Cooper nodded. "They were kind of Maddox's idea."

Guppie knew that expression. It was the same one he'd seen on the faces of his fellow soldiers when one of their friends went down and didn't get back up.

"He'd be impressed with what you've done," Guppie offered. It was the only thing he could think to say.

Cooper shrugged and pushed past the subject. "This is Frankenstein-ing stuff right here. I'm just taking the DARPA equipment and bolting onto it."

"I think you're selling yourself short."

"I modified a few things after trying to ride the Clankers." He hauled himself up onto the back of one of the robots, powered it on, and leaned over its back like a jockey. "You can ride 'em upright when you're traveling, but when you're in combat, there are a couple of tricks I built in. The engineers who'd been messing with this tech left all kinds of cool toys behind."

"None of the finished products, though," Guppie observed bitterly. Johnson had gone on quite the rant about how the best tech had been shipped off to Washington, along with most of the equipment and all but one of Camp Keystone's tanks.

"Maybe so, but I have plenty to work with." Cooper waved toward the far end of the workshop. "The mechs are a lot closer to the kind of engineering we worked with at the Country Duke, if you can believe it, but I've made some upgrades. Check this out." He reached down and pulled up a curved section of the Jackal's underbelly. It locked in place on the far side, shielding his hips and back from attack, while still allowing him to look forward. "Then, if I need to abandon ship, I can roll out the back."

"*You* can," Guppie agreed. "I don't have that luxury."

He slid the shield back into its usual place along the mech's underside. "Settle down, gramps, I'm getting to it. Now, check this out." Cooper pulled in a lever, and the Jackal's whole torso spun around, so that he clung to its belly instead of its back. "Pretty cool, right?"

"I suppose," Guppie agreed.

Cooper pulled the lever again, and the torso rotated back to its starting point. "See, what I love about these things is that they're adaptable. We can use them for basic recon, we can use them for combat against Clankers *and* humans, they're effective transport. *And* they're adaptable."

"Power source?"

"That's the best part. These DARPA super gen batteries can juice up on solar and go for *weeks* on a single charge." He swung off the machine's back and pointed to the one at the far end of the row. "This one's a little different."

Guppie followed him down to the Jackal in question. From a distance, it seemed identical to the one Cooper had ridden, but when he examined its back more carefully, he realized that it included what looked like a saddle, complete with leg braces.

"What's this?" Guppie ran his hands over the exosuit. "How'd you build this?"

"I didn't. I took it." Cooper wiped his nose on his sleeve. "From Johnson."

Guppie glanced up in alarm. "You took it off a dead man?"

"I'll tell you one thing, it's not bulletproof. There's a reason I didn't keep the chestpiece." Cooper bared his teeth in a bloodthirsty smile that didn't suit him. "The gyroscope works a little differently on this one, and it's harder to dismount, but I think you'll like it." He indicated the attachments for the exosuit. "This will keep you in place, but I've included joints at the hips and knees, so you won't be stuck in the same position twenty-four-seven. If you need to stretch or adjust your seated position, no problem, but there's a pin-lock system that means you can pin the braces in a fixed position if you need to. I'm not sure if you'll be able to move your legs on their own, so I included handles here, here, and here so that you can adjust them manually, and—Guppie? Are you okay?"

The retired soldier sniffed and rubbed his palms a little too hard against his cheeks. "I'd have been fine with a harness, you know. I could make it work. It doesn't have to be all, you know, *fancy* and shit. We're in the middle of a war. There are bigger fish to fry. You could have been using your time better..."

Cooper squatted down beside the wheelchair, so that he was shorter than Guppie again. Both dogs came over to lick his face, and he waved them away. "What's a better use of time than taking care of my friends?" He gripped Guppie's shoulder and squeezed. "I'd like to get you up in this thing and see if there's anything else I need to adjust. I'd like to give you some practice with the controls, too. But I gotta ask... does it bother you to be using Johnson's suit, all things considered?"

Guppie snorted as he knocked his knuckles against the hollow armor. "That bastard is the reason I don't have working legs anymore, isn't he? Seems only fitting that I should be taking his."

"Cold, but fair."

"Not a lot of justice in the world these days. Gotta take it where we can. Come on, kiddo, give me a hand up."

It took both of them to get Guppie up on the Jackal's back, and even with Cooper's help, Guppie ended up on his belly mid-climb and nearly toppled off the far side. Unlike the machine Cooper had demonstrated on, most of *this* one was hollow, and it gave Guppie plenty of room not only to adjust his legs, but to fold himself down inside its hollow body. It wasn't exactly *comfortable,* but nor was the chair, and the sense of autonomy he felt at being able to move under his own power more than made up for it.

Once he was settled, he laid his hands on the controls, trying to figure out what all the buttons and dials and fiddles were for. The machine operated like a piece of heavy equip-ment, with the same controls he'd used on Bobcats and hydraulic diggers.

"So I can move, and I'm shielded," he observed, "but what happens if I'm attacked? How do I fight back?"

Cooper's grin widened, and he shook his head. "Oh, Guppie," he sighed happily, "you haven't seen anything yet. Come on, let's put this critter through its paces."

In the old days, he'd gotten frustrated with smartphones, with their myriad bits and bobs and their tiny screens that didn't seem to fit his clumsy hands. As Cooper walked him through the Jackal's options, he felt the same sense of overwhelm that had consumed him every time he walked through the doors of the Briar Grove AT&T to ask why his phone, which had 'smart' right in the *name*, wasn't doing what it was supposed to do.

If it meant getting out of the chair, though, he'd do whatever he had to do to make it happen, even if it meant writing the uses for all the buttons out in Sharpie.

4

COOPER

COOPER'S FAMILY was long gone, but as he patiently explained the layout of the control panel for what felt like the eightieth time, he could have been right back in Little Creek teaching his dad the basic principles of Google.

"Okay," Guppie said, "I think I got it!"

"Want to give it a whirl?" Cooper was already planning his exit from the garage. He was fairly confident that the Jackal wouldn't explode if Guppie messed up the controls somehow, but he'd also been fairly confident that it was impossible to accidentally delete the OS from a laptop, and his mother had proven him wrong a few years back. Even now, knowing that his mom was gone for good, he felt the usual mixture of annoyance and wonder at the memory.

After Maddox's death, he'd had all kinds of awful dreams about everyone dying. A memory of Nate's death bled into imagining Len in that same situation, battered against the roof of the Jeep until his bones gave way. A nightmare about Maddox lying on the cooling concrete became a premonition of Vera staring with blank eyes, until she became Guppie, or Pammy, or his mother. He hadn't slept much the week after they took Camp Keystone.

It helped, he was finding, to remember the good days. They made the hard nights easier to swallow.

Guppie drummed his fingers on the controls. "Okay. I'm going to try taking her out through the doors."

"Works for me. Come on, boys." Cooper whistled, and the dogs followed him outside, where Guppie couldn't accidentally trample them in the Jackal if he got confused.

He had to squint against the sun. He spent most of his time in the workshop where it was cool, and where he could make things rather than destroy them. He walked all the way to the building on the far side of the street and stood in its shade with his back to the wall, waiting to see what Guppie would do.

A few strange noises came from inside the garage, then a loud curse, followed by another clatter.

"Probably shouldn't have left him in there with all the equipment," Cooper mused, crossing his arms over his chest. "I should never underestimate the power of an old person to misuse technology."

The dogs whined and wagged their tails, ignoring his quip. Phobos got to his feet and yipped in greeting.

Len and Estes were coming down the street; Estes carried something over his shoulder. Cooper's stomach bottomed out. It looked like a body, and there was an awful lot of blood. *Who is it now? Who were we too slow to save?*

They were only a few paces away when he realized that the body wasn't human.

"What happened?" he asked, jogging over to them. "Are you hurt?"

Len knelt down to greet the dogs, who licked at his hands. "I'm fine," he said. "It isn't our blood. We brought dinner."

Cooper examined the deer with relief. "I'm surprised the Clankers missed one."

"I wouldn't say they did," Len remarked, rising back to his feet. "We had a little run-in with—*whoa!*" He lifted his arms and lowered his chin, falling into a defensive stance as a dark shape scuttled out of the workshop.

Guppie whooped in delight as he emerged from the garage, sending the Jackal running across the street and up the side of the building without pause. He maneuvered onto the roof, then yanked a couple of levers so that the machine lifted its fore-limbs, the way a Clanker did when it was poised to attack.

"Can these things jump?" he yelled down to Cooper.

"I wouldn't try it," Cooper called back. "The machine would be fine, but there's no reason to break your neck!"

The machine lowered its limbs, returned to the edge of the building, and began its vertical return to land. Cooper hadn't given the old man enough credit. He'd taken to the controls like a natural.

At last, Guppie pulled up alongside them and sat upright. "Best damn present anyone's ever given me. If I could get it to play a little classic rock, we'd be golden." His smile transformed him into a younger man. "Feel like my old self again."

Estes whistled, adjusting his grip on the deer. "Dang,

Cooper. Maddox said there was some crazy shit down there, but he never mentioned anything like that."

"Never underestimate the propensity for cool military toys," Cooper agreed.

"Especially war toys," Len muttered.

"Too bad I'm gonna be driving the transport truck," Estes said. "Those things look a lot more fun. Excuse me, folks, but this thing's starting to stink, and I don't want the meat to spoil. Looks like we'll be eating fresh meat for our last supper in camp." He strolled off toward the cantina, although Cooper caught him eying up the Jackal as he passed it.

We'll have access to better scrap in the city, Cooper mused. *Maybe I can build an even better model there to help defeat the hivemind. Or after it's defeated, when we're trying to figure out how to move forward, I can improve the design.*

It was impossible, though, for him to imagine what would happen if and when the hivemind was toppled. There was no going back to the way things had been before. The Clankers would still be there: perhaps less aggressive, but still numerous and hungry. Would they all end up as neighbors, with fragile truces keeping them from falling on one another? Or would there be more truces like the ones Pammy had made?

He couldn't begin to guess.

"Cooper!" Vera's voice echoed off the buildings, and all three of them turned toward her. She stopped short when she saw Guppie, gripping a large sheet of rolled paper to her chest. "Whoa, where'd you get *that*?"

"You like my new ride?" Guppie bent back to smack the

back of the mech with his palm. "Pretty sweet, huh? I'm gonna call her Chelly."

Vera's brow wrinkled.

"Like Michelle Pfeiffer," Guppie explained. "But with a shell. Oh, hell, you think Michelle Pfeiffer survived the invasion?"

Vera squeezed her eyes shut. "I... guess? Listen, Cooper, I wanted to talk to you. We'd planned that route to D.C. before we left Little Creek, but circumstances have changed a little. I'm not sure that we need to avoid the highways anymore, and I'd like to know what you've got planned for transport. Can we go over it?"

Cooper nodded. "Sure. When are we leaving?"

"Tomorrow." Vera licked her lips. "There's no point in putting it off anymore, and Pammy..."

She fell silent, and none of them spoke. Cooper had never stopped thinking of her as part of their group, but while the four of them had gotten closer over the last three weeks, Pammy had drifted away, keeping to herself more.

"You think she blames us?" he asked in a low voice. "For killing Johnson?"

"That might be part of it, but it's not the whole story." Vera gripped the map tight in one fist. "She's not well. Physically, I mean, and mentally..."

"We need her to keep it together," Len said, a bit too bluntly for Cooper's liking. But he wasn't wrong. "She'll be the one leading the Clankers."

"That's the problem," Guppie observed. "We get caught

between looking out for her health and safety and knowing that we need her as a translator even when she's sick."

"She's more than a translator," Cooper murmured. "She's the only reason this plan has any chance of working." He pointed to the workshop. "Come on, Vera, let's look at the map. Guppie, spend all the time you want with, uh, *Chelly*. I'll help you off when you're ready."

He and Vera headed inside, leaving Guppie and Len to some muttered conversation, the topic of which he could only speculate on. Pammy wasn't the only one he was worried about lately. Between Guppie's injuries, Len's missing eye, and Vera's slow descent into depression, Cooper had come to feel that he was the only thing holding their little group together.

The last surviving member of the Lutz family. The last healthy member of the Little Creek Five.

His life in Little Creek had revolved around surviving the everyday humiliations of being the weird outsider. These days, survival meant something else entirely.

It meant protecting the people he cared about.

No matter what.

5

PAMMY MAE

THE SUN WAS JUST COMING up over the horizon when Pammy Mae stirred. It was impossible to say if she'd managed to sleep at all. Whenever she closed her eyes, her thoughts drifted away from herself and into the tangle of a million consciousnesses, all of which centered around the intelligence at the center of the hivemind.

More often than not, she was incapable of making sense of the hivemind's thoughts. Its memory was too deep and too broad. When she tried to seek out certain information, she got lost. It was different when she allowed herself to drift at random, letting images wash over her in an unordered wave. The Clankers lived and died like anything else, but the hivemind was different, more like a virus that was constantly adapting to its environment, defined by its collective rather than by individual organisms.

In the night, she had watched a man and a woman descend

into dark passageways below a ruined city and approach the hivemind. Only the man had emerged, but Pammy had the sense that he was more than he'd been when he entered, hosting some dark passenger that made his blue eyes glimmer like dying stars.

It might have been a dream, but she doubted it. So little of her mind was her own anymore, and whenever she resurfaced from a dip into the hivemind, her own consciousness felt raw and scraped clean.

Pammy rubbed her eyes with one knuckle and stood up. Her stomach was empty, her mouth was dry, and Vera had told her that this morning was different.

The march would begin today. The beginning of the end.

PAMMY WAS in charge of the Clankers, but Vera was the one who spoke to people. Pammy was glad that the unenviable job fell on someone else's shoulders. She had no patience for people anymore. She couldn't get in their heads, the way she could with the aliens.

As the assembled audience bit into their tasteless MREs, Vera got to her feet. "Good morning, everyone. As you know, today we'll begin our march toward D.C." There were angry mutters, as Pammy had known there would be, but she kept eating and ignored them.

Vera lifted her hands, ever the peacemaker. "Please, allow me to explain. Anyone who's willing can come with us. We're launching an offensive on the central hive in Washington, D.C. following Pammy Mae's intel."

One of the civilians snorted. "Right. We'll just follow Johnson's niece into battle alongside the aliens. Great plan."

Her hands tightened of their own accord, causing the wrapper of the MRE to crinkle. At her side, Emma Jean shifted closer, as if her skinny body would be enough to protect Pammy from the man's tone. Like her daughter, Emma Jean was wasting away, although the reasons for her slow decline were different. She'd been upbeat and delusional when Pammy Mae had first arrived. Since Uncle Kevin's death, however, she'd pivoted toward darkness and despair.

It would have been impossible to sleep in that house, even for someone who *did* sleep. She'd tried once, and only once. Better to sit on the wall and wander through the dreams of the hivemind than to spend another second beneath that roof, where her mother's desperation pooled like rising water in every corner and cranny.

Even Vera bristled at the man's words. "You can do what you want, Chris. That's why I'm giving the option. Just hear me out, all right?"

The man took another bite of his MRE and, mercifully, kept his mouth shut.

"Those of us who go to Washington will be taking the truck, the DARPA bots Cooper has modified, and the Keystone Hive. We'll leave the tank for anyone who wishes to stay, to help them defend the camp. The rest of the supplies, including food, weapons, and ammunition, will be divvied up according to our numbers."

A woman at the back of the crowd called, "What's to stop more Clankers from showing up and swarming the wall?"

"Good question, Ellie." Vera stepped back and nodded to Cooper. "Care to explain?"

Cooper got to his feet, and the sight of him compressed Pammy's chest. He looked more like Nate than ever, but older, more man than boy. Nate would never get that far. She'd tried to accept that he was gone for good, but it was so *hard* some days.

Emma Jean rubbed a small circle on Pammy's back. She had to fight her instinct to push her mother away. It had been a long time since human touch made her feel anything but sour and resentful.

Cooper offered the crowd an awkward wave. "Hey, everyone. So I've been working on a soundboard, with Pammy's help. It's not perfect, but if any other Clankers do show up at the walls, all you'll have to do is hit play. It'll sound like there's a hive here, a strong one, one that loners shouldn't challenge. The whole thing is solar-powered with a backup battery, so it won't matter if you don't need it for months."

"It won't last forever," the grumpy civilian observed.

Cooper's smile turned brittle. "It'll last longer than the food supplies, though."

Pammy lowered her head so that nobody would see her grin. It wasn't polite to laugh about the fact that they were all in deep shit, but at least Cooper wasn't sugarcoating things anymore.

"Anyway, that's the plan." Cooper shrugged. "And like I said, it's not perfect, but we're not leaving anyone out to dry. If you want to come to D.C. and make a last stand with us, we'll appreciate the assistance. If you want to stay here and try your luck inside the walls, nobody's going to stop you. So, um. Back

to you, Vera." He dropped down to the ground again. Beside
him, Klarie offered him a high-five.

"Those are your options," Vera said. "Take them or leave
them. We'll need a headcount of who's coming so that we can
finish loading. Time to make your choices, folks."

Guppie wheeled forward, with Len right beside him.
Cooper got up, and Klarie too. Pammy climbed to her feet, and
Emma Jean immediately reached for her.

"I'm not staying, Mom," she whispered.

"I know, baby," Emma Jean said. "Just give me a hand up.
I'm coming too."

Pammy pulled her mother to her feet, and the two of them
went to stand with Vera, hand in hand.

She had wondered if there would only be a few of them, but
Estes was already moving, and an Asian-American soldier who
seemed to know Guppie. When Peachey got to his feet, a few
people groaned.

"You can't take both doctors!" someone called.

Peachey stopped in his tracks and turned, adjusting his
glasses as he did so. In his cool, dispassionate voice, he said,
"You heard Vera. We all get to make our choices. Yes, I'm a
doctor, but I'm a military man first. I'll divide the medical
supplies the same way we split everything else, but I've made
my choice." He drifted over toward the group, and more people
followed him, either out of real conviction or because they saw
the scales tipping in a new direction.

Vera's pleasure was obvious, and even Pammy experienced
a small thrill of satisfaction at the size of their group. People
believed in them. That meant something, even now.

"All right, folks. Everyone coming with us, report to Estes for a headcount. Everyone staying, figure out who's in charge, and let me know your numbers so that we can be sure everything is fairly dispersed. Cooper, you're in charge of assigning people to the transport vehicles. And Pammy..." Vera turned to her and held up her fist between them. "Time to rally the troops."

Pammy lifted her fist to Vera's, brushing their knuckles together. "Yes, ma'am," she said. Then she turned on her heel and stalked toward the gate of the encampment and the woods beyond, where her ravenous subjects awaited the return of their queen.

6

CARLA

"LET ME GET THIS STRAIGHT." General Greene waved to the *homoptera invadenda* inside its glass case. "You think all those ugly buggers are connected by some sort of... fungal infection."

"There's scientific precedent, sir," Nathan insisted. Out of all of them, Nathan and Dr. Sharma were the two most reasonable speakers, and he'd volunteered to run Greene through their working theory. "Even on Earth, there are several types of fungi that can essentially drive the biological functions of their hosts. We believe it's possible that the *invadendae* carry a similar chemical compound in their bodies. Whether it's due to a fungal infection or a virus of some sort is difficult to say, but we'd like to run some tests to prove our theory. With your permission, of course."

Greene grunted, then turned to face them. "And the rest of you are on board with this?" he asked.

Stew, who was sitting with his feet kicked up on the edge of one of the desks, nodded. Carla did, too, although she couldn't bring herself to meet the general's eyes.

"We're in agreement, General," Sharma said.

"It's an interesting theory." Greene laid one hand on the glass. Behind it, the glittering alien only stared at him. "But it has nothing to do with your assignment."

Sharma frowned. "General, you asked us to discern anything we could about the invaders. If we're right, this could be *huge*."

"I *asked* you for a way to fight back." Greene turned to them and folded his hands behind his back, scowling at each of them in turn. "We were hoping to develop a Plan B, but that's no longer necessary. As of this morning, your team has been deemed non-essential."

"But sir!" Nathan intertwined his fingers and shot a desperate frown Carla's way. "This isn't the only thing we've learned from the message. We just need a little more time." It was obvious that he was hoping for backup, but Carla had nothing to say.

Greene waved a dismissive hand. "We're *done* here. And I would like to personally express my disappointment that this team was so utterly useless. We've wasted valuable resources, and you've made so little progress."

"*Disappointed?*" Stew lurched out of his seat. He would likely have tackled Greene if Sharma hadn't blocked his way. Of course, he'd be shot a moment after that. Being deemed *non-essential* could have gotten Carla fired in the old days. Now, she was pretty sure it was a death sentence.

Stew didn't physically press forward, but his anger was palpable. He jabbed a finger at Greene. "Don't tell me that you're *disappointed* in us, like we volunteered for the job. You brought us here. You *held* us here. We were the ones who parsed the message in the first place. We *warned* you people what was coming, and you twiddled your thumbs while the world burned."

Greene didn't so much as blink in the face of Stew's accusations. They were never going to get an apology. Stew had always thought of himself as a major player, a future hero, but Carla knew the truth. They were like the *invadenda* sitting in its glass terrarium, slowly starving as the war outside the bay played out. The huge insectoid alien sat perfectly still and watched as the humans raved and raged beyond the barrier. It didn't so much as move a limb. It was biding its time, conserving its energy, waiting for its chance to strike out against death one last time.

"We did what was necessary for the survival of the species," Greene said coolly. "As a scientist, you should be familiar with survival of the fittest. Yes, the world has burned, but America the beautiful will rise like a phoenix from the ashes."

Sharma looked dumbfounded. "That's never been the position of any—"

"Doctor, please. Things are more complicated than you might realize."

Something about the way he said it sent a shudder down Carla's spine. Even though she suspected there was a rogue element to what was going on, this was as close as she'd seen Greene to acknowledging it. Was there even official leadership left at all?

"That's some pretty friggin' poetic language, General, given that what you mean to say is *we let all the civilians die because we knew we wouldn't win the war.* This is what happens when things go according to plan, huh?" Stew waved his arms at random to encompass the whole ship and everything beyond.

"That's enough." Greene arched one salt-and-pepper eyebrow. "You'll receive your new assignments shortly. The less trouble you make in the meantime, the better." He nodded to his men, and the three of them left the little lab, closing the door sharply behind them.

"Son of a *bitch.*" Stew turned and drove his fist into the wall, bruising his knuckles against the slate-painted steel wall in the process.

"What are we going to do?" Nathan's lip trembled as though he might cry. "They're not going to have a new assignment for us, are they? This is it."

"They should have just put a bullet in each of our heads back in the day," Stew snarled. "It would have been kinder."

"Well, they didn't." Dr. Sharma adjusted her glasses and squared her jaw. She was by far the shortest of them, but her no-nonsense attitude had impressed Carla from day one and scored her Stew's respect, which was no easy feat. Her rich brown skin had taken on an ashen pallor in the wake of Greene's revelation, but as always, she'd managed to keep things in perspective. "We're alive now, and we have valuable information. If anything, this has been a litmus test for our theory about the infection. Greene barely batted an eyelash when we told him, which suggests that they already know. I wonder how many others know."

"How would they?" Nathan asked.

"Maybe he's infected too," Carla said. It wasn't a cogent argument, more of a thought that she had blurted out. "Maybe they all are."

Nathan, Stew, and Sharma all turned to stare at her. She'd been so quiet, they seemed to have forgotten that she was still in the lab.

Sharma frowned. "There's nothing to suggest our species would be susceptible in a similar way."

"It's *alien*," Stew said. "There's nothing to suggest it can't."

"My God..." Nathan said.

"This is just speculation at this point," Sharma said. "May I remind all of you that we've also learned a confirmed way to counteract the aliens?" She bent over one of the computers and opened the song file they'd made by shortening the frequency of the *Stark*'s original message. The sound was awful, like nails on a chalkboard, but the sudden pain that spiked through Carla's head was nothing to the *invadenda*'s reaction. As it had every time they played it, the alien went into overdrive, battering itself against the glass in an attempt to escape the sound even after the file stopped playing.

"I'm not sure how much good this information will do on its own," she said over the sounds of the alien's pounding limbs, "but I have to believe that there are other survivors out there. And maybe they could benefit from this information."

"Yeah?" Stew demanded. "And how are we going to get it to them?"

"It's obvious." Sharma straightened up and pushed her

glasses back onto her nose. "We need to find a way off this ship. We have to escape."

"Yeah, great." Stew rolled his eyes. "Solid plan. Just one problem, though... even if we figured out a way to escape, these asshats would shoot us before we made it ten feet."

Carla cleared her throat, and the three of them once again turned to look at her. She nodded to the alien still writhing against the glass.

"Not if they were busy trying to shoot something else."

BELOW WASHINGTON

Crystal City Metro Station

Agent Dante followed the Ambassador deeper into the veins and arteries below the city. He could hear the thrumming and rustling of the Akrido around him. His organization had devised other names for the creatures, but all of their knowledge— including that of Team II, which had managed to make contact with the aliens early on—was purely theoretical. Dante was the only one who had descended into their nest. He would be the first to make contact. The first go-between.

He would be the one to orchestrate humanity's rise to true power.

The beam of his floodlight bobbed along the walls, scattering yellow reflections as they bobbed off the living walls. The tunnels seemed to be getting narrower.

No, he realized. *They aren't narrowing. The Akrido are moving in layers now. There are more of them here than in the upper levels of the metro.*

"Are you frightened, agent?" The Ambassador turned her head slightly, and the light caught her profile. Her eyes were like the shells of the aliens, a sleek darkness full of glittering stars, with nothing human left in them.

Dante hesitated for a moment before answering, "Yes."

"That is wise. Your honesty is appreciated." She spread her arms to encompass the opening of the hall. "The Akrido have helped us conquer worlds more advanced than yours, but your foresight impresses us. Other advanced species have tried to make deals with us, but only when it is too late and they are overrun. By then their numbers are scattered and their focus divided, but *your* species was proactive. Even so, you are right to be afraid. We could always change our minds about you."

"Are you threatening me, Ambassador?"

She laughed, and the sound echoed back to them from deep in the tunnels. "What would you do if we were?"

Over the years, Dante had engaged in many games of cat and mouse. He'd sat through shows of power and one-upmanship, of empty threats and subtle flexes. He had never gone into a situation blind before, and he'd always had a trick up his sleeve. In the bowels of the WMATA metrorail system, however, he was helpless. This many aliens could strip the flesh from his bones in a matter of seconds if they put their collective minds to it.

"Very little," Dante said. "Although my death would benefit you almost nothing, while my life might help you a great deal. I think I'm more valuable to you with my organs intact."

"We shall see. And your strength, too, will help determine the longevity of our association. Your species is hardy, but your minds are too complex. It makes them more prone to breakage."

He could imagine, certainly, how lesser men might waver and crack under the pressure of an intellectual challenge. Dante had broken enough men in his time to know that most people could only guess at their mental fortitude until it was truly tested. Hopefully he hadn't overestimated himself, but it was too late now for such concerns.

A distant light appeared at the far end of the tunnel, and Dante's steps faltered. "What is that?"

The Ambassador chuckled. "It is the ninth circle of Hell, agent."

Dante almost stumbled in his surprise. "Does that mean something where you're from, or...?"

"We have taken up residence in a few of your species already. Some of them knew your literature. Not every apex species has managed poetry, you know. You should be proud of humanity's accomplishments, such as they are." The Ambassador chuckled, as if her condescending tone wasn't grating enough. "Do you understand our reference, agent?"

Dante bit the inside of his cheek and swallowed. The light grew brighter with each step, casting a watery, limpid glow along the tunnel where the alien hosts now stood three layers deep, maybe more, narrowing the tunnel to the point of claustrophobia. He would have to touch them in order to pass through the arch.

His voice would *not* tremble. He wouldn't allow it.

"Yes," he rasped, "I know the reference. The ninth circle is reserved for traitors."

"Indeed. Which is why it will be *your* circle, agent, since what are you if not the greatest traitor of all? You have betrayed your whole species. Your whole world."

There had been times over the course of the passing years when Dante had questioned whether his organization was in the right. Millions of people, billions of them, were dead. The aliens had swept across the globe more effectively than any virus, any pandemic, any plague or army. Humanity had indeed been brought to its knees, but there was a reason for all of it.

"I haven't betrayed them," he said. "I've *saved* them. Earth could survive without us, but *we* couldn't survive here, not the way we have been. Humanity turned its eyes to the stars a long time ago. An alliance with you brings them within our grasp. Individuals will die, but that was inevitable."

"And you shall be their hero." The Ambassador's tone was taunting.

"The living will view me as a savior," Dante told her. "And the dead will keep their opinions to themselves."

The Ambassador stopped in her tracks and turned to him, only steps away from the doorway. "Whatever becomes of your species, we believe you will thrive among us. Your thought process is *so* like ours. Anything can be justified if it means our continued survival. Anything." She reached out one hand to him. He tried not to flinch as her fingers, with their broken fake nails and dried blood, closed over his. "Come. Let us meet at last, without this cipher to connect us."

Dante switched off his light, let the strap rest over his shoulder, and then followed her into the chamber beyond.

After well over a mile of sloping tunnels, the sight of the enormous vault beneath the city would have stolen his breath if the cramped and airless room hadn't done so already. Half a dozen tunnels converged around the great room, whose honeycombed ceilings weren't cut from stone this time, but built out of some waxy material that reminded Dante of a flaking wasp's nest.

Despite the cluster of alien forms amassed in the hallways, only a few of the Akrido moved about in this room. Instead, it was largely taken up by a pale, shifting form that dominated the space. Anchors thick as cables, but evidently woven from something like spider silk, bound it to the ceiling. The main structure of the alien mass sagged against those lines, rippling with a phosphorescence that emanated from its core.

"Oh." Dante dropped the Ambassador's hand and took a swaying step toward the bulbous excrescency. There was something nightmarish about its size and shapelessness, and the way it gently pulsed with what might have been a heartbeat. Its glowing heart, however, mesmerized him. *This* was what he saw in the eyes of the aliens each time they fixed him with their piercing gaze. "You're a *star*," he murmured.

"Not quite." The woman behind him was still speaking, although her voice sounded different here. It echoed back to him from all directions, as if more than one voice had joined in chorus. From the halls beyond, the Akrido began to hum. "We are made of star stuff as you are, agent. Every planet in this universe is our destiny and our birthright. We are the hunter, and the lesser beings are our harvest. We spread in order to claim our inheritance, world by world."

Dante placed his palm against the membrane that surrounded the mass. It gave slightly beneath his touch, and he could feel the hum that echoed outward from it. "And I could be... part of you?"

He felt the answer radiating outward from its physical confines. The Ambassador didn't need to speak now. He was close, so close to understanding, so close to being engulfed in the only *real* power.

To pair with us is to know and be known, it told him. *You will end, but you will not be diminished. You will be absorbed, and you will grow with us, if you are resilient enough. Only the strong survive. Are you strong, agent?*

"I will be," he whispered.

Beneath his palm, the cell wall began to weep with a sticky amber substance that gathered in great drops at each pore. Each bead shimmered with its own bioluminescence, glistening like gems. The few Akrido within the room immediately altered their routines and began to collect the drops. They gathered them so gently that the little spheres of nectar didn't burst.

Dante didn't hesitate. He bent his head toward the cell wall and licked at the glittering drops. They burst in his mouth, thick as honey, but with a bitter aftertaste that made his temples throb and his throat constrict.

Ambrosia, he thought. Despite the bitterness, he lapped again at the supple tissue that gave like skin beneath his tongue.

It took a moment for his stomach to cramp, but when it did, the pain was so intense that it brought him to his knees. He clenched one arm across his belly and bit his tongue to keep from crying out. Satisfaction swept through him, but the sensation wasn't his own. The palm that he'd pressed to the alien's thin hide was stuck there now, all but glued in place by the substance that coated his tongue.

Sweat broke out on his skin, and Dante leaned forward, accidentally pressing his forehead into the nectar-slick surface of the alien as he did so. Its light rippled around him, and it seemed to drip into him, filling his skin like starlight and poisoning his veins. He retched once.

Close your mouth. The thought wasn't his, but he obeyed it anyway, almost without thinking and certainly without question.

His vision dimmed, darkening from the center outward, as if he was watching a movie at the middle of his line of sight and only the periphery remained his own. He saw the world as the alien before him did, through thousands upon thousands of borrowed eyes. He could see himself, slumped against the floor in a pathetic heap, and he whimpered.

Don't fight it, he thought. *Accept it. This is what you wanted.* He couldn't tell whether the thought was the alien's or his own. There was no difference. This time, they were in total alignment.

Dante stopped fighting, and the pain eased. He sank back into himself, gasping for breath, but he was more now than he had been before. There was no boundary between himself and the invader. They were one and the same.

"What are you?" he breathed.

The answer floated to the top of his mind like a single bubble of air rising from the lightless depths of an infinite ocean.

We are the throng. And now, you are one of us.

7

PAMMY MAE

PAMMY PRESSED her knees to either side of her Clanker mount as it strode along. She had worried that it would be difficult to convince the creatures to let her ride them, but this migration wasn't so different from what they did on their home world in the marshy season, when the otherwise solid ground of their native territories turned spongy and damp beneath their hives. Then the Clankers would lay their eggs and retreat to the drier uplands, with their Hive Queen and their stores of royal jelly in tow.

After weeks of preparation, the hive had been prepared to move out the moment Pammy gave the command. The last of the eggs had hatched, and the smallest of the baby Clankers were just strong enough to leave the water, cleaving to their matrons' underbellies. Those who weren't tasked with carrying the young split apart the honeycomb structure in which their nectar was stored and carried it with them. Those carrying their rations walked ahead, while those with the Clanker-fry walked behind, since their young could swim if the water rose behind them. Each of them hummed with the intensity of their purpose, like soldiers singing in time to mark the tempo of their steps.

Pammy couldn't say with any clarity how much of her understanding of the Clankers came from her tenuous connection to the hivemind and how much came from her conversations with the aliens themselves. With each passing day, she seemed better able to understand them.

Her dreams had become increasingly strange. Maybe it was only her imagination, but they'd had more depth in recent weeks, as if her mind was flitting across the world, witnessing Earth's collapse through the eyes of the Clankers as she slept.

Beside her, Cooper rode one of his Jackals alongside Guppie's modified mechanical. At least they didn't have engines that rumbled like the transport truck, or the commercial flatbed that was hauling spare Jackals and their supplies. They'd also hitched up the old Cessna to the back and were towing it along like they were just some crazy tourists dragging their car behind their fancy RV, except it was an *airplane*. The plane was a gas guzzler, and they weren't planning to use it until they got closer to D.C.

The constant rumble of the motors grated on her, as did the voices of the men as they talked.

"How long did you and Vera reckon it will take to get there?" Guppie asked.

"Ideally, we'll get there by tomorrow night. It's hard to say, of course, how much ground we can cover with these machines.

We're not going as fast as we would in a car, but it's better than traveling on foot by a long way. And what happens if we meet a roadblock, or get in a fight? Plus, we'll need to camp..."

Pammy Mae squeezed her eyes shut. *Why can't they stop talking, even for a few moments? They're exhausting.* She took a few deep breaths to try and relax and rubbed her temples.

She didn't open her eyes again, but all of a sudden, she could see. Rather than viewing the world from her own position, however, she was looking at herself, watching from outside of her body as she crouched over the black bulk of the Clanker, with a commingled army spread out behind her.

Immediately, her eyes popped open, and she strummed a single note on her stolen tymbal. The Clanker-song around her died, and the soldiers and workers alike came to a standstill.

The other humans took a moment to register what had happened, and Cooper's mechanical mount nearly collided with her before he registered the fact that she'd drawn to a halt.

"Is something wrong?" he asked.

Pammy swung down from the Clanker's back and took a step forward before rotating on the spot in the middle of the road. There was a small overpass above them, but she hadn't seen herself from directly above. She held up two fingers and tried to imagine where someone would have to be standing to see her as she'd seen herself. As her fingers traced the angle of sight to forty-five degrees, she paused.

"There," she said. "Right there."

Cooper leaned over the saddle of his mount. "*What's there?*"

"Clankers," she said. "And they're not our friends." Her

palm struck the tymbal again, and as the pad of her thumb danced over its ridges in a warning call, the answer came from the very spot she'd pinpointed.

She didn't need to translate for her hive. The soldiers surged forward, while the workers gathered in a defensive cluster, bracing their reinforced backs outward against any future onslaught. Pammy pulled herself up onto her mount's back as it took off in the direction of the challenger.

"Wait here!" she called to her friends.

The human members of Keystone's blended army held back, shouting questions to one another that were mercifully difficult to make out over the Clanker battle cry. She left them to sort out their own business and rode forward into the fray. Vera could give whatever commands she liked, so long as she stayed out of Pammy's way.

Pammy's Clankers swarmed toward the off-ramp, ignoring the rules of the road. The metal girders that kept vehicles from swerving into the ditch on either side of the divided highway, much less into oncoming traffic, did nothing to deter the Clanker mob from going in whichever direction suited them.

They were crossing the far side of the highway when Pammy realized that she wasn't alone. Cooper rode beside her, crouched down in the shielded compartment of the robot's body.

"What are you doing?" she snarled. "I told you to stay back!"

Cooper shook his head and tapped his finger against one ear, which was a crock of crap. He could hear her just fine. Even more annoyingly, Guppie was on their heels. How was she supposed to keep them safe when they wouldn't obey her?

Friends aren't supposed to obey you, an old part of her brain reminded her. The new part of her, the one that had been born on the wooden floor of Stoltzfus Antiques, could only accept fealty. Her vision was wider than any of theirs. She knew better. They should do as they were told.

There was no time to stop and argue. A handful of Clankers descended the slope, leaping over the concrete barrier on the edge of the overpass. They were grossly outnumbered, but their song was a call to action, which implied that there were more out there somewhere. The Keystone hive was a small one, by Pammy's estimation. She couldn't tell how far away this one was, nor how fiercely guarded. If it rivaled Keystone's, she could lose Clankers in the fray, shrinking the numbers of their army long before they reached the city. Where there were more people, there was more food; the D.C. hive would be much larger than anything they passed out here.

The more hives we conscript, the more soldiers we have... and the harder it will be to control them.

An instant before Pammy's army clashed with the newcomers, she changed the tune of her command. *Surround, don't kill. Incapacitate, but do not slaughter.*

The Clankers obeyed, circling the interlopers in a maelstrom of limbs and carapaces. Pammy's Clanker pushed to the front of the group. She signaled a cease-fire, then turned her attention to the attackers.

Song was the Clanker's primary form of communication, but the longer that she spent among them, the more she understood that there was a form of grammar in every performance. There were subtle differences in the melodies with which strangers should be addressed, as compared to those from within one's own hive. Pammy Mae changed her melodic syntax accordingly and addressed the newcomers. According to the sign on the overpass, they weren't far from Parkton. Easy enough, then: she would think of them as the Parkton Hive.

We are not invaders, she told them. *We are merely passing through. We don't want to challenge your territory.*

The Parkton Clankers conferred with one another for a moment as their attitude shifted from hostile to mistrustful.

The King, one of them said.

The King, they agreed, until all of their little scouting party took up the same call.

"What's going on?" Guppie asked. "Should we shoot 'em?"

"No," Cooper said, before Pammy could respond. "She's talking to them." His face was set in grim determination, and when Pammy turned to glance at him, there was wariness in his eyes. She'd have to get used to that sooner or later. The humans suspected her connection to the aliens, and the aliens sometimes struggled with the fact that their new queen smelled a great deal like dinner. The Keystone Hive had never turned against her, but another ruler might feel differently. Even if they didn't see her as a snack, they might see her as a *threat,* which was just as dangerous.

"They want to parlay," she said.

"Like you parlayed with the old queen in Keystone?" Cooper asked.

Guppie grunted. "As I recall, that didn't turn out so well for her."

The other scouts from the Parkton Hive were approaching. They would be easier to pick off in groups. They could fall into formation here and draw out Parkton's defenses until it was safe to pass.

Or they could try to recruit a new squadron. Nothing risked, nothing gained, after all. If their first attack on the hive-mind in the capital failed, they wouldn't get a do-over.

"I'm going," she said, even as she played the same message to both hives of Clankers. "If I can't stand against another small hive, there's no point in going to Washington. If I have to challenge the local king, so be it."

"Then I'm coming with you," Cooper said.

She shook her head. "No, you stay here. Go back and tell Vera the plan. If I don't meet up with the convoy again, keep going."

Cooper set his jaw. "No way."

"I don't know this hive yet," she snapped. "What if they turn on you and I can't stop them?"

"Better the two of us than the whole convoy," Guppie pointed out. "This plan only works if we can fight together, remember?"

"And if I get killed?" She tried to stare them down, glowering at the pair of them.

"Then we go back to Vera and tell her that our treaty with the Clankers is dissolved," Cooper said. "I'm not leaving you."

Back in Little Creek, Cooper's loyalty had saved her life several times over. At the moment, however, she couldn't shake the feeling that he wanted to stick to her out of something more than camaraderie.

He doesn't trust you out of his sight.

Pammy snorted and turned away from him. *And maybe he shouldn't. After all, you're no longer sure how much of your head is still* yours, *are you?*

Better not to dwell on it. Instead, she urged her mount forward and let the Parkton Clankers lead her to their king.

THE PARKTON HIVE, she soon discovered, wasn't actually located in Parkton itself. Instead of heading toward town, the Parkton scouts led them overland. Without the workers and their burdens to slow them down, they made better time, scurrying through the woods in an undulating stream of jointed bodies. Cooper and Guppie's mechanical counterparts struggled to keep pace with her mount, and she wished that they would fall behind for good and turn back to the human portion of the convoy where they belonged.

Unlike you.

It wasn't until they reached the water that Pammy realized just how grossly she had underestimated the size of the Parkton Hive. The town itself was small, but a hive's size was dictated by the size of its freshwater breeding pools, even more than its food supply. The Parkton didn't have a pond, or even a lake. They had a whole reservoir full of coves and inlets in which to hatch their fry.

"Oh, God." Cooper finally caught up with her and stared

down at the foaming water in silent horror. "How many of them are there, do you reckon?"

"Five times as many there are on our side. Maybe six." Her hands trembled on the shell of her mount. As soon as the fry could emerge from the water, their number would double. Pammy wasn't sure exactly how long a Clanker could go without water, since their grasp on time was slippery at best. A long time, she reckoned. Months, at least. That was how they'd managed to cross the vast reaches of space without stores, and why they'd been so ravenous when they finally landed. If the Parkton Hive diverted all of its fresh catches to their young, their numbers could swell indefinitely before the colony faced collapse.

Guppie came to a stop on her far side. "We could go back." When she didn't answer, he shook his head. "But you won't do that, will you?"

"I can't," she said.

Guppie raised one grizzled eyebrow. "Can't, or won't?"

The water foamed, and Pammy allowed herself to float into the minds of the fry for a moment, letting herself see through all their half-formed eyes at once. If she wanted, she could turn back now, but she would never be Pammy again.

Might as well accept that you're long gone, Miss Butter. She could hear Sean Hawes' voice as clearly as if he was perched on the Clanker alongside her.

Great. Now she was seeing ghosts.

"Can't," she repeated, and urged her Clanker toward the Parkton Hive.

The scouts led them along the shoreline away from the dam,

where the water was thick with algae and very nearly stagnant. Hundreds of Clankers swarmed across the banks. As Pammy Mae and her company passed, they paused to look up.

Back in Keystone, the old Queen had lived in a heavily damaged house, one side of which had collapsed. The Parkton King, however, had been forced to build his own castle. Segments of walls and roofs were interspersed with downed trees to create a shelter. In addition to the makeshift building, the Clankers had amassed a junk pile of their own.

"What's that?" Guppie nodded to the mound of bottles and old bikes, rusted chains and broken umbrellas, lawn chairs, bird-feeders, whirligigs, pots, pans, broken dishes, and even a pile of rain-soaked paperbacks whose pages swelled with mold. "Hoarders, are they?"

"They're studying us," Pammy said. "Wait here. I mean it this time."

Astride his Jackal, Cooper stared into the depths of the house with his shoulders hunched and his eyes narrowed. With a confidence she didn't feel, Pammy mustered a smile.

She left her reinforcements behind and approached the haphazard structure. *Greetings,* she played. *I come as an equal.*

From beneath the browning evergreen branches and flaking panels of sheetrock, several long limbs emerged. The King of Parkton hummed in greeting, although there was a note of pride in his hum. *We are not equals. I am the master of this place. And you... you are...* His eyes sparkled among the shadows. *You are one of* them.

I was. She didn't have to lie. Time was a difficult thing to convey on the tymbal. She had yet to determine whether the language of the Clankers didn't allow for it, or if there was something subtle that eluded her in the intonation.

Why are you here?

I want to... Pammy's fingers stilled on the tymbal as she chose her tune carefully. *I want to make a deal.*

The King of Parkton shifted forward. The Queen of Keystone Hive had been swollen and bulbous, but this monarch was all lean, sharp lines with cruel edges and razor hooks. *We do not deal.*

Then we will be the first. I wish to...merge. There was no word for an alliance in their language.

The King of Parkton's rattle didn't sound like laughter, although it meant the same thing. *And who will lead them? Will I bow to you? Or will your hive settle here and merge with mine?* He stepped entirely free of his composite nest. Behind Pammy, Cooper sucked in a breath so loud her own lungs constricted at the sound.

The King circled her. His long body reminded her more of a silverfish than any of the other Clankers she had thus far encountered. Pammy closed her eyes. In the darkness, she saw the image of a thousand white lumps, mounds of foam beneath each of which a human corpse softened, its flesh ripening to feed the generations of Clankers to come. She couldn't tell if it was real, or if the King of Parkton only longed for it to be real.

What do you ask from me?

Some of your soldiers, Pammy replied.

And what will you give me?

She'd been raised on stories of small children stumbling into fairyland and making deals with unkind spirits. As a little girl, she'd thought the children in those tales terrifically stupid. Now, she understood that they were desperate. Desperate and proud.

When she didn't answer at once, the King slid closer. *Give me meat. You have brought two meals with you. For each one of them you give me, I will give you ten of mine.*

She would never hand over Guppie and Cooper. Never. But there were soldiers in the convoy whose names she didn't know. There were civilians who would likely be useless in the coming fight. Even Emma Jean, who barely knew how to fire a gun. One Clanker would gain her a lot more ground in Washington than any *one* of them, never mind ten.

The King of Parkton circled closer, waiting for her answer. How did the children in those stories ever survive? The same way pageant queens convinced the judges that they were perfect.

They lied.

Ask why I am marching. Ask what awaits us. Pammy's fingers flew across the tymbal. *There are more of them where we are going, more* meals *like me, enough to feed your offspring until the next migration. There will be a harvest unlike anything you can imagine.*

The words weren't hers. They were the same promises that the hivemind had made when it had absorbed the Clankers untold generations before.

The King of Parkton stopped moving. *This is true?*

Yes.

He considered her. *And you will lead us?*

Yes.

His long, slender limbs reached out toward her, prodding at

the Clanker armor she wore. If he wanted to, he could spear her clean through without a second thought. There would be a battle, but the Parkton Hive would surely triumph.

Pammy didn't flinch. If he killed her, it would be the end of everything she'd endured. She could stop worrying about the coming battle and rest.

Then my soldiers will come with you. And so will I.

Pammy backed up a step. When he didn't try to stop her, she retreated to where her colony awaited her, along with Guppie and Cooper.

"You're alive," Cooper said. "So I take it that went well."

"Yup. He's coming with us to D.C. to help fight the hive-mind." Pammy kept her eyes down when she spoke, just in case Cooper was able to read the truth in her expression. One way or another, the Clankers were going to demand payment, and the only currency they traded in was flesh.

She only hoped she'd be able to control them when the time came.

8
VERA

"THEY'VE BEEN GONE TOO LONG," Estes said as he peered over the side of the truck. They'd killed the engine on the truck only minutes after Pammy Mae and her Clankers took off without explanation. Vera had been braced for the sounds of battle or screams, but all she'd gotten was a distant snatch of Clanker-song as it receded into the woods.

"Maybe they killed her and took off," one of the other soldiers suggested.

Vera shot the man a filthy glare. "We'd have heard them," she said. "And Cooper and Guppie would have come back."

"Unless the Buggers got them all," the soldier suggested.

Vera scowled. "Enough. They're *fine*."

"And how long are we gonna assume that, without proof?"

Len lifted one hand. "Quiet."

"Look, I know you Little Creek folks are close, but that girl is—"

"*Quiet.*" Len tapped one finger to his ear, then pointed at the sky. Beside him, Phobos whined, and Deimos sniffed the breeze as his hackles rose.

At first, Vera thought it was a Clanker. The low, dull thrum reminded her of their song. The angle wasn't right, however. Len was right. It was coming from the sky.

"Helicopters?" Estes hopped out of the truck bed, eyes fixed on the gray sky above them. There was hope in his tone, although Vera didn't feel it. "Helicopters mean *survivors.*"

Vera met Len's eye. She knew exactly what he was thinking. After they fled Little Creek, they'd been thrilled by the idea of finding other survivors, only to be met with hostility in Keystone. Now, Vera didn't trust anyone who still had access to resources.

"Funny," she murmured, "how I'm starting to trust the Clankers more than other people."

Len nodded. "'Cause Clankers are predictable, and people aren't."

They followed Estes out and stared toward the heavens as three black specks hovered over the convoy. Estes waved his arms over his head.

"They're coming in," Len said.

Klarie's head appeared around the corner of the truck. "Is that a good thing?" she asked nervously.

"I don't know." Vera grabbed one of the ThunderGen guns and slipped out of the truck. She'd been toying with the idea of having Len take the Cessna up — it turned out he had some training, like Cooper — to see if he could spot anything going on with Pammy and the others. But now she was glad she hadn't.

When Phobos tried to follow her, Len grabbed his collar and pulled him back down into the truck bed. "I suppose Pammy's recruiting Clankers, and we ought to see if we can bring anyone else on board. Estes, do you know anything about helicopters? Who do they belong to?"

"Silhouettes look like Apaches," Estes said.

"That'd make 'em attack choppers," Len grunted. "Not transports."

Vera braced her feet apart and stared up at the cloud cover, with one hand shielding her eyes. "Let me handle this, okay? We're not making any deals with *anyone* until we know more. I don't want a repeat of the situation with Johnson."

More people emerged from the vehicles, including Dr. Josiah Peachey. Emma Jean Johnson was right behind him. She was holding a rod in both hands; the thing was almost as tall as she was.

Vera knew that weapon. It was the rod Johnson had used to fry Dylan Maddox. *How did Emma Jean get her hands on that thing?* She usually thought of Pammy's mother as confused but relatively harmless, but not when she was holding a weapon that powerful. She could hurt herself.

Or someone else.

Soon enough, all sixty or so of them were standing in a cluster, staring up at the late afternoon sky. The helicopters were coming lower, but Vera got the sense that they were waiting for something.

"Back at Camp Keystone, we had orders to turn away survivors who tried to force their way into the camp," Dr.

Peachey said. "Those orders came down from Washington." He cast Vera a sidelong glance.

"Heard and understood, Doctor," she said.

"When I say *turn them away...*" Dr. Peachey's words were interrupted by a sharp *ping* as something struck the ground near Vera's feet. At first she thought it might have been a raindrop or a hailstone, something benign dropping from the clouds. Then she saw the chunk of tarmac go flying.

Not raindrops. Bullets.

They're shooting at us.

"Get down!" Vera screamed.

A few dozen feet away from her, one of the soldiers cried out as a bullet tore through the top of her shoulder, only to exit below her right shoulder blade a fraction of a second later.

Good thing it was her right, Vera thought dully. *She might live.* Her medical training should have had her scurrying toward the other woman, but instead she lifted her ThunderGen to her shoulder and took aim.

"What the hell?" Estes exclaimed. He'd already dropped to his belly and rolled under the truck. "What are they doing?"

"Trying to kill us!" Len called from beneath the reinforced canopy of the truck. "They can see we're not Clankers, Estes. This is entirely intentional."

The lowest helicopter was dead center in Vera's scope. Her finger twitched on the trigger.

It always surprised her how quiet the weapon was, and how little kickback it had to it, all things considered. Whoever had designed the recoil on these things must have come up with a pretty clever mechanism. Vera fell back half a step.

At almost the same time, the helicopter was blasted upward. The metal frame of its cockpit buckled under the force of the blast, and only some clever maneuvering by the pilot of the next closest machine kept the two aircraft from colliding. Vera let out a hiss of triumph.

Her shot had more than one consequence, however. As the first pilot struggled to regain control of the vessel, the other two had clearly determined that Vera was the biggest threat. Bullets rained around her, and she had to drop to her belly and roll under the truck with Estes to avoid getting shot.

Estes thumped his fist against the tarmac. "They've gotta have some sort of machine gun on board. How is it so damn quiet?"

"Smart, though," Vera observed. "The Clankers rely so much on sound... imagine how much damage a sniper could do with a weapon like that if they were on *our* side."

"I can see for myself." Estes nodded to the road, where three of their people lay on the tarmac. Vera's stomach clenched. Every death on this excursion would be *her* fault, *her* burden. She was the one who'd talked people into coming.

First, do no harm...

It felt like a hundred lifetimes since she'd taken that oath.

Above them, something hissed. "Look out, folks!" Klarie's voice called from the depths of a black plume of smoke. Two canisters bounced off the ground and rolled away, one in either direction. Within seconds, Vera couldn't see the helicopters overhead.

Which meant that they couldn't see what was happening down here, either.

"Anyone with a weapon, let's move now," Vera called into the smog. "Head to the periphery of the smoke. I want those helicopters *down*. If this is the kind of greeting we're going to get, we don't want their home base to know our location. Understood? *All right, move!*" She slid forward, pulling herself out from under the truck before she stood. She had to guess where everything was based on her memory of the landscape. Somehow, she managed to avoid knocking her head against the underside of the truck. She dipped sideways to follow the line of the truck and almost collided with another person.

"Sorry!" Emma Jean's voice was faint and distressed. "I'm a bit turned around."

Vera didn't bother responding to her. Instead, she kept moving, with the ThunderGen clenched in both hands. Her mind churned as her feet pounded the pavement. *The blast was strong enough to dent the helicopter. If you aim for the tail, you might be able to bring it down.* Her conscience twinged at the idea of killing the passengers, but not enough to stop her.

By the time she reached the edge of the smoke, she could feel the thrum of the engines in her chest, humming through her blood. There was relief in adrenaline, she found. When she was on edge, she could almost forget how hopeless she'd felt since Johnson's death.

Vera hovered at the edges of the smokescreen, tracking the helicopters as they descended. Evidently, they had stopped firing when the caravan was blacked out. *Probably conserving ammo, like us.* The two undamaged machines were closest. They were so low that their propellers sent the smoke spinning around in little vortexes. Vera's heart leapt to her throat. Forget the tail.

Vera lifted the ThunderGen to her shoulder and took aim at the rotor.

This time, when the gun went off, Vera was thrown to the ground—not by the recoil, but by the rush of wind as the whole rotor was blown backwards, sending the body of the helicopter on a mad descent toward the road. It crashed into the overpass and crumpled before bursting into flames.

"Yeah!" Vera howled. "Take that!" Lying on her back, she fired another shot at its companion, but the other helicopter was already rising toward its damaged counterpart, turning back the way it had come. She missed, and the recoil sent her shoulder and head slamming into the road. Stars danced in her vision.

Before she could get back to her feet, a figure emerged from the smog with what looked like a sword gripped in both hands. It uttered a terrible cry and swung the sword like a baseball bat. A long, rippling arc of blue lightning leapt from the figure toward the rising helicopter. Vera could *feel* the engine die as the aircraft's rotors stopped spinning and the engine stuttered, shorted out by the current. It dropped like a stone on the far side of the divided highway and sent shrapnel scattering in every direction, blown outward from the gout of flame that accompanied the impact.

"Good *God*." Vera struggled to sit up, gaping at the wreckage that littered the road.

Above her, Emma Jean Johnson lifted the lightning rod again, but the last helicopter was too far away. When she swung the rod a second time, the current fizzled out, filling the air with static long before it could hit home.

"Sorry," Emma Jean said vaguely. Her eyes were still somewhat vacant as she lowered her weapon and reached down to take Vera's hand. Her teal-framed glasses were askew, and her pale blonde hair floated around her head in a staticky halo. "If I'd moved faster, I might have been more useful. I'm always too *slow*." Her hand closed over Vera's with surprising strength.

"I appreciate the help," Vera said, although she still didn't entirely trust Pammy's mother. There was no denying that she'd been useful, however. *Can't afford to pick and choose our allies these days, can we?*

The smoke was dissipating now, and Vera could get a better sense of the damage the helicopters had done. Peachey was already bending over one of the injured members of the convoy, and Len was crouched beside the truck with the dogs at his side. Above them, the last of the aircraft was just a distant speck against the sky.

She wished she could have brought it down. It rankled to know that there were more enemies out there, waiting for the chance to take their pound of flesh.

At last, her medical training kicked in, and Vera hurried to the side of the woman she'd seen fall. She was bleeding heavily, but when Vera touched her shoulder, she opened her eyes.

"I can't move my arm," the woman said, sounding almost puzzled.

"Breathe for me." Vera laid her head against the woman's chest. From what she could tell, the bullet had missed the woman's lungs. She might get lucky for now.

Yeah, and what happens when the other pilot comes back with friends?

"I'll be right back," Vera said. "Emma Jean will stay with you. I'm just going to get some supplies from the truck." She stood up and jogged over toward where Len was kneeling.

"Bad news," he said. "They managed to hit one of the tires."

"Seriously?" Vera paused to examine the deflated rubber. "Do we have backups?"

"Yeah." Len gestured to the sky. "But it's getting late. By the time we get the tire changed out, we'll need to start looking for cover. And there's no sign of Pammy and the others."

Deimos sniffed at Vera's hand, and she patted the bloodhound's head absently. "Always something, huh?" She tossed the ThunderGen into the back of the truck and grabbed a medical kit instead. "Fine. Change the tire, and then we'll look for a place to make camp tonight. If Pammy and the others are still AWOL, we'll have to go without them for now." One day in, and their plan was already going to hell. They needed help, and instead, they only seemed to find more enemies.

She jumped when a hand landed on one shoulder. "You're doing just fine," Len told her. "None of this is your fault. We'll regroup, and the next time we see helicopters, we'll know to arm ourselves."

"Yeah," Vera muttered. "And then some new problem will crop up that none of us know how to deal with."

"Like that?" Len gestured toward the woods at the side of the highway.

Vera turned to see where Len was pointing, and her heart

stuttered. Masses of skittering shadows boiled over from the treeline.

"Yeah," she rasped. "Like that."

9

COOPER

COOPER WAS BEGINNING to suspect that he was losing his mind.

Pammy was already nuts, and the rest of them were fraying at the edges, but he wasn't quite sure how to quantify himself. He didn't *feel* crazy. His mental health in high school had taken a turn for the worse, and he'd been more than a little alcohol dependent that last year in Little Creek, but this felt different. He was spinning out. Probably just hallucinating.

For whatever reason, he was starting to think he could understand Clanker.

The Keystone Hive stood still around him and Guppie, forming a fortress of their own bodies around the two humans in their midst. He didn't think for a second that the Clankers were fooled by his attempt to recreate a likeness of them, but they seemed to have accepted the two men, much as they had accepted Pammy Mae.

Unless he was very much mistaken, one of the Parkton Hive aliens stopped beside their group and made a curious, hungry noise in Cooper's direction.

And he must have been imagining things when he thought that one of the Keystone Hive aliens replied, *Ours*.

"You hear that?" Guppie asked.

Cooper turned toward his friend. "You hear it too?"

Instead of staring at the Clankers, however, Guppie's face was turned skyward. He was squinting at something a long way off, but the canopy only allowed them glimpses of the cloudy heavens.

Pammy stood at the edge of their group, watching as the Clankers went about their business. After a long moment, she turned to the two men.

"We should go back and tell Vera to find someplace to wait until tomorrow. In Parkton, maybe. Not here." She shot a suspicious glare back toward the burrow where the King of Parkton had retreated.

"Don't trust the local hive, huh?" Cooper asked.

"Don't fully trust any of them." Guppie leaned over to spit on the ground.

Pammy leaned against one of the Keystone Clankers for a moment before pulling herself up onto its back. She looked as though she might collapse at any moment. "Let's just go. Tomorrow, we can—"

An echoing *boom* resounded through the trees, and Cooper flinched. "Sounds like one of the ThunderGens."

"I agree." Guppie's hands flew across the controls, and soon his Jackal was bounding between the trees with all the grace of a drunken grizzly bear. Cooper had been able to repair the base machines, but they'd never been particularly elegant. He urged his own mount toward a run, too.

The Keystone Clankers overtook him in a matter of seconds, with their armored bodies rippling around him as they swarmed back toward the highway. Being around the aliens when they were like this always left Cooper nervous, but even that sensation had dulled with time. He didn't think about Nate so much anymore. It wasn't as though he'd *forgiven* them for everything they'd done, but hating a whole alien race for what they had done to his hometown would have been as exhausting as hating humanity for what Johnson had done at Keystone.

This time, he was too distracted to be afraid. All around him, with every movement, he swore he could hear the Clankers whispering to one another, communicating in the subtlest brush of leg against tymbal, indicating their next move, their next step, their next plan.

You've spent too much time with Pammy, he told himself. *You don't understand them, you're just picking up on their phys-ical cues like she used to do back in Little Creek. After every-thing we've been through, it would be reasonable to crack just the tiniest bit... Right?*

All thoughts of the alien language were driven out of his head as an earth-shaking boom radiated from the direction of the highway. The alien swarm pulled up short, but Guppie didn't stop, and Cooper had no intention of being left behind. The two men rode on as the sounds of battle intensified.

It was a final deafening collision, followed by absolute still-ness. Cooper's heart hammered against his ribcage as he tried to imagine what they would find when the trees yielded to the traffic corridor.

To his immense relief, they emerged near the overpass to find the convoy largely intact. A few injured soldiers were being gathered up onto the trucks, and Estes and Len were in the middle of changing a tire. In Cooper's experience, most folks didn't bother with tires if things were that bad.

Guppie made a beeline for the vehicles on his mechanical mount, but Cooper was more interested in the helicopters that had crashed along the highway. One of them was blown to pieces, but the one alongside the overpass was partially intact. There was, at least, enough undamaged cockpit to make him wonder what else might have survived. He rode his Jackal over to investigate.

Cooper slid off the back and padded over to the downed chopper. On closer inspection, the cockpit wasn't as intact as he'd assumed; the interior had been burned out. The smell of pulled pork and burning hair confused him for a second, until he saw the remains of the two crew members inside. They were almost unrecognizable as people. He grimaced and pulled the neck of his shirt over his nose and mouth before averting his eyes and turning toward the back of the chopper.

What little experience Cooper had with planes evidently wasn't going to carry over. He could *recognize* the engine, but he wasn't sure exactly how it worked, much less what he'd be able to do with it.

I should have gone to a VoTech, he thought, and then wondered where that idea had come from. It was a little late to be worrying about what he should have done before the world went to shit. There were a lot of things he'd have done differently if he'd realized that the clock was running out.

Is that true, though? Time is always against you. How many experiences did you let slip by just because you were afraid of getting them wrong? The first time you were really brave was when you asked Kat to that stupid meteor-watching party, and look how that turned out.

"Salvage?" someone asked behind him.

"Yeah, that's what I was thinking." Cooper shook himself back into the present. "I'm not sure I can use any of this, though. If we were back in Keystone, with the workshop, maybe I—"

He turned around to see who had approached, and trailed off. He'd expected one of the soldiers from the caravan to have come up behind him, but instead he found himself facing a Clanker. It was watching him curiously, standing perfectly still against the side of the chopper, its forelimbs folded down in an attitude of rest.

"Hello?" he called, hoping that a human voice would answer him.

None did. It was only him and the alien. The alien he could have sworn he just heard talking to him.

Cooper stared down at his grease-smudged palms. *We need at least one sane person in this party, or the campaign's doomed.*

THE TOWN of Parkton wasn't far, and there were still a few hours of daylight left. The convoy rolled into town well before dusk, and began a sweep of the buildings to see where they should settle for the night.

"I'm not even sure what we're looking for anymore," Vera admitted. "People? Clankers? Seems like anyone could be a threat these days."

Parkton was nicer than Little Creek. Wealthier, too, and closer to a major highway. From what Cooper could tell, that hadn't helped the residents survive.

"Did you find anyone yet?" he asked.

Vera shook her head. "Not that I was expecting to run into a lot of people. With a hive as large as the one you described set up just down the road? My expectations weren't high. Although I suppose it would have been easier for the residents to evacuate."

"Yeah." Cooper scuffed the toe of his boot against the tarmac as they walked. "And then what? Johnson was a dick, but at least he let people in. Sounds like most had orders to turn civilians away."

"I'd heard that."

"Vera?" Cooper came to a halt, and Vera doubled back to stand beside him. In the close quarters of Camp Keystone, they hadn't gotten many opportunities to talk frankly, and Cooper didn't want to be overheard. "I wanted to ask you something. Since we're kind of the, uh, optimists of the group, you know?"

Vera snorted and adjusted her grip on the ThunderGen she was carrying. "Are we, now?"

"Last I checked, yeah." Cooper bit his lip. "Well, we used to be. Pammy's falling apart, Len would self-destruct if it meant getting revenge, and Guppie's—well, I guess he's not doing too bad, all things considered. But back in Little Creek, we were the ones who planned for the future. For an *after*."

Vera stared down at her boots. Like Cooper, she'd grown leaner over the last few months. When she'd run the Little Creek Garden Center, she'd been a beacon of hope for him. She was proof that someone could thrive where they took root, even if they didn't quite fit. Cooper had never told her in so many words, but she'd always struck him as kind of a badass.

"I don't know," she said at last. "I guess we cross that bridge when we come to it?"

Cooper was tempted to push back, but one glance at her was enough to tell him that she was exhausted. "Sure," he said instead. "No point in wasting time on what-ifs when we've got choppers targeting us and a billion Clankers breathing down our necks."

"Vera?" Estes came jogging over. "We've finished the sweep. We haven't found anyone, but there's a church that's still standing. I figure we can hole up there for the night. There's plenty of room on the lawns to set up a three-hundred-and-sixty-degree watch."

"Great. If you can set up a watch rotation, I'll take point on handing out rations."

Estes jogged back to the caravan, while Vera wrapped one arm around Cooper's shoulder.

"Listen," she said in a much gentler voice. "If you have any ideas, I'd love to hear them. But we don't know what we're going to find in D.C., and I can only fight one war at a time, okay? You're the one who's good at building stuff. Maybe you'll be good at *rebuilding,* too." She patted his arm once before releasing him. "In the meantime, come get some dinner."

Cooper glanced back toward the caravan. "Actually, I think I'm gonna hang back for a minute, okay?"

"Just make sure you get some dinner." Vera lifted one arm in farewell as she followed Estes toward the church, where they were setting up camp.

Dusk was setting in. It occurred to Cooper that time, in the traditional sense, had lost all meaning. There was no schedule to keep, no hour of designated dinnertime. They were moving with the weather now, and the cycle of the seasons. It would have driven his dad up a wall. David Lutz had always been a real stickler for time.

Instead of heading toward the others, Cooper went in the other direction, wandering down a sloping, grassy hill for a bit of silence. It was a risk, he supposed, heading off on his own like that—but if the Parkton Hive decided to turn on Pammy, there would be no safety in numbers. If he was going to risk his life just by *existing,* he might as well have a moment to himself.

He was halfway down the slope before he realized that someone was calling him.

A Clanker was waiting in the tall grass. There hadn't been anyone around to mow for months, so the hillside had gone to seed. Some of the plants reached as high as Cooper's waist, but even so, he could see the alien long before he finished his descent.

He stopped in his tracks and glared at the dark figure, a patch of night that gleamed brilliantly black in the twilight. "What do you want?" he demanded. Unless he was very much mistaken, it was the same Clanker from earlier, the one who'd approached him outside of the helicopter.

The alien didn't move except to hum. Cooper couldn't make out any words this time, but the beast didn't move as he skidded through the dewy grass down to its level.

"Just tell me what you want," Cooper said. "You're freaking me out. Are you stalking me, or am I just losing my shit?"

The Clanker extended its forelimbs, and he realized that it held something pinched between them. An offering. He had to take a few more steps forward before he recognized what it was: a single cell of royal jelly, taken from the supplies that the Keystone Hive had carried with them when they set out that morning.

Cooper stared down at the offering. "What am I supposed to do with this?"

The Clanker shifted. "*Eat.*"

Cooper winced. "No, no, I'm not *talking* to you. This is insane."

Now that he thought about it, though, he'd been able to understand them for a while. Not their full language, not like Pammy could, but hadn't he been able to pick up on the broad meaning of their language even as they stormed the walls of the camp?

"Oh my God." Cooper bent forward, bracing his palms against his knees. "No, no, no, this isn't happening. I don't want to understand you. You bastards *ate my family.*" He let out a shuddering gasp as he remembered his last view of Nate before his brother was dragged through the roof of the Jeep.

"*Eat.*" The alien bobbed its mouth again, then held out the cell of jelly.

"Oh, screw you!" Cooper snatched the papery hexagon

out of the alien's grasp. "If this is what it takes to tell you to piss off, fine." He dug a finger into the jelly and raised it to his lips.

His first thought was that it tasted like the worst Jello cup in existence. As he tried to swallow it down, he revised his opinion; it was more like eating a handful of sweetened lard. He almost choked on the honeyed animal-fat taste of it before it finally slid down his throat.

"God, that's *awful*." He gagged and pressed his fist to his mouth, but for better or worse, it stayed down.

Now that he'd swallowed it, though, he could feel it shifting around in his belly. It made him feel strangely warm, like neat whiskey on an empty stomach.

"Are we good with this, like, hazing ritual or whatever?" He giggled and swayed on his feet. "Are you trying to poison me? 'Cuz this is kinda better than the crap I used to drink. I mean, tastes like shit, but it's..." He ran out of words and settled for giving the Clanker a thumbs-up.

The Clanker swayed back and forth before turning its back on him and scurrying off into the darkness.

"Hey, man, come back! Aren't we gonna talk now?" His own voice echoed back to him. When he tried to follow, he tripped over his own feet and went sprawling across the grass. He giggled again and rolled over on his back, staring up at the night sky. There were so many stars up there, more than he remembered there ever being before. When he closed his eyes, he could still see them, spread like glitter across the inside of his eyelids. He lay there for a while until the warm, drunk feeling turned into a dizzy spell and he had to close his eyes. Within moments, he was tumbling through the stars like a meteor charting a path between worlds.

Oh, he thought, *I get it. This is how it starts. It ends when we crash.*

And this is the only way to fight back.

10

CARLA

CARLA STOOD in front of the tank containing the *homoptera invadenda*. "How much longer?"

Nathan, who was keeping time, checked his watch. "Four more minutes. I dunno, are you guys sure about this? We could give it a little longer. Think this through..."

"We've been over this," Stew snapped. "The sooner we move, the more surprised they'll be. Dr. Sharma was pretty clear on her timing, and we know the routines. I'll bet you any damn thing you like that Greene'll be back right after shift change to dispose of us. So grow a spine, Nutty, and stop whining."

"Hey." Carla frowned at Stew and shook her head. "Not cool."

"Sorry." Stew pressed his palm to his knee, which bounced more erratically with each passing second. "I'm a little *tense* right now, for some reason."

"I'm just saying, this is suicide," Nathan said.

Stew raised one eyebrow. "It's one alien, Nutty, and we already have a plan for that."

"He's not talking about the alien," Carla said. "He's talking about Greene. The man who's already made it clear that he's done with us." She held out her hands. "We're already dead, as far as he's concerned. As I see it, this is our only chance to make it out in one piece—no matter how slim the odds."

Nathan pursed his lips. "Hmm. Fair enough. Fifty-seven seconds."

"You know what that sounds like to me?" Stew asked. "Sounds like close e-damn-nough."

"Sharma might need the next minute," Carla said. "Make a plan. Stick to it."

"Since when did you become the strategy gal?"

"Since you started getting twitchy."

Nathan stared down at his watch. "Twenty seconds."

"You ready to hit play?" Carla asked.

Stew held up the work tablet and swiped his finger across the screen. "Ready when you are, Bone."

Nathan's voice was barely a whisper. "Ten seconds."

Carla knelt before the terrarium controls and pressed her thumb to the release. The door of the lab was open. Sharma's twenty minutes were up.

Here goes nothing, she thought.

Nathan squeaked, "Now."

With one last deep breath, Carla punched the release.

As the reinforced cylinder rose, the alien stayed perfectly still. It must have used up so much of its energy in the early days that it was reluctant to expend any more until it was sure that it would be worthwhile.

Carla backed away toward the others, keeping her center of gravity low. Once the *invadenda* started moving, she didn't like her odds against it. She'd seen how badly it could batter the glass, and the video feed from the day of the invasion played through her mind on loop.

The alien shuddered and extended one leg over the edge of the podium where the glass had been.

"Ready," Carla muttered. "Set..."

The *invadenda* surged forward, rattling as it came, its long proboscis unfolding from beneath it even as its pointed legs skidded on the floor of the lab. Carla lifted her arms over her head instinctively, knowing full well how useless the gesture would be when that serrated mouth descended.

Stew hit play, and the speakers of the tablet let out a high, shrill alarm. It was the sound created from the message they'd intercepted, infinitely looped so that instead of a three-second shrill, the wail looped infinitely. The alien had hated the sound the first time they'd played it back, and evidently it hadn't warmed up to the noise in the meantime. The alien fell back and shuddered, almost losing its footing in its desperate attempt to get away. It retreated to the door of the lab and burst out into the hallway.

"See which way it went!" Stew called.

Nathan darted to the door and peered out before spinning back to tell them, "Left! It went left!"

Stew killed the sound and shoved the tablet into the over-sized pocket of his lab coat. "So we go right." The mad glint in his eye made Carla feel, just for a moment, that things had come back to the beginning. Their first attempt to flee from trouble all those years ago had started with one bad decision and an ill-planned and ill-fated escape attempt. It was fitting that it should end that way, too.

Carla only hoped that this try would be more successful than the last.

EVEN BEFORE THEY reached the main deck, the ship was in chaos. Most of their attention was aimed outward in an attempt to defend the ship from anyone who might attack. They weren't expecting an attack from within.

The three of them thundered over the metal, which echoed beneath their feet with every stride. Carla tried to ignore the cries from behind them. It wouldn't take long for someone to bring the alien down, but in the narrow corridors of the aircraft carrier, it might be able to do a fair bit of damage before the end, and hopefully it would buy them some time.

'Fair bit of damage.' That's one way to describe an other-worldly monster killing people. A monster you set loose on them. It was hard to feel that guilty about it, all things considered, after having seen the government stand back and watch the monsters ravage the world and barely lift a finger. Then again, she now believed that was more to do with a small group at the top, not the everyday soldiers around her. But that wasn't a distinction she could afford to make right now.

The old Carla would have felt guilt anyway. She wouldn't

have kept score, wouldn't have played tit-for-tat. Apparently, old Carla had died when the world went to hell.

They were nearing the top deck when two soldiers blocked their path.

"What's going on?" one of them asked.

Nathan ran one hand through his hair, using the other to point behind him. "Aliens! Loose in the ship! Not sure how many there are, but—"

"Oh shit," one soldier said, while his partner looked down at their lab coats and gasped.

"There really was one onboard?"

"Yes, and now it's loose!" Carla shouted. She ran forward, splitting the two soldiers and practically smashing her shoulder into one as she went.

"Hey," the closest one said, making a halfhearted attempt to grab her arm, but missing.

"Oh shit," his friend repeated, staring straight ahead.

Stew and Nathan followed Carla, and they left the soldiers standing dumbstruck in the corridor. The men didn't call after them, and Carla didn't look back.

They made their way up to the main deck, where Dr. Sharma waited with her husband and daughter. She held a rifle awkwardly, and handed it immediately to Stew. He wouldn't have been Carla's choice to be armed, but now wasn't the time for a discussion. Besides, Sharma's husband produced a second one and gave it to Carla.

"Is it still loose?" Sharma asked.

Stew shrugged and held the rifle close. "Let's not stick around and find out." Some of the other guards on duty had taken notice of their weapons and were already turning toward them. "We need to get *moving*."

Dr. Sharma's teenage daughter clung to her mother's arm. "What's the plan?" she asked in a shaking voice.

Stew had the look of a madman about him as he sprinted toward the helicopter landing pad on the far end of the deck. "We're done with the ocean," he said. "Time to fly, baby!"

11

GUPPIE

AFTER A FULL DAY of riding in a mechanical contraption, Guppie hurt like hell. While the rest of the caravan set up camp in and around the church in Parkton, Guppie struggled to extract himself from the leg braces that held him in place.

"Having trouble?"

Guppie looked up from his efforts to find Travis standing next to him. "I can handle it," he lied.

Travis grinned and tapped his finger to his chest, where Guppie had dug a bullet out of him a month ago. "I appreciate that, Mr. Martin, but I can still help. I owe you one, remember?"

Grudgingly, Guppie leaned back. "If you could just finish helping me with these latches, I got most of 'em. And, uh, I wouldn't mind if you wanted to lift me down."

"Where's your chair?" Travis asked.

Guppie felt the heat rise in his face. "In the truck. I forgot to grab it, I was just so damn ready to get out of this stupid thing."

He reached down to pat the side of the machine. "No offense, Chelly. I just hurt like hell."

Travis chuckled to himself and turned to call over his shoulder. "Hey, Klarie, mind helping out here? Mr. Martin left his chair somewhere."

"On it," the girl's voice said from somewhere to their right.

By the time Travis and Guppie had the buckles undone, Klarie was back and wheeling the chair with her. "Got you, gramps," she said with a cheeky grin.

"Have you been talking to Cooper?" Guppie demanded. "Kids these days. No respect."

"You got your panties in a twist the last time I called you Mr. Martin," Klarie pointed out.

"You don't like it?" Travis asked.

"Nah." Guppie allowed himself to be lifted down. "Makes me feel older and more useless than I already am." As much as he hated the chair, he sighed with relief. It was a lot more comfortable than the braces on the mech.

"Want me to wheel you inside?" Travis asked.

Guppie swatted his hands away. "I can wheel my own self, thank you very much. You're a good kid, though."

"Maybe if you stop calling us kids, you won't feel so old," Klarie said.

Estes jogged by and pointed at Travis. "You're on first watch. Ten minutes. Grab some supplies if you need 'em and take the two o'clock post."

"I can pick up some rations, for you if you want to get settled." Klarie rolled her eyes. "Estes says I'm too *young* to stand guard. I think he's forgotten which one of us started the uprising back in Keystone. I was the one that saved *his* butt."

"You mind grabbing two sets?" Guppie asked. "I'd like to watch with you, Travis, if you don't mind."

If Travis wondered what use an old man in a wheelchair was going to be, he was polite enough not to ask. Instead, he headed to his post, walking slowly enough that Guppie could keep pace.

"We've got to work on your arm strength," Travis said. He flexed and kissed his bicep. "Get you *swole*. You ever see Murderball? Those dudes were jacked."

Guppie chuckled. "My New Year's resolution was to keep the world from ending."

"Assuming there is a next year," Travis said casually.

"You Millennials are so jaded," Guppie scoffed.

Travis rolled his eyes. "Okay, Boomer."

Guppie tried to laugh. He'd felt normal for a second there. Of course that couldn't last.

"Hey." Travis stopped at his station and sank down against the wall of the church. "You know that there's nothing wrong with needing a chair, right? It's not the end of the world." He seemed to realize what he said before the words left his mouth, and he waved to the ruins of Parkton, with the burned-out houses and the overgrown yards. "Like, yes, *this* is the end of the world, but there's no shame in getting all busted up."

"I know. It's frustrating, though. Like being a baby, learning to walk all over again, except that I'm too old for this crap."

Klarie returned, passing each of them a water bottle and an

MRE from the pile she held in her arms. "Nobody's seen Cooper, so I'm going to go look for him. Have fun, guys." She saluted sarcastically as she backed away, then jogged off into the darkness.

The two men ate in silence for a while. MREs still tasted like trash, but for once Guppie wasn't feeling inclined to joke about it.

"What's got you all mopey?" Travis asked at last.

"That thing you said before. *Boomer.*"

Travis crinkled up the trash from his MRE and broke open the seal on his water bottle. "Seriously? Did I hurt your old-man ego?"

"Nah. It's just something my nieces used to say." Guppie set his unfinished meal in his lap.

"Aw, man." Even without asking, Travis seemed to understand that he was talking about people who were no longer around. That was one of the side effects of the invasion. People acknowledged loss without having to poke the old wounds too much. "You want to talk about it? 'Cuz we've all lost people, you know."

Guppie managed a half-smile. "It was from before the invasion. Plane crash. The older one, Francesca, would have been about Pammy's age. Klarie's age. Just makes me wish I could do more, you know?"

"You never said," Travis murmured.

"Never talked about it much. No point." Guppie crumbled a dry cracker between his fingers. "I tried to get over it, and people have lost so much, you know?"

Travis let his head rest against the wall of the church. "It's funny, but I kinda forgot that there used to be tragedies before all this. Private ones, that people who didn't know you well enough would never guess. Now we just assume that everyone's been through hell and back."

We should always have assumed that, Guppie thought. *Most of the time, we would have been right.*

One of the stars shifted above them, and Guppie flinched. He half-expected the sky to collapse again, the way it had when the Clankers first arrived, but the light didn't fall. It simply moved along a trajectory.

"Hey," Guppie said, pointing to the sky. "When was the last time you saw a satellite?"

But even as he said it, the trajectory shifted, and he knew immediately it was no satellite. There was only one thing it that could be.

"Son of a bitch," Travis muttered. *"Look out, people, we've got enemy at two o'clock!"*

His exclamation was followed with a sound like hail striking the wall behind them. Travis dropped to his belly, and Guppie didn't stop to think before he did the same. He hit the ground with a grunt before realizing he didn't have a weapon on him.

"What kind of bastards attack an encampment at night?" he demanded.

Travis lifted himself onto his elbows and snatched up his ThunderGen. "You know the answer to that one as well as me." He scrambled to his knees and fired a few shots at the clouds, almost at random.

There were more lights now, almost a dozen of them. *Where are they coming from?* Guppie wondered. *Do they really want us dead that badly?*

Estes' voice echoed off the church wall, and Travis took off running, leaving Guppie where he lay.

"Dammit," Guppie hissed into the grass, but not loud enough that Travis could hear. The kid had work to do. And if Guppie was going to stick around, he needed to be able to help himself.

He dragged himself back into his chair as the choppers descended, then turned toward Chelly and began to wheel himself forward.

Cooper had built him a custom weapon, after all. He was damn well going to use it.

12
LEN

LEN WAS HALF-ASLEEP under one of the church pews when he heard the screaming. Both dogs lifted their heads, and Phobos let out a *whuff!* of warning. Len opened his eye and lay perfectly still, listening. To his relief, most of the yelling sounded like orders being shouted, rather than cries of pain.

"What's happening?" someone asked from a few feet away. It was too dark to see who was talking, and Len had no intention of turning on a light and attracting unwanted attention from whoever was outside.

"I think we're under attack," he said. "Come on, boys. *Heel.*" He rolled out from under the bench and took his weapon with him. Other people were doing the same, and he heard the same questions being asked all throughout the building in a ripple of sound. The boom of ThunderGens and the steady thrum of engines was loud enough to reduce the words spoken around him to a mere blur.

He didn't wait around to find out the plan. There wasn't time. Instead, he ran for the street. When he reached the door, it wouldn't open, and he threw his weight against it. *Please tell me they didn't lock us in here,* he thought desperately, but on his second try it opened a crack, and he understood the problem. Wind. Or rather, air pressure caused by helicopters coming in at close range.

Len swallowed hard and glanced down at the dogs.

"Change of plans, boys!" He had to shout to make himself heard. "Sit. *Stay.*" Deimos obeyed, but Phobos whined and tried to paw at the door. Len grabbed him by the collar and tugged hard until the German shepherd finally sat. "*Stay,*" he said again.

For the first time since he'd trained Phobos, Len wasn't sure he would obey.

He threw his weight against the door and stumbled out into the midst of a firefight. The blast from the helicopter rotors was strong enough to push the door closed behind him before Phobos could make a break for it.

Not only were there a handful of helicopters hovering above the road, but black-clad soldiers in reflective helmets were already dropping onto the tarmac. All of the helos boasted brilliant floodlights that nearly blinded him when he glanced upward. These *were* larger helicopters, probably Black Hawks or something similar. Len watched as one of the soldiers fired on a Keystone private, hitting the man and dropping him like a stone. The shooter turned his gun toward Len.

Before the soldier could fire, a shadow moved behind him,

and someone sank a Ka-Bar blade into his spine, where the protective dome of the helmet met his body armor.

Len lifted the ThunderGen to his shoulder and fired on one of the choppers, blasting it back toward one of the trees that lined the street. Its rotor blades snagged in the thick branches. It spun out of control and crashed against the hillside.

One of the attacking soldiers grabbed Len from behind and flung him to the ground. "Where are the Buggers?" he bellowed. "We know you're with them."

Just for that, Len shot him point-blank in the nuts. With a high-pitched shriek, the guy was lifted off his feet and flung backward into one of his allies. The man he'd hit curled up into a ball, and his friend turned on him. Len was about to fire again when a black spear-tip emerged between his ribs, disfiguring his armor as it went.

Guppie had arrived.

"You okay, Len?" he called as he fiddled with the controls of the mech. A corresponding limb of his ride shuddered, and the soldier's body slid to the ground between them.

"Yeah." Len got to his feet and aimed the ThunderGen at the head of the soldier he'd already incapacitated. When he didn't see movement, he lowered it. "Yeah," he snarled, louder this time. "I'm doing *great*. I just love being attacked in the night by my own kind."

Guppie's mech had attracted more than its fair share of attention. More soldiers were headed toward them, evidently baffled by what they at first thought was an alien. To Len's surprise, they held their fire.

Johnson was told not to attack the alien forces, but the guy who went after me just now wanted to know where to find the hive. Are they looking for the aliens? Or for something else?

He had an ugly feeling that he knew what they were after, and that their *real* target was all too human.

"We gotta bring down as many of those helicopters as we can," he told Guppie.

He lifted one hand to keep the light of the nearest helicopter from blinding him. "You got it. *Giddyup, Chelly!*" He threw the mech into motion, charging at the side of the church. Soldiers scattered in an attempt to get out of his wake, and Len seized the moment of chaos to bolt down the road and try for a clear shot at another chopper. He'd only made it a few dozen yards when Guppie reached the top of the church spire and leapt through the air. His battle cry echoed down the road and only ended when, with a mighty clang, the two machines collided midair.

Len fired two more times before the thrum of the rotors was undercut by the rattle of Clanker-song. This time, when the floodlights reflected off a Clanker-shell, it wasn't a mech in the road, but the real thing. Dozens of the beasts swarmed over the carcasses of the ruined Parkton homes, whipping their long tongues at the helicopters overhead. One Clanker alone couldn't have brought them down, but they worked in fluid unison to orchestrate an attack. In less than a minute, all of the helicopters were dragged to ground-level and swarmed with frenzied aliens. One by one, the floodlights died, and the screams of soldiers were cut short. Len was left standing in the darkness, unable to make out a single thing.

His adrenaline kept pumping, but instead of fear, Len was

buoyed by manic delight. *That'll teach 'em,* he thought, *to try and shoot us in the back when we're not looking. That will teach them to underestimate us.*

One of the Clankers brushed past him without so much as stopping to sniff. The military might not be on their side, but the local hives were. They were no longer powerless.

Next time we meet, you won't be coming for us.

We'll be coming for you.

IT WAS dawn before the caravan was able to take stock of the damages. They'd lost another ten soldiers in the night, but most of the dead lying in the streets of Parkton weren't theirs. Deimos wandered around, sniffing each body experimentally, but Phobos stayed glued to Len's side.

The Clanker's reasons for helping clearly hadn't been altruistic. The dead from both sides had been split open and drained, but judging by the wounds on the corpses, none of the Keystone soldiers had been *killed* by aliens.

"Is it wrong that I almost don't care?" Estes asked, rubbing his forehead. "We'd have lost more if the Clankers hadn't come."

Len glanced over to where Guppie was being treated by Dr. Peachey. The veteran had taken a beating during his little stunt drive, but other than a few bruises sustained during the crash, he didn't seem much worse for wear. If anything, he looked a lot more cheerful than he had the day before.

"If I get killed, they can eat me," Len said absently. "I won't care at that point."

"Same here." Vera crossed her arms, a deflated expression on her face. *She needs to toughen up,* Len thought, *or she's going to fall apart the moment we need her most.*

"What I want to know," Vera went on, "is why they're so intent on killing us."

Peachey spoke up. "Whatever issues we had with orders coming from Washington, there were no orders to send out hunting parties like this. Of course, orders could have changed over the last two months, but that's a big waste of resources."

"You want to know what makes us special," Len said. "I think I have an idea, given that they must have known we were coming."

Vera bit her lip. "I'm not so sure. The helicopters we saw yesterday afternoon could have been a routine scouting mission. It might have been a coincidence."

"Hm." Len forced an ironic smile. "Maybe. But three choppers for one scouting path? That's a lot of resources to waste on the regular for a few months, unless our timing was just that bad."

Vera glanced at Estes, and the soldier shrugged. "I'm not following his logic, either."

"I'm just thinking about who came up with this plan," Len said. "Pammy was the one who decided we should attack the main nest. But do we really believe that Pammy Mae's the only one on Earth who's managed to make contact with the aliens? And here's another question for you." He met Vera's gaze, then Estes'. "If she can see into this all-powerful alien hivemind thing and use its own knowledge against it... what's to keep it from using her right back?"

Vera bit her lip. "Pammy said—"

"Does Pammy seem particularly stable to you right now?" Len demanded. His friends' expressions gave an answer as plain as any words. "That's what I thought. And I'm not saying that I'm right, but I do think we need to acknowledge that it's a possibility. It might be wise to proceed accordingly."

"What does that mean?" Vera asked. "That we start leaving her out of the loop? Treating her as hostile? I don't like it, Len. She's been with us from the beginning. She's one of the Little Creek Five." She dug her palms into her eyes.

"You don't have to like it," Len said. "But you *do* have to be smart. You're in charge of too many lives right now to value friendship more than facts."

"I know. And you're right." Vera lifted her head again. She was more tired than Len had ever seen her, and she appeared to be on the verge of tears. "She's managing the Clankers now, anyway. We can just... be careful what we tell her."

Estes nodded. "I doubt she'll notice. She's been in her own head a lot lately."

Vera shifted from one foot to the other. "I don't think we should tell the others, either," she blurted. "Put it in their heads, I mean. Guppie would hate the idea of shutting her out as much as I do, and Cooper's always been closer to her than the rest of us. He might let something slip. Accidentally, of course—"

Len put her hands on Vera's shoulders. She felt frail, like she might fall apart if he shook her. "I'm not accusing anyone of turning against us, okay? We're fighting a war against forces we don't fully understand. Let's hedge our bets where we can. It doesn't have to be some huge secret. We'll just play our cards a little closer to the vest."

Vera seemed comforted, and Len was glad that he'd kept one secret of his own. He wasn't convinced that Pammy had already betrayed them, but he could say with absolute certainty that if any of the Little Creek Five was going to turn against them, it would be the girl.

BEYOND WASHINGTON

Longyearbyen
Svalbard, Norway

Una had never intended to stay in Svalbard. It was a joke that she'd come at all, if she was being completely honest. When she had first filed for divorce eight months ago, she and her girl-friends had joked that she should quite literally freeze out her ex. Besides, she hadn't needed a visa to visit, and there had been a kind of symmetry to a northward migration. She and Claud had gone to the Mediterranean on their honeymoon, back when she was young and naive and believed he would never cheat on her.

The world had changed a lot since then, and Una had changed with it. She had loved the idea of endless sun on the ice, and found it strangely charming that rifles had been deemed mandatory in case of polar bear attacks. *Polar bear attacks.* Who would have thought? Claud would have hated it there. He despised the cold; in fact, he avoided personal discomfort of any kind, and the idea of being mauled by a bear would have made his skin crawl. All the more reason to buy a ticket northward and celebrate the fact that she was legally free of him.

These days, Una would have paid money to be attacked by a polar bear. They could use the meat.

She adjusted her visor and stared out over the Longyear Valley. The days were still impossibly long, and even now the temperatures rarely rose above freezing. She could only imagine what life would be like as the midnight sun gave way to endless night. At least the permafrost kept the aliens at bay, for the most part.

A rustling behind her made Una jump, but it was only Barry climbing over the edge of the roof.

"You're early," she told him.

"Yeah." Barry dropped down beside her. She and the American were on the same rotation. At first, she'd kept her distance from him, but the Minnesotan was aggressively friendly. It was easier to tolerate him than to keep putting him off, and he'd gradually worn her down.

She knew him well enough by now to guess what brought him around before the start of a shift. "What did you get this time?"

"Shot a couple reindeer this morning. I traded one to the folks at Karlsberger." Barry nudged her with his elbow. "Guess what I got?"

"Another of your fifty-year-old whiskeys," Una said drily. Barry was nothing if not predictable, and the local pub was known for having one of the finest whiskey collections in the world. Probably the finest, by now, since the rest of the world had apparently gone up in flames.

"Nah, even better." Barry tugged a bottle from inside his jacket and held it out to her. "Ichiro's Ace of Spades. Do you have any idea how much this stuff was worth?"

"Spare me the details. Is it any good?"

Barry hugged the bottle to his chest. "How *dare* you? *Any good?* This is a once-in-a-lifetime opportunity!"

"Yes, because our time is short," Una told him. "Everything is once-in-a-lifetime now."

"All the more reason to *carpe* the *diem,* dontcha know?" Barry opened the bottle and held up to his nose, taking a deep breath. "Ooh, would you get a whiff of that aroma! Apple, mint, maybe a bit-a bergamot..." He held the bottle out to tantalize her.

As always, Una gave in, unable to resist the pull of his enthusiasm. She coughed. "Smells like liquor."

"You're a monster," Barry said, as though they hadn't seen real monsters with their own eyes. He sniffed again before taking a draught of the amber liquid. After a long moment, he swallowed and let out a dreamy sigh. "Thick. Sweet. Yup, yup, citrus. A bit of, hmm, maybe anise? Lordy, that's good."

"Would you admit if it was bad?" she asked.

Barry clicked his tongue at her. "What's the point of surviving at all if you don't take joy where you can find it?"

Una groaned. "Next you'll be saying *Live, Laugh, Love.*"

Barry chuckled. "Not quite. I'm just saying, Una, I got a plan. I'm gonna live long enough to try all my bucket-list whiskeys before the long night sets in, 'cuz once that happens, I'm done for. I don't mind the cold, but I hate the dark. That's what keeps me going, and this?" He held up the bottle so that the contents sparkled in the icy sun. "This right here is one of the finest damn malts on Earth. I'm living the dream, baby. You sure you don't want a snort?"

"You'd waste the king of liquors on an ingrate like me?" She couldn't stop herself from smiling.

"Sharing is caring," he told her.

"Give it here." She took the bottle from him and downed a sip, letting the spicy liquor settle on her tongue. Una had never understood Barry's rambling descriptions of the drinks. To her, it all tasted like fire, but at least this one was a *smooth* fire.

"Whaddya think?" Barry asked.

She swallowed. "Tastes like whiskey."

"Good Lord, you know how to hurt a guy." He took the bottle back and helped himself to another sip. "What about you, Una? What gets you up in the morning?"

She snorted and hugged her rifle closer to her chest. "My ex-husband used to tell me that I couldn't survive without him. That I needed him."

"Hard to picture you needing anyone," Barry said.

A movement in the corner of Una's eye brought her to her feet. She stared out across the barren plains of permafrost. It had risen above freezing, and there were gaps in the blinding snow that made it harder to tell what she was seeing. Another reindeer, perhaps?

Then the creature moved again, and she saw that it was one of the nuckelavee.

"Is that what I think it is?" Barry capped his bottle and set it aside, scrambling to his feet beside her.

"You see him?" Una had already lifted her gun to her shoulder.

"Yeah I do. Shoot 'im!" Barry fidgeted with his own rifle. "Or I can do it..."

"I'm the better shot," Una told him. "Patience. I only see the one."

Back when the radios were still working, their contacts farther south had told them that the nuckelavee needed fresh water sources to breed. They didn't take well to the cold, either. After the first few days, Longyearbyen had been largely untouched by the invasion.

"Whaddaya think brings the sucker up here?" Barry whispered.

Una kept her scope fixed on the solitary nuckelavee as it traipsed across the plain. "Hunger," she said. "They've gone through their food supply down south."

Barry gulped. "Callin' people *the food supply* is mighty unchristian of you."

"I used to think my husband, Claud, was obsessed with women," Una said. The alien stopped for a moment, but it was still a little out of range. No point in startling it or wasting the ammo. It would come close soon enough. "But then I realized he was only interested in what we gave him. He didn't care about me. He was chasing a feeling. He wanted that feeling of *fullness*, or *satisfaction*. He wanted release. I'm used to feeling like a piece of meat, Barry. And you know what's funny?"

"I'm afraid to ask," he said.

"Claud stayed down south with his pretty new girlfriend. So who's the piece of meat now?" She let out a bark of laughter and fired three precision shots just as the nuckelavee came in range. Its dark blood spattered the barren earth, and it collapsed in a heap where it stood.

"Christ on a cracker." Barry scratched his head through his hat. "You're a little terrifying."

"I'll take the compliment." She held out her hand. "Give me another sip of your what's-it-called."

"Ace of Spades," Barry said as he passed the bottle her way.

The second sip left her warm and buzzing, and Una helped herself to a third. "You're right," she said. "Bergamot. Maybe a hint of leather."

Barry laughed. "I knew there was a whiskey-drinker in there somewhere."

"You want to know what keeps me going?" She hooked her thumb toward the hill above the airport. "That does."

"The planes?"

"The seed vault. See, I figure those things are more like Claud than not. When his luck ran out with one woman, he moved onto another. The nuckelavee are going to get hungry, and then they're going to leave as quick as they came, and I'm still going to be here. He couldn't stop me from taking my life back, and these bastards won't, either. I'm going to plan for that future, and when they're gone, I'm going to start over. It isn't as hard as it sounds."

Barry held his hands above his head and hooted. "Preach, Una!"

She offered him a thin smile. "Shift change, Barry. Stay sober enough to shoot... and thanks for the whiskey. Let me know when you get a new bottle."

She climbed down to ground level and headed toward her quarters. It was amazing how much a person's perspective could change in the span of a year. Asking Claud for a divorce had felt like the end of the world. Now she'd experience the real thing, and she'd survived both.

Coming to Svalbard had been the best decision of her life.

13

COOPER

COOPER WOKE to the worst headache of his life. Someone was shaking his shoulder, and each jostle made his stomach lurch.

"Stoppit," he groaned.

Above him, Klarie's face swam into view. "I thought you were dead," she said. "What happened? Did you get shot last night?"

"Shot?" Cooper rubbed his throbbing temples. "When?"

"Uh, during the attack?" Klarie squinted at him. "Cooper, your eyes are messed up. Are you drunk or what?"

"I'm—" A piece of that papery casing fluttered in the grass beside him, and Cooper's stomach jolted. The memory of the night before came back in a rush. He rolled over and gagged against the grass.

"Coop?" Klarie rubbed his back. "It's okay, I'm here.

Dammit, where did you even get booze? You could have shared, you know—"

"Not drunk. My head..." he groaned. He was *not* going to be sick, he told himself. For one thing, that jelly crap would taste so much worse coming up. For another, he *wanted* to be able to understand the Clankers. It would be good, wouldn't it, for another one of them to be able to at least comprehend what the aliens were saying?

Klarie's breathing hitched. "Oh my God, are you concussed? Should I get Vera or Dr. Peachey?"

"No." Cooper sat up and waved her away. "Can you, uh, get me some water maybe?"

"Of course. Wait here." She hurried away, and Cooper sat balled up in the grass with his head on his knees. He'd been dimly aware of something going on around him the night before, but whatever his senses had gleaned from the real world had blended with his dreams until he couldn't tell one from the other.

Klarie returned with a bottle, buzzing with news about the attack. Cooper listened and let her draw her own conclusions about what had happened to him the night before. He couldn't fully explain it yet, so he held his peace.

And besides, he was reluctant to confess to Pammy what had happened. Ever since she'd cut a deal with the King of Parkton the day before, he'd wondered about the details of their conversation. It hadn't felt right, even if he hadn't been able to follow the conversation.

If she didn't know that he could understand her better now,

she wouldn't be able to stop him from overhearing the next time she made a pact.

IT STARTED DRIZZLING before they finished breaking camp. There was a chill in the air, and Cooper hadn't modified the Jackals to run in wet weather. The mechanisms could obviously handle it, but their riders would be exposed to the elements unless they spent the whole time hunched over under the back shield, or riding upside-down between the robot's legs. Guppie had begrudgingly accepted a nudge to ride in the transport. Len and Klarie had as well, even though they wanted to take the Cessna up to try and scout ahead. But they needed to conserve the plane's fuel, especially considering the elements.

"Are you going to ride your mechanical critter in this weather?" Vera asked.

Cooper lifted on shoulder. "Might as well. The only covered truck is going to be full, so I'm getting wet either way."

Vera accepted his explanation, leaving Cooper with a guilty knot in the pit of his stomach. He wasn't *lying*, exactly, but he had other reasons for wanting to ride with the Clankers. He just wasn't ready to explain them yet.

The general mood of the caravan was one of grim determination. Knowing that they could be attacked at any time by any*one* left the human contingent in a sour mood. They followed the highway back out to where the choppers had come down, only to have the mood shift again when they found the Parkton Hive waiting for them.

"Goddamn," Cooper breathed. There were a lot more of

them than he'd expected, including the King himself. Pammy rode one of the other monsters. She didn't look like she'd slept.

He could imagine why. There was a cockiness to the members of the Parkton Hive that set his teeth on edge. He'd sensed it the day before, but today it was far more obvious. Today, he couldn't just feel it. He could *hear* it.

Evidently, eating the royal jelly had worked. He could understand more of the Clanker-song than before, but there were so many voices all around him, it was like being at the fairgrounds on a 4H weekend, or standing at the dead center of a crowded Pittsburgh club. It was impossible to pick out any one conversation among the din.

There was a common theme, however.

Hunger.

The song must have carried, because although Pammy never broke off from the main army, Clankers continued to join them as they went. As they followed 83 southeast, a steady stream of aliens found their way to the main procession via cross-streets and on-ramps.

They left Leesburg behind well before noon. A few times, Cooper saw Len's biplane pass overhead to signal a route change so that the army could avoid barriers and blockages. When they passed over one of the many Potomac River tributaries, hundreds more joined them, all singing that same hungry song.

Cooper didn't need to speak Clanker to sense the shift in power. Pammy was at the head of the group, riding alongside the other Kings and Queens who had joined them.

If she thinks she's still the one in charge here, she's a fool.

And even if she can bargain enough to keep the other royalty in line, what happens when the hivemind realizes it's under attack? They go right back to being our enemies again.

Eating the jelly had given him exactly enough insight to recognize that humans and Clankers working together was the only way either species would have a future on Earth.

Whether long-term cooperation was possible was another matter entirely.

14

GUPPIE

THE CLOSER THEY'D gotten to D.C., the denser the houses had become. Guppie had never felt comfortable in cities at the best of times, but as they ventured toward the heart of the capital, it hit him all over again how dire things had become. The entire population of Heartland County wouldn't have been enough to fill one of the neighborhoods, and now they were utterly abandoned.

"How are you holding up?" Vera asked.

Guppie tried not to scratch at the bandages Peachey had applied in the night. Taking out that chopper had given him a momentary high, but he was paying for it now. The impact had been powerful enough to drive the rough spots on his braces right through the skin. He'd done something to his neck, too, and he couldn't turn his head all the way. "I hate being old."

"It's better than the alternative. Be careful what you wish for."

Both of the dogs were lying tight against Guppie's side, and Phobos started to growl without lifting his head. They'd been getting more and more skittish as the Clanker army swelled, and Deimos kept nudging Guppie's elbow in an attempt to garner comforting chin-scratches.

They were only a few blocks into Shepherd Park when the truck stopped short. Outside, the Clankers fell still as well. A moment later, Peachey's face appeared around the back of the truck.

"Um, Vera?" He shoved his glasses up his nose. "You're gonna want to see this."

Vera got up and jumped out of the truck bed. From where he sat, Guppie watched as her eyes widened.

"What's going on?" Guppie demanded. "Is there another attack?"

Vera shook her head and pointed to the roof of a nearby building. It took some maneuvering for Guppie to get an angle that allowed him to see what was going on. Three people stood on the roof of a building far above the street. One of them was waving a large white flag, while the other two squinted down at the army that filled the street. The Clankers shifted uneasily, but Pammy was playing something on that little instrument of hers, so they didn't attack.

"You think they want to negotiate?" Estes asked. Judging by his posture, he wasn't thrilled with the prospect.

"Only one way to find out," Guppie said.

"Hold on." Estes scowled at him. "We've just been attacked *twice* without precedent. You want to stroll up to some strangers and cut a deal?"

The three figures were dressed in ragged clothes, most of which looked as though they'd been scavenged from the streets.

Guppie turned to Vera and spread his hands wide. "Look, I know we've had problems when we've trusted people, but they don't look like military folks. They look more like... well, like us. Back when we were in Little Creek, just trying to stay alive. I say we hear 'em out."

Vera's smile was somewhat bemused. "And Cooper thinks *I'm* the optimist."

"We can't just go in shooting every time we meet a new group of survivors, Vera. At some point, we're going to have to extend a little trust."

Vera's gaze bounced between him and Estes. "Don't look at me. I'm not going up there, but I'm not going to stop you, either."

When Vera continued to hesitate, Guppie reached for her hand. "Send me," he said. "If you have to think that hard about it, I'll go. I'd rather find out that they're the kind of people who'd shoot an old man in a wheelchair than tell Pammy to set the Clankers loose on 'em and never know if we did the right thing. Johnson was paranoid in the end, Vera. He saw enemies everywhere. We can't be like him. We *can't*, dammit. We have to make the choice to be better."

"Fair enough." She squeezed his fingers. "But I'm going with you."

Estes scowled. "You sure about this?"

Vera nodded. "We let Pammy run off to parlay with the local Clankers, and she's the only one who can do that. I'm replaceable. As of right now, Estes, I'm leaving you in charge."

"Vera—" he began.

Vera squeezed Guppie's hand again before reaching for his wheelchair. "I'm sure about this, Estes. Besides, you're a better soldier than I'll ever be."

When Guppie was settled in his chair with a ThunderGen in his lap, Vera pushed him forward. The dogs followed, shrinking away from the Clankers at every opportunity, but unwilling to stay behind.

"I'm not coddling you," Vera whispered. "I figure it's better if they underestimate us, don't you?"

"Three strangers with little guns against the two of us and the dogs?" Guppie scoffed. "Please. We could take 'em with our eyes closed." He caught Pammy's eye as they rolled past, and she nodded to him in acknowledgement.

"They could try to take us hostage," Vera pointed out.

He twisted in his seat to pat her hand where it rested on the handle. "Good thing we're both replaceable, I guess."

Cooper rode his Jackal over to them as they approached the base of the building. "Do we have a plan?" he asked.

Guppie shook his head. "We're flying by the seat of our pants."

"The usual strategy, then."

The Clankers pulled back to make room for them, and the three of them stopped on the sidewalk below the building.

"Hello!" Vera called up.

A shaggy head appeared over the edge of the building. The guy who looked down at them was wearing a battered hoodie over a pale ribbed tank that was now more gray than white. The rain had let up, but he'd obviously been outside for a while; the hoodie clung to his skinny frame. There were black stains on it that were almost certainly dried blood, although Guppie wasn't sure if it was human or Clanker.

"Hey there." The man crouched at the edge of the building and lifted one hand in greeting. "Nice little army you got there. Are you lot with the floating fortress?"

"Never heard of it." Vera squinted up at the man above them. "You wouldn't happen to be with the folks who've been sending helicopters after us, would you?"

"Helicopters?" The man snorted. "Hell, no. Although, this..." He waved toward the mass of Clankers. "This is new. Can't say we've seen anything like this before. If you folks aren't Army, who are you?"

Vera hesitated, and Guppie cut in, "We're survivors. I'm Guppie Martin, this here is Vera Khan, and the kid is—"

"Vera Khan?" The man cocked his head. "Holy shit. No way. Are you folks from some raggedy-ass little town in West Virginia?"

Cooper leaned back in the saddle on his Jackal. "Couldn't have put it better myself, sir. How do you know about Little Creek?"

The man was still staring down at Vera in bewilderment. "Hold on a minute." He stood up and disappeared again, presumably conferring with his companions.

Cooper swung his head around to stare at Vera. "Holy crap. Your family's from D.C., right? You think there's any chance they're here?"

Vera kept staring skyward, although her jaw had gone a little slack and she didn't appear to be focused on much of anything. "I suppose it's *possible*," she murmured. "But someone would have had to warn them what was coming, unless they got incredibly lucky. It's not like we have any connection to the military. They ran a neighborhood bookstore, for heaven's sake."

Deimos whined and wagged his tail, nudging Guppie again.

"You're a good boy," Guppie muttered as he scratched the dog's floppy brown ears. Vera had been right when she'd called him an optimist. At the moment, it was taking all of his willpower to stay optimistic about whatever was going on above them. He wasn't, for example, feeling jealous that Vera might have people waiting for her in the city. He also wasn't worrying about the last family reunion that had almost gotten them all killed. Either of those thoughts would have been pessimistic and selfish, and even if Guppie wasn't always feeling himself these days, he was still smart enough to know that Vera deserved every ounce of happiness she could get. They all did, and he hoped like all hell there was a little spark of joy awaiting her in the carcass of the capital.

The man's face reappeared. "We're not sure what to think, and the walkie's on the fritz. You mind coming with me? Just you, mind. Your, uh, army stays here."

Cooper raised his eyebrows. "Smells like a trap, don't you think?" he asked in a low voice.

"Maybe," Vera admitted. "But he definitely recognized my name."

"Or figuring we were from a shitty town in West Virginia was a lucky guess. *Or* he was thinking of Keystone, and he knows something about Johnson." Cooper pulled a face. "Okay, I can tell that you're not listening to me."

"I have to go with him," Vera insisted. "I have to know." For the first time in a long time there was fire in her eyes, and her enthusiasm loosened an unnamed tension in Guppie's chest. He'd been worried that the old Vera was gone for good.

"We'll come with you," Guppie called up, "if you'll take both of us. And the dogs. Everyone else stays."

The man on the building gave a lazy two-fingered salute. "You got it. I'll meet you back in the alley. Anyone else comes with you, and our deal's off." He disappeared again.

Cooper slumped forward. "Lovely. So, how long should I wait before I tell Estes to avenge your *alleyway murder?*"

"He's not going to kill us," Vera said with a great deal more confidence than Guppie felt. "Tell them to break for lunch. If we're not back in two hours, keep moving without us."

"Right." Cooper backed up his Jackal and rotated it so that he could look out over the thousands of Clankers standing silent guard behind them. "A lunch break. We'll just have a nibble and hope these guys don't get any ideas." He shook his head and rode off, muttering to himself under his breath.

"All righty, kid." Guppie wheeled himself forward and whistled for the dogs. "Let's meet our guide and see if we've made new friends, or if we're just a couple of moon-eyed idiots too simple to take off our rose-tinted spectacles."

Lord Almighty, but he hoped it wasn't the latter.

15

CARLA

THEY WERE HALFWAY to the landing pad when the first soldiers tried to bar their way.

"Stop, by order of General Greene!" one of them barked.

Nathan let out a strangled cry and clung to Carla's arm, but Stew planted his feet wide apart and aimed his rifle at the sky. "Get out of our way!" he cried. "We have guns and we're not afraid to use 'em!" Just to prove his point, he fired into the air.

Instead of a blast of gunfire, the weapon emitted a low whir as it powered up. Stew shrieked when it shot a jet of green light high into the air and almost dropped it in surprise.

"Lasers!" he squeaked. "You got us lasers! Oh shit, man, that's *hot*."

Dr. Sharma's daughter blinked twice before murmuring to her mother, "Your colleagues are idiots."

"Believe me," Sharma said drily, "I am well aware."

As the first of the soldiers took aim, Carla dropped to a

crouch and braced the rifle against her knee. For the second time in her life, she pulled the trigger on a weapon she was holding, pivoting as she did so. Since it didn't fire individual shots like a normal gun, she was able to sweep the laser beam across the deck in the hopes of hitting something. The soldiers scattered like bowling pins; fifty feet away, the railing around the edge of the deck fizzled and melted. Carla released the trigger, gritting her teeth against the burning in her palms. Stu was right. The guns got hot when fired.

More soldiers were coming now, running out of the door that led belowdecks. Carla could only assume that the *invadenda* belowdecks had been killed by now. She almost felt sorry for it. Like them, it had never stood a fighting chance.

"Keep moving," she barked, nodding her head toward the helicopters. She could feel the throbbing in her temple giving way to a preternatural calm. Let them come for her. She'd been waiting for this opportunity for half a decade. They'd ruined her life.

She owed them one.

As the others kept moving, Carla fired another long, sweeping shot in the direction of the main bridge. It would have been absurdly satisfying to have the whole structure give way and slide into the sea, but unfortunately her weapon was only strong enough to sear a mark into the surface of the metal. She cursed and shuffled back, firing another shot in the general direction of the crowd of soldiers as they closed in. One of them returned fire, but Carla was already moving backwards by the time they did.

"Why aren't they shooting us?" Nathan asked, echoing the question that was already in Carla's mind.

"Don't wanna risk it," Stew panted. "They could damage the ship. No point, anyway. All they have to do is, *huff*, keep us grounded."

Stew's words sparked something in Carla's brain. The soldiers needed the ship intact going forward, but they didn't. *We've got nothing to lose if this whole thing goes down.*

"Why are you smiling?" Nathan demanded.

Stew paused to point at her. "I know that look. The woman's got a plan, huh?"

"Yeah." Carla felt the grin creeping across her face. "Yeah, I guess I do. If you can get us a ride out of here, I'll keep them distracted."

The words were barely out of her mouth before a brilliant streak of light arced over their heads.

"I thought they weren't shooting at us!" Mr. Sharma cried.

Carla didn't have time to answer him. She dropped to the ground and rolled onto her belly, turning to face the soldiers. *Good luck hitting me without damaging your ship,* she thought, propping her gun against the ground. She didn't need to hit anyone. Hitting the ship would do just fine. In fact, it might be more effective in the long run.

There were roughly a score of soldiers coming after them now. Carla weighed her options for a split second—her morals, or her life?—before taking another sweeping shot at the soldiers' legs. She grimaced when the beam met a soldier's thigh with the same popping sizzle of a marinated steak hitting a hot barbeque.

The soldiers screamed and collapsed. *But he's not dead,* Carla reasoned, even if it didn't really feel like a moral victory.

Several of the other soldiers cried out and fired on her, but Carla tucked and rolled. Their lasers left deep scars in the metal, with edges so hot that they glimmered molten for a few seconds after.

She heard shouting behind her from the direction Stew and the others had gone, but Carla didn't turn to look. Her adrenaline was going haywire, and her sense of calm vanished just as suddenly as it had set in. Instead of moving in slow motion, the world had sped up. She understood it only in glimpses: a shot, a flash of charred bone, a soldier's cry, brilliant flashes like emergency lights.

A scorching pain in her shoulder brought the world to a halt. As a girl, she'd once laid her hand on the hot burner of the gas-fired stove right after her father finished cooking, and she'd given herself blisters that made her hand swell to twice its normal size. This pain was different. The laser blast was hot enough to cauterize the wound, searing straight through two layers of clothing and eating into the meat of her bicep. She stared over at the injury in wonder. It looked as if it had been scooped away with all the efficiency of a melon baller.

She was still staring at it when a shadow fell across her. Carla rolled onto her back with the laser gun still clutched in both hands and stared straight up into the face of one of the soldiers. They were caught on the event horizon of a black hole, and Carla weighed that question again: *your body, or your soul?*

The soldier's eyes widened as she pulled the trigger.

"Sorry," Carla whispered.

She couldn't make herself look at the man's face when the body dropped to the deck. Carla gasped for breath, unable to process what she'd done.

You're no better than them. No better than Greene. What happened to the moral high ground, Carla?

Her heart thrummed in her chest, and it took her a moment to realize that it was echoing a sound outside of herself. Somewhere across the deck, one of the helicopters had come to life.

The sound was greeted by more shouting as the soldiers surged forward, passing right by Carla in their haste to get to the evacuees. She rolled upright and took aim at one soldier's back.

There's no honor in this, she thought, but it had been so long since honor had factored into any aspect of her life that she couldn't bring herself to care. These soldiers were only doing their job... but the job was *wrong.*

It was far too easy to use the laser gun. It didn't require any talent. All it took was *point, aim, click.*

The soldier in front of her collapsed in a heap, already dead before Carla took aim at the next target.

The running helicopter sat on its landing skids at the outermost edge of the flight deck. A few other aircraft stood between them, although Carla had only ever seen helicopters come and go from the deck. Carla could only assume that they were waiting for her, but there were too many people between them. It would only take one well-placed laser blast to bring the aircraft down.

Come on. You can do this. You're not going down here. She

lifted herself to her feet, squeezing her eyes shut as she went, dizzy with pain. She maintained her grip on the gun, and when a soldier turned to her, Carla fired point-blank without a second thought.

She hadn't had a plan for how to reunite with her labmates, even though she could hear someone calling her name. Stew? Or someone from the other side, telling her that it was all right to give up?

You don't get to tell yourself that you're the hero now. You don't get to pretend that you're the good guy. Still, she kept moving forward, putting one foot in front of the other despite the pain that radiated out through every inch of her. *Len would be horrified if he could see the woman you've become.*

Another engine started up; she was still at least fifty feet from the chopper, but even as she watched, it began to lift off. Two figures stood in the doorway, firing lasers. They must have found another one along the way, because Stew and Mr. Sharma stood shoulder to shoulder, taking potshots at the figures below. Mr. Sharma's jaw was set, but Stew was cackling like a lunatic. The guy had watched too many G.I. Joe cartoons as a kid, apparently. Someone was running the artillery, too, someone with terrible aim. Nathan, maybe? Although it was hard to imagine him threatening *anyone's* life. Then again, it was equally hard to picture him flying a piece of equipment like that. Speaking of which, who the hell was on controls?

Stew waved to her and called her name again, but they were too far off the ground to reach now. The other chopper was rising, too, already taking aim at them. The pilot of the getaway helicopter was either a genius or a madperson, judging by their evasive maneuvers.

Instead of running toward her friends, Carla watched as the other helicopter rose higher. *It's susceptible during takeoff.* She lifted the laser rifle to her shoulder quickly. She'd never been the type of kid to tear the wings and legs off of insects; hell, she'd once broken her arm in the process of climbing a tree to return a downed fledgling to its nest. For the first time in her life she could understand the cruel and reckless thought process of causing harm just to see what happened when she did.

She fired on the second chopper, hitting one of the rotor arms.

Stew stopped firing to raise his arms in a victory cheer as the other chopper spun out. Instead of just dropping, it spun madly above the deck until it crashed into another aircraft. Glass and metal went flying, and people on the deck ran for shelter.

Carla, however, just ran. Her lungs burned and her head swam and her shoulder screamed, but she ignored them all. Stew was still beckoning to her from well over twenty feet above the flight deck. Carla pushed herself harder, pumping her arms and forcing herself to keep her breathing steady. Gunfire came from her left, laser fire from her right. When she crossed a sharp chunk of shrapnel on the deck, she leapt over it, nearly twisted her ankle, and kept moving. She didn't bother looking up anymore. Instead, her eyes were fixed on the gray expanse of sea at the end of the deck. Across the Chesapeake, Washington had long since stopped burning. It was a shell of its former self, but it was still there.

You and me both, she thought grimly. The saltwater breeze

gave way to a rush of wind that buffeted her with such force that she almost closed her eyes.

Don't do it.

Eyes open, Carla, no matter how much it hurts.

Give me your hand.

Give me your hand.

"Give me your hand!" Stew bellowed from above her. The chopper had swung low, so that the open side of the cockpit was only a few feet away. Close, but not quite close enough to jump. He was about to run out of deck.

At the last moment, Carla pitched her weight forward and jumped.

For a moment, there was nothing between her and the water below or the sky above. She held out one hand toward Stew, but she was too low, falling too fast. She hadn't calculated her trajectory correctly. Her fingers slipped past Stew's, and her chest collided with the landing skid, knocking the breath out of her. She would have plummeted into the sea then if she hadn't hooked her arms over the metal bar.

"Reach up here!" Stew called as the chopper began to rise. Deliriously, Carla lifted her laser rifle above her head. "Not with the gun, you idiot! Drop it. Drop it and give me your hand."

Carla swayed, but she didn't budge. They were going to need weapons where they were headed, or this whole thing was pointless. She'd traded her conscience for her life, and was beginning to suspect that neither was worth very much anyway.

"Stubborn!" Stew yelled, and took the gun.

Her shoulder was on the verge of giving out, so Carla wrapped her arms around the skid and caught her breath.

"*Now* give me your arm!" Stew called.

They were higher up now, with both the fortress and the sea far below them. Carla laughed at the sight of the soldiers below, scurrying around like ants after their nest had been kicked.

"Stop laughing, you freak, and give me your hand!"

Carla lifted her arm again, and Stew's hands descended to meet her. He was holding what looked like the nylon cord of a ratchet strap of some kind tied like a slipknot, and he wrapped it around Carla's wrist before grabbing hold of her. The knot tightened, and Carla gasped in pain as her hand went numb, but an instant later she was being hauled up into the cockpit.

"Sorry about that," Mr. Sharma said, bending over her. He held the other end of the nylon rope. "I thought it would be better with both of us."

"Thank you." Carla wiggled the rest of the way up into the cockpit and lay on the floor, gasping for breath. Dr. Sharma's daughter was clinging to the guns and staring at her with an ashen countenance, and her similarly shell-shocked mother sat in the gun turret.

"I'm a Buddhist," Mr. Sharma whispered. "And I just shot at *people*. What if I hit one?"

Dr. Sharma spoke to her husband in another language, wrapping one arm around him and the other around her daughter. Carla looked up at Stew, massaging the sensation back into her wrist. "Am I to infer that *Nathan Nolte* is flying this thing?"

Stew nodded to the front of the cockpit. "Not exactly."

Nathan's shaking hands weren't on the controls. Instead,

they were clenched around the butt of a handgun aimed at a woman Carla had never seen before.

Stew bowed as if he was speaking to the two of them over high tea, rather than in the midst of a hostage situation. "Bone," he said grandly, "it is my pleasure to introduce you to Merry Clark."

16

VERA

WHEN VERA HAD first set out from the bunker in Little Creek, she'd still been clinging to the faint hope that her family had survived the invasion. Camp Keystone had destroyed that expectation. It was impossible to imagine Burcu or Harun fending off a wave of Clankers with...what? The newest releases in the children's section? A stack of science fiction paperbacks? They were anti-gun, anti-violence, anti-racism. Despite the friction surrounding her career change and her departure from the city, Vera had been proud of her family's stances on most things. That said, their pacifism didn't exactly make them prime candidates for surviving the final war.

But neither was I, remember? I'd have been toast without Len. Running into him was pure luck. Maybe my family got lucky, too.

As she and Guppie rounded the corner of the building, the man who'd waved from the roof stepped out into the street. He immediately crouched down and held out his arms. "Hello, loves, and who are you?"

Phobos stuck to Guppie like a limpet, but Deimos trotted over to the man and immediately started licking his face.

"The dogs never liked Johnson," Guppie muttered. "That's a good sign."

As the bloodhound licked his face, the stranger waved to them. "I didn't introduce myself, did I? You can call me Felix." Initially, she'd thought he was white, but now that she could see him a little better, Vera wasn't so sure. The name sparked something in her memory.

"Hold on." Her words caught in her throat. "Are you Nazarena's son?"

Felix's smile widened. "Sure am."

Guppie glanced between the two of them. "Who's Nazarena?"

"A friend of my family's. She owned the bodega around the corner from where I grew up." Vera clutched at her chest. "Is she here, too?"

"Sure is." Felix beamed as he got back to his feet. "I can't believe there are people still alive out there. Come on." He waved them forward, through the familiar grid of roads near her old neighborhood. Vera had seen old photographs of London after the Blitz, and walking through Brightwood Park in the wake of the Clanker invasion wasn't much better. Some of the buildings had been razed to their foundations, and only the rough layout of the street served as proof that the city she remembered so vividly had ever existed.

"I'm shocked that there are people alive *here*," Vera murmured.

"Most folks weren't as lucky as we are." Felix raked a hand through his hair. Like Vera, he had no distinct accent to give away his immigrant heritage. He was enough older that she hadn't played with him much, but he'd been closer to Alfie when they were kids. *Is he alive?* she almost asked. *Are any of them alive?* But she held her tongue. Hope was bittersweet, and if her family hadn't made it, she just wanted a few more minutes of hope to tide her over.

"How did you make it?" Guppie asked suspiciously. It was probably good that he'd come along; he'd be able to be more objective if it turned out that something wasn't right.

"Funny story," Felix said. "So there's this old *gringa* who moved into the neighborhood, like, fifteen years back. I don't remember her, but I guess she got in good with just about every-one. She was kinda eccentric. Had a whole, you know, *alien conspiracy.* I remember my mom talking about her a few times. This one day, she came around with fliers, right? Like, *In the event of the end times, meet here, bring this, pack a go-bag,* blah blah. And everyone thinks she's out of her mind, but she's rich and she seems normal, and she just brings it up in casual conver-sation whenever she comes around. It's the city, right? People are weird."

"Sounds familiar," Guppie murmured.

The overcast sky, the gutted streets, the wreckage and ruin in every direction... none of it was enough to stop Vera from smiling. There were other survivors. People she *knew.* There was something worth fighting for left in the world.

"Well, I guess we should have been nicer to the crazies," Felix said. "Seeing as how we owe them our lives and all."

It was only as they navigated Park View that Vera finally realized where they were headed. "Felix," she gasped, "are we going to the MedStar?"

He nodded. "Sure are. Getting our hands on it was a pain, but you'd be surprised how easy it's been to defend."

Approaching the hospital complex was another kick in the gut. Vera had worked in the MedStar's trauma and emergency care center during her time as a doctor. For a long time, it had felt like a cage. An obligation, not a passion. As they approached the fence that surrounded the complex, however, it felt a little bit like coming home.

"Aye, Felix!" Someone on the far side of the metal bars waved as they approached. "Everything copacetic? I'm getting some wild reports from the other teams. You should have heard the ruckus when your staticky shit message came through, dude."

"All good." Felix waved his hand to the two of them. "Wild, though. We're gonna have to have a long talk with the Commander."

"I thought you *weren't* Army," Guppie said.

Felix shook his head. "We're not, but—"

"*Şekerim!*" A short, squat figure forced her way between the little crowd gathered at the fence. "Vera! Is that you?"

"Mummy." Vera's voice cracked, and she pressed her palm to her mouth to hold back her tears. Somewhere around the time that they'd taken Camp Keystone, Vera had told herself that she didn't deserve to get her family back. She had broken all of her old oaths, she had lost her business, and she'd changed so much that she barely recognized herself.

And yet, Burcu recognized her, so she must not have changed as much as she thought.

The metal gates opened, and her mother flung herself through and wrapped her arms around Vera's as she pulled her down into a crushing hug. In a raw voice, she rasped, "*Dandini dandini danadan, bir ay doğmuş anadan...*"

The old Turkish lullaby was one that Vera had heard often as a child, and having it repeated back to her now, when the world had been turned on its head, was almost more than she could bear.

"I missed you, Mummy," Vera whispered.

She was dimly aware of other people talking, and Guppie trying to ask a question, and the dogs snuffling eagerly at her sides.

"My little girl, my little girl." Burcu trembled under the weight of her emotions.

"I've done things, Mummy. Bad things. I'm not sure you'll forgive me when I tell you."

Her mother backed away and cradled Vera's face between her palms. She looked different, too. Vera had never seen her so thin and so pallid. There were bruises on her cheeks and hollows beneath her eyes.

"Of course I will," Burcu said. "You're my baby. Nothing will ever change how much I love you."

Vera had managed to hold back her tears, but it was as if her mother had given her absolution, a release from all the guilt and sorrow she'd carried with her since the fall of Little Creek. Unable to restrain herself a moment longer, she burst into tears.

17

LEN

"YOU THINK it's been two hours yet?"

Estes jiggled his knee so that the ThunderGen bounced erratically against his thigh. "I don't know. Gotta be close, right?"

"I can't believe they took my dogs with them." Len knocked his fist against the side of the plane. "Why? Why would they do that?"

Klarie rolled her eyes. "Yeah. You're definitely just worried about your *dogs*."

Her point was fair. It was easier to be angry that his friends had taken liberties with his pets than to admit that Vera and Guppie could be in danger. Walking off alone with a bunch of strangers? Classic naïveté. He'd thought they were past that by now. What if they never came back? What if they became two more people whom Len knew were *gone* without ever finding out the details?

"Hey." Cooper swung up off the end of the truck. "Something's coming."

"Something?" Len turned to see what he was talking about, but the only difference he could pinpoint was a slight rustle among the Clankers.

Klarie frowned. "You sure about that, Coop?"

"Yeah. Can't you hear anything?" Cooper raked his hand through his hair and averted his eyes.

"Better not be another chopper," Estes muttered darkly.

"Nah." Cooper craned his neck in the direction of a cross street. "I think it's something on wheels."

Len shouldered his ThunderGen. Now that he was listening, he could hear it, too. And there were voices.

All the Clankers had turned in one direction now, and Len followed their gaze, glaring into the scope. They were too close to the city now to be turned back. A fight was coming. A big one. He could feel it in his bones with the same certainty that old-timers could predict changes in the weather.

When his dogs came charging down the road, tails wagging, Len exhaled and lowered his gun. Vera and Guppie weren't far behind. Around and behind them came a whole parade of people dressed in shabby street clothes, toting homemade weapons of every variety.

"Huh." Estes scratched his head. "That's... unexpected."

Vera was grinning from ear to ear, and she had one arm thrown around a woman who looked astonishingly like her. A man walked beside them, deep in conversation with Guppie.

"Oh." Emma Jean had wandered over, clutching the electronic rod she'd carried the day before. "Those must be her parents."

Klarie whistled. "What are the odds of being reunited after all this time?"

Emma Jean adjusted her teal glasses and glanced toward Pammy Mae, a lone human figure in a sea of alien soldiers. "Slim," she murmured.

The Clankers drew back to let the procession through, although more than a few of them extended their proboscises as the humans passed. There were a lot more people in the new group than in the Keystone caravan, perhaps three hundred of them, and they'd brought a handful of ambulances, too. Len was trying to work out what might be inside them when a woman at the front of the group raised her arms above her head.

"Len Bonaparte, as I live and breathe! You made it out!"

Len squinted as the woman jogged toward him, arms outstretched in greeting. He didn't recognize the woman at first. She wasn't family, and Len could count on one hand the number of older white women in D.C. whom he could have reasonably called a friend. Even when the woman pulled him into a bear hug, Len stood rigid in the circle of her arms.

"I looked everywhere for you." The woman held her out at arm's length. "I thought they must have taken you, too, or made you disappear. Do you have any idea what happened to Carla?"

Len tilted his head to one side. The woman's face was unfamiliar, but her accent was familiar. She sounded more New York than D.C., and the way she said Carla's name nudged at something buried deep in his memory.

"Wait." He reached up to grab the woman's arm. "Lavelle? Lavelle Steward?"

The woman beamed back. "The very same."

IT TOOK a handful of people talking over each other to explain precisely how the MedStar Stronghold had been established.

"See," Lavelle began, "it all started when I found Jeremy's flash drive thingy in the catbox scoop."

Len made her repeat herself twice more before he could believe it. Evidently, Jeremy Steward—whom Len had only met a handful of times, but whom Carla had complained about constantly—had managed to get a message to the computer in his mother's basement. The computer had been quickly confiscated, but apparently it was a half-assed job, because Lavelle had found Jeremy's remote backup upstairs. And she'd taken it to some experts.

"Not these sellout government scientists, either," a man with an impressive mullet chimed in. "She brought it to *us*."

Len stared at him helplessly. "And who are you?" she asked.

"UFO experts." The man crossed his arms and grinned. "Some of us had already seen the Steward Message from the original postings, before they got scrubbed from the web, so we knew she wasn't some crackpot or faker."

Lavelle nodded eagerly. "So these nice young fellas helped me get the word out, and then we got to translating. And some of them are real good hackers, too, you know, so they were able to learn all kinds of things about the government's plan."

"The *aliens'* plan, really," said another. "Pretty clearly they're calling the shots now."

"Excuse me?" Len said.

"Classic signs of enemy infiltration," the UFO specialist said. "If the plan was basically *bend over and take it*, then it's pretty clear that wasn't coming from our side without outside influence."

"So you're saying—"

"It's not important," the man called Felix chimed in. "The point is, we made a new plan. Well, Lavelle did." He nodded in her direction. "She started recruiting folks in the neighborhood. Most of us didn't take her seriously, but she kept at it."

"And then when it all started, she waited for us, and we managed to take over the hospital before the aliens did." Vera's mother, Burcu, hadn't let her daughter go since they'd reached the caravan. "Everyone who came to us for help, we accepted. Mrs. Steward saved our lives."

"It was the least I could do," Lavelle said modestly. "After all, I built myself a little community in the city. And Jeremy made sure that I got that message, so the least I could do was help my neighbors with it."

Len wasn't sure Jeremy had actually meant for his mother to get that message, but he wasn't going to quibble with a miracle. "Did you ever find out what happened to him?"

Lavelle shook her head. "Sorry, honey. That's top secret. Even Greg and his little friends couldn't work that out."

The mulleted UFO enthusiast rolled his eyes at her terminology. "Yeah, me and my schoolmates from MIT. But we *did* figure out something about the message."

"I remember Johnson mentioning the Steward Message," Estes interjected. "Wasn't it some kind of dark web thing? He always made it sound like it was something getting shared around by traitors and terrorists." When Lavelle glared at him, he raised both hands in self-defense. "I'm not saying he was right. I'm just wondering what it actually is."

"It's a warning," Lavelle said.

"And a roadmap," Greg added. "And get this, the alien is actually a hivemind!" He held his hands out wide and beamed, clearly awaiting awed gasps from his audience.

"Yeah, dude." Cooper bobbed his head. "We worked that out, like, six weeks ago."

Greg pursed his lips. "Okay, *dude*, but did you work out how to kill it?"

Four members of the Little Creek Five exchanged curious glances. "No," Cooper admitted. "At this point, our plan was to bring the army of aliens, attack the main nest, and hope we could work the rest out."

"Well, then, I've got some good news for you." Greg rubbed his hands together. "We figured out how to kill it. We've even developed a weapon that should work. Only trouble is, we need to get it all the way to the hivemind, and we haven't figured out how to do that without getting turned into meat Slurpees the instant we approach the nest."

Len swiveled around to look at Pammy, who was deep in conversation with one of the largest Clankers in the swarm. "I think we might be able to help with that."

18

PAMMY MAE

THERE ARE MORE *humans here now,* the King of Parkton complained. *We are hungry. My people must feed. You promised us...*

I know. And don't worry. Pammy gestured deeper into the city. *You'll have plenty of opportunities to gorge yourselves when we get where we're going.* The attacks yesterday had proved that there were still humans in the city whom she could reasonably count as enemies, and who could be sacrificed to the Clankers without any lingering guilt.

One of the queens who'd joined that morning let out a deep hum. *These humans are ripe, and they are here. Smell them. Smell them.*

Her call was taken up by the larger group, and the hair on the back of Pammy's neck rose as the aliens chorused, *Smell them. Smell them!* As their song reached a fever pitch, she bit her cheek to keep from yelling at them to stop. Human beings didn't have the same sense of ingrained community that the Clankers did, and even among a more individualistic species, a mob mentality could result in calamity. The Clankers were already itching to rebel against her plan. The added pressure of their growing hunger only made them angrier.

Control your hive, she told the King of Parkton.

The alien's segmented body undulated and folded in on itself, like an Escher painting come to life. *My hive obeys me. They do not answer to you.*

Pammy gritted her teeth. Her headache had come back in full force, like the worst kind of migraine. If the Clanker hives rebelled against her now, in the open streets of the city, the human contingent of the caravan wouldn't stand a chance. They'd be killed within seconds.

And would that be so bad? she wondered. *They are fodder for the throng, the sustenance upon which their betters feed, little more than protein chains destined either to decay back into the earth without purpose, or to fuel the expansion of a species too vast for them to comprehend.* The questions came from her own head, not the King of Parkton's tymbal, but they didn't feel like her own thoughts.

She'd experienced intrusive thoughts when she was younger, mostly in the form of self-doubt, especially during times of pressure. Were they mere doubts, or were they being put in her head by something else? She would have given anything to know.

"Pammy?"

She jumped at the sound of Cooper's voice and spun around to face him. He sat behind her on his Jackal, flanked by several members of the Keystone Hive. Evidently, they had taken it upon themselves to ensure his safety.

"Cooper. What are you doing here?" Her voice came out sharper than she'd intended, and she realized how long it had been since she'd spoken to another person. Her fingers ached from so many strums across the rough, slatted surface of the tymbal.

"Just, uh." His gaze darted around the Clankers, whose chants of *smell them* had faded into a mere whisper. "Just coming to get you. New plan. Gotta catch you up, right?"

She swung down from her mount and took a step toward him, squinting up at his eyes. "Are you okay? You look..." *Like your eyes are bloodshot. Like the Clanker-song puts you on edge.*

Like your head hurts as badly as mine does right now.

"I look like I slept like crap, like we all did, because this could very well be our last day on Earth. Come on. Do you want to know the new plan, or what?" He twisted away from her, so that she couldn't see his face anymore.

That hurt more than she'd expected. If Cooper had started to understand the Clankers, she wished he'd tell her so. It would be such a relief, to share the burden of knowing and seeing on behalf of everyone. Right now, her insight was an anchor around her neck, pulling her down into the depths of the infinite darkness from which the hivemind had first spawned. It would be such a wonder to ask someone else if she was going crazy and get an honest reply.

"Right," she said stiffly. "Let's talk." Before she withdrew, she pointed to her own eyes, and then to the King of Parkton. *I'll be right back. Keep them in line for a few more minutes.*

Then we'll find you a feast great enough to feed every hungry mouth among your hive.

The King of Parkton lowered his belly toward the road. *We will wait a little while. But not long, Queen. Not long.*

STANDING in a circle of other humans, especially humans she didn't know, was incredibly disorienting. All of them were looking at her, and there was fear in many of their faces. Only her mother and the rest of the Little Creek Five seemed to regard her as anything other than a madwoman dressed in Clanker shells.

That wasn't as comforting as it should have been. After all, her mother was known to be more than a little delusional when it came to family. Maybe majority rule was more accurate right now. She didn't trust her own mind these days, and she wasn't sure that anyone else should, either.

"So you can actually *see* into the hivemind?" the man who'd introduced himself as Greg asked.

Pammy nodded. Her throat seemed to have closed up.

As if she could sense her daughter's nerves, Emma Jean laid one hand on Pammy's shoulder. She had to fight the impulse to shrug it off. Casual contact had long since stopped soothing her. These days, it only served to remind her that her skin no longer fit right.

"Wow." Greg's eyes bulged in his skull. "That's wild. So you know where it is? And you can get close to it?"

"I guess we'll find out," Pammy croaked. "I'm either going to kill it, or it's going to kill me."

Greg opened his mouth, then closed it again. His gaze slid toward Lavelle Steward. "Well," he said at last, "correct me if I'm wrong, but we're all in the same boat, right? This is it. The final push. Unless we want to wait until tomorrow? Plan a little more thoroughly?"

"No," Pammy and Vera said at once.

Greg raised his eyebrows. "Okay then."

"Someone's tracking us," Vera explained. "We've been attacked twice already. The closer we get, the more trouble I expect we'll find. The longer we wait, the more likely we are to be targeted again, and the more time they have to prepare."

"And the Clankers are getting restless," Pammy added. "If they stop listening to me..." She trailed off and closed her eyes. The generational memories of the Clankers were only a breath away. Recollections of swarming through the stars and consuming everything foolhardy enough to stand in their way danced across her mind's eye, a litany of battles that ended in full bellies and countless species wiped wholesale from the universe.

Greg whistled. "Right. Yeah. Solid motivation. So let me show you what we've come up with."

He led them over to the nearest vehicle and threw open the back doors. Instead of a gurney and a bank of medical equipment, the interior contained an arsenal of weapons and a hard-sided Pelican case.

"So *ophiocordyceps* is our closest parallel to this hivemind organism, right?" Greg pulled himself up into the back of the ambulance and threw open the crate. A protective layer of black foam padding covered whatever lay inside.

"And that is...?" Cooper asked.

"Basically a fungus that grows on insects," Vera said.

"Exactly," Greg said. "It's *way* less evolved, obviously, but it operates kind of the same way. Think of our *ophiocordyceps* as a minnow. Compared to that, the hivemind controlling the aliens is like a Great White. More complicated, more dangerous, but all related. Now, the thing about funguses is, they operate in the body differently than other infections."

Vera was already nodding. "They're harder to eliminate. Most of the things that will kill a fungal infection will harm the host as well."

Greg aimed finger-guns at her. "Bingo, the lady knows her stuff."

Peachey, who was leaning against one of the open ambulance doors, adjusted his glasses and glared at the newcomer. "We're doctors. We probably understand it better than you do."

Greg blew a stray curl of hair out of his eyes. "So you already know that a fungus doesn't just have a vaccine or a comparable antidote. You have to disrupt mycological organisms on a cellular level. Killing the infection in an individual alien will kill the alien, too, and the hivemind will carry on just as it always has. But if we kill the 'seat' of the hivemind?" He wiggled his eyebrows.

"Then the rest of the infections don't matter," Pammy murmured. "Kill the source, cure the host."

"*Ding ding ding ding!*" Greg waved one arm over his head. "We have a winner! And on that note, allow me to present to you the Big F.U." He flipped open the Pelican case to reveal two glistening silver orbs. "Stands for the Biggatel Fungal Underminer, named after yours truly, but with a bit of poetic flair." He scooped one up in his arms like a baby and passed it into Pammy Mae's arms. It was lighter than it looked. "All you have to do is get up close and personal with the big bad, fold back this cover, flip this switch, and run like hell for the thirty seconds it takes to go off. After that, you're golden." He spread his hands wide. "Easy peasy, am I right?"

Pammy nodded, then tipped her chin toward the one that still sat in the case. "What's that one for?"

Greg's brow wrinkled. "Have you watched a movie, like, *ever?* What's the number one rule of horror films?" He waited for her to respond, and when she didn't, he threw his hands in the air. "The double-tap! There are so many things that could go wrong, even with a foolproof device like this. You gotta have backup."

"Mm." Pammy hugged the device to her chest. "Good idea."

"You're gonna want this." Greg held out a drawstring sports bag. He opened the top, and Pammy slid the disruptor inside, taking care not to jostle it. When it was safely stowed away, she swung the bag onto her back.

"Got it," she said. "Disrupt the hivemind and get out, preferably in one piece." She gave Greg a thumbs-up, then turned on her heel. The longer she left the Clankers alone, the more likely they were to act out.

She'd only made it a few steps when Vera caught her shoulder. "Pammy?"

She turned back. "Yeah?"

Vera's smile was brighter than it had been in a long time. After a moment's hesitation, she pulled Pammy into a hug. "If this works," she mumbled against Pammy's shoulder, "maybe you'll start to feel like yourself again. Once the hivemind is gone, it won't be in your head anymore, right?"

Pammy stood stiff and rigid in the circle of Vera's arms. "Yeah," she said. "I guess."

"Take care, okay?" Vera released her at last, but she kept smiling, watching Pammy Mae as though they were old friends and not virtual strangers. As if Pammy was still the girl she'd been back in Little Creek, rather than a monster who could barely keep her fellow monsters in check.

Guppie rolled up, too. He held out his hand for a high-five, and Pammy went through the motions, slapping her palm against his with just enough force to be convincing. Cooper held out his fist, and she brushed her knuckles against his. Even Len pulled her into a one-armed hug.

"See you on the flipside," Cooper said.

"Take care, kiddo," Guppie added.

"It's the Little Creek Five," Len reminded her, holding out a hand with all five fingers extended. "Don't mess up the nickname, mmkay?"

"Yeah." Pammy glanced past the group to where Emma Jean was standing by the open door of the ambulance, watching her daughter's departure with a small sad smile. "Yeah, I'll see you later. Take care, everyone."

She left them there in the street, trying not to let them see how smothering she found their optimism. Each stride became longer than the last, quickening her pace from a walk to a jog. Surely they knew that this was the last time they would all be together? Pammy could fight. She might even win. What she couldn't imagine was a future in which she was made whole again.

She didn't stop running until she reached the King of Parkton. *Come on,* she told the Clankers, raking her nails across the rough surface of the tymbal. She swung up onto the back of one of the Keystone Hive members. *Feeding time.*

The swarm thronged around her as she led them into the city, carrying humanity's last hope on her back.

She couldn't help but wish that humankind had chosen a better champion.

BEYOND WASHINGTON

Floating Fortress Survival Outpost
Chesapeake Bay

Sergeant Kyle Mathers stood on the deck with his hands clasped behind his back, surveying the damage that the scientists had done on their way out. He would never have guessed that they'd have the balls to go through with that little stunt, much less the skill to carry it out. He saluted as General Greene arrived. He'd been the general's right hand for the last 18 months, and thought he could read him well. He expected seething anger. Instead, he saw only what he'd increasingly seen for the last few months from Greene: a passivity bordering on indifference. When he'd first come aboard the floating fortress, it was the last thing he would expect from a superior, but it was something he was getting used to encountering aboard the ship.

Behind the general, a man whom he'd never seen before introduced himself as Agent Dante. He didn't reveal what agency he was an agent *for*, and Mathers didn't ask. He didn't need to be told it was classified.

"Problems?" The agent's voice was easygoing, but Mathers knew better than to let his guard down. The general wouldn't have escorted him down here to see this mess if he didn't expect answers.

"We've had a situation with one of the research groups," he said.

To his surprise, the agent didn't seem angry. In Mathers' experience, men from mysterious units weren't known for being understanding. "How tiresome it can be to learn that the things we think we can control are the ones in charge." Agent Dante smiled to himself. "There will be no more room for error, General. From now on, we will communicate more directly, which should help us avoid any future... surprises. We will host a final meeting with the members of your ops team before they deploy."

"Deploy?" Mathers tried to bite back the question a moment too late.

"Yes, Sergeant, please try to keep up." Dante's smirk widened. "We have a situation on the ground in the city. An army of Akrido... of *invadendae* are marching on Crystal City, with a human contingent at their rear. They've been making problems for us. They are to be eliminated."

Mathers glanced at Greene, but his face remained passive. *OK, so this guy is in charge.*

Mathers was already running through the list of stockpiled weaponry: the exosuits, the thunder cannons, the wardogs, the jets, and the laser rifles; never mind the experimental tech that they'd been sitting on for months. They had plenty of gear to arm all the teams, but there was only so much manpower to go around. Soldiers were more expensive to keep in the long term, especially now, when food production was more or less a thing of the past.

"Two armies," he said slowly. "Do we have a primary target? Because the *invadendae* are powerful, sir, and if we're waging a war on two fronts, we'll need to divide our troops."

Agent Dante waved a dismissive hand. "You'll focus on the human forces. Your last efforts left a great deal to be desired. It's not enough to send a handful of ships here and there. This unit's efforts have been, ah, *unprecedented.* The matter has become personal. Furthermore, they have a weapon that needs to be neutralized." The first hint of doubt crossed his cold features. "It is an unimpressive effort, but so far they have been tenacious. And *lucky.*" He squeezed his eyes closed and rubbed his temple. "As for the other army, consider it handled."

"But Agent—"

Dante lifted his head, and Mather's mouth snapped closed. There was something wrong with the man's eyes, an empty, inky blackness that had engulfed his irises. Come to think of it, so were Greene's.

"We'll be communicating differently from now on,

Sergeant," Greene said. "It will allow us to operate more effectively as a team."

More effectively as a team? "Sir?"

Dante reached into his pocket and produced a small bottle of amber liquid. When he turned the bottle over in his fingers, the substance clung to the glass like thick honey. "I think you'll find that once you grasp the basics, the rest is fairly self-explanatory. Once we're all on the same wavelength, we'll find it easier to coordinate our efforts." He pressed the bottle into Greene's hands. "That dose is for your sergeant here. There's plenty for everyone."

Greene frowned down at the bottle, then handed it to Mathers, who took it warily. It was light as air.

This wasn't part of any plan he'd heard of. He also didn't get the impression that Dante was *asking*. But when had things last been *ordinary*, anyway?

"Drink it." The agent watched him with a crooked smile. "Then call up your crew. One more little rebellion needs to be put down, and after that, we'll expand our efforts. We'll reestablish our foothold on land, and with the help of the Akrido, we'll make our way overland to a launch point."

Launch point? Mathers glanced up at him in disbelief. "Am I to understand that we've had a mission success in Crystal City?" he murmured.

"Indeed." Dante nodded. "One way or another, this ends today."

Mathers uncapped the bottle and lifted it in the air. "I'll drink to that," he said. The details of the operation had been withheld from him, but he knew the outcome. Humanity, or what was left of it, would leave Earth behind. That must be why Dante wasn't worried about the alien horde. His overtures of alliance must have been accepted.

Mathers lifted the vial to his lips and drank. Whatever sat inside was bitter medicine, but if a little bitterness was all it took to justify everything they'd sacrificed, he'd swallow it gladly. The masses had been swept away, while the worthy rose to the top.

By the time Mathers wiped the back of his hand across his lips, there was no more room for sentimentality. He had been consumed.

The throng had grown by one.

PART 2

JUDGMENT

19

GUPPIE

GUPPIE MARTIN HAD NEVER BEEN MUCH of a city driver. He liked the long, undulating roads of the backwoods, with their unexpected turns and startling vistas. A deer leaping out of the cornfields that backed up to the road? No problem. A horse and buggy appearing over the brow of the hill on a country highway? Easy. He'd even gotten used to the roundabout that had been installed outside the new medical facility in Eastplain.

But God help him, if he ever met the inventor of one-way roads, he was going to lose his mind.

"It doesn't matter," Cooper called to him when Guppie drew up short at a triangular intersection.

The kid had a point, what with it being the end of the world and all, but he'd gotten stuck going the wrong direction on a one-way street precisely often enough to have hang-ups about it. There were rules, dammit, even if they were dumb rules.

"How do we even know where we're going?" he demanded.

Cooper was too far ahead to answer. He probably had a dang GPS installed in his head. That was what came from the youth spending so much time on their little tech gadgets. With a grunt, Guppie pushed his mech back into action.

Len had finally gotten his wish and taken Walk's old Cessna up to scout ahead. As far as Guppie was concerned, following Len's guidance was good enough. Then again, the plane hadn't looped back in a good ten minutes, and Guppie couldn't help worrying that something had happened to him already. Splitting up was a terrible plan. Still, Cooper seemed to understand where he was headed, so Guppie followed.

The battle plan, such as it was, had been kept fairly simple: find a place relatively close to the Crystal City metro station, with three-sixty views that would keep anyone from flanking them, and hold that position. Ideally, their proximity to the underground would allow them to draw some of the heat off of Pammy, since they'd be acting as live bait; and if the human forces responsible for sending helicopters returned, they'd be able to hold them off Pammy's tail. Nobody had said so explicitly, but Vera's mannerism had suggested that there was another reason for sticking close to Pammy and her army: if their girl wasn't able to detonate her disruptor, they could send in the backup.

She'll get it, Guppie thought. *She's one tough cookie. She's not going to let a little thing like the hivemind stop her from enacting her plans.* All the same, she wasn't invulnerable. Having a backup plan wasn't the same as mistrusting someone. It always paid to have insurance.

It hadn't been particularly difficult to determine the site of their last stand. Lavelle Steward had opened a pamphlet map of the city and dropped her index finger right on the perfect location—the Washington Monument, on its wide open hill, just across the Potomac from Arlington. It seemed a fitting place for their battleground. The only trouble lay in getting there.

The truck engines rumbled behind Guppie as they marched south toward Le Droit Park. The reservoir just below the hospital had been emptied of Clankers, although whether they were on Pammy's side or not remained to be seen.

He had just bucked his lifelong fear of one-way roads when a whistling shriek echoed across the sky.

"Jets!" Guppie bellowed to nobody in particular. "We've got jets!"

A trio of white planes sailed above, leaving perfectly parallel tracks across the sky. It wouldn't have surprised him in the least to learn that they were drones, given their precise formations. Human pilots weren't that exact, were they? He'd made his fair share of cracks about the Air Force in his day, but truth be told, he had little enough experience with planes.

I hope they didn't get Len, he thought bitterly, then stopped the thought in its tracks. He couldn't let himself fall down a rabbit hole like that. *Just pretend everyone else is okay and go from there. You can worry about how they're doing once we complete this phase of the mission. Otherwise, you're going to lose your marbles.*

Rather than waste any more time on grim thoughts, Guppie drew his ride up short and examined the buttons. At Klarie's suggestion, he'd gone over his Sharpie labels with black nail polish to keep them from smudging. It was a good hack, he had to admit.

In a split second, his gaze bounced between the three long-range buttons, which he'd shorthanded as *Zap, Whap,* and *Boom.*

"Okay, Chelly," he muttered, "time to put you through your paces." He brought the modified Jackal back on her heels and fixed his crosshairs on the middle jet. When he was confident that he'd gotten a bead on their trajectory, he slammed the pad of his thumb against *Boom.*

Cooper had warned him that there were only a dozen or so rounds of any given ammo on board, but if taking down a jet wasn't a special occasion, what was? Guppie watched gleefully as a trail of light fizzed through the air like a Fourth of July Roman candle.

His aim had been good, but evidently the jets were flying a little high for Chelly's range. The two-stage explosive flare Cooper had nicked from the Keystone armory burst before it reached its target. For a moment, Guppie thought his shot had been a waste of perfectly good ammo. As the jets looped back to target him, he braced for gunfire that never came. They dipped low enough to enter the flare's range. He couldn't see exactly what happened; the delayed second stage of the explosive must have gotten sucked into the rightmost jet's fuselage. It burst apart over a row of townhouses, knocking the middle jet off-target. The two surviving planes had to spin to keep from crashing, very nearly colliding as they did so.

"Good work, Chelly!" Guppie crowed. Next time, he'd head for the rooftops before making a shot.

He was in the midst of trying to determine which of the nearby buildings looked the most stable when something hit the road behind him with such force that the pavement cracked. Guppie whirled to find what reminded him of an old comic book supervillain climbing to its feet. The figure was larger than a man, bulkier in every direction, and made almost entirely of metal. At first he thought that it, too, might be a drone, but when it turned toward him, he could make out a dazed human face through the shield of the helmet. His eyes widened. He knew that suit, or at least a shitty prototype of that suit. At the moment, he was *wearing* it.

"Hell in a handbasket," he muttered. It was a good thing Johnson had been stuck with the outdated version of this tech. Otherwise, who knew what kind of damage he could have done?

The figure in the upgraded suit dropped into a crouch and slapped one huge, gloved knuckle into their open palm. The new exosuit was less of a skeletal upgrade and more of a one-man tank. It stood nearly eight feet tall, and with every motion, the joints let out a hiss of hydraulics. Guppie barely had time to think, *Oh, shit,* before the soldier pushed off, charging right at him.

He didn't stop to think before throwing Chelly into reverse. He scuttled backward, hinging when she hit the wall of an apartment building and climbing backwards, vertically, without breaking stride. The suit's fist slammed into the wall with more force than Guppie would have thought possible, sending bricks scattering in every direction. As the soldier pulled their fist back through the hole in the wall, the fist retracted.

Great. Not only is it built like a friggin' war machine, but it throws punches like a jackhammer. Lovely work, everyone. Guppie's mobility was somewhat hampered by the connection points of his own suit, but his adrenaline was running high, and he was getting mad.

Well, his enemy wasn't the only one with toys. He used the controls to send one of Chelly's limbs whipping out with lightning speed. Most of Cooper's augmentations had relied on upgrading the main design of the original DARPA war beasts developed in Camp Keystone. Chelly's Clanker parts were mostly for show, and the arm that grabbed at the exosuit's throat was more houndlike than alien. It wasn't strong enough to crush the exosuit's neck, but it could hold it in place. Guppie glared right into the face of the soldier as he brought his palm down on the *Zap* button.

Whoever had designed the exosuit hadn't thought to ground it. Cooper had managed to strip one of the two-ended electrical rods, like the one Johnson had carried, and install their power sources in the Jackals. The instant Guppie activated it, the soldier's eyes rolled back in his head, and a spark of blue energy danced through his helmet like the voltage on a Tesla coil. Guppie let go of him, and the soldier crumpled to his augmented knees.

"Son of a bitch," Guppie growled. "If I had a suit like that—"

The thought was only halfway out when he stopped. He was supposed to be guiding the caravan, but he'd already lost track of the foot soldiers from the hospital. Falling another five or ten minutes behind wouldn't hurt, would it? Not if it meant he'd actually be *useful* again.

He brought Chelly back to street level. The soldier in the exosuit was already getting to his knees, and he lifted both arms in a defensive fighting posture.

I've got to find a way to take him out without damaging that suit, Guppie thought. Using the *Boom* button would decommission it for sure, and too many *Zaps* might fry the circuitry that kept it running.

Whap it was, then.

According to Cooper, the weighted chain he'd installed near the mech's 'mouth' was pretty low-tech. The Clankers' whiplike tongues had been his source of inspiration, and although the chain wasn't as accurate as a prehensile tongue, it could certainly pack a punch. The first blow sent the soldier staggering back and left a sizeable dent in the chestplate. Guppie took a few seconds to consider how he'd aim the next blow. It would be nice to knock the soldier down altogether, maybe snag him by the knee—

Landing two hits in a row had evidently made him cocky. He wasn't braced for the soldier's punch, which landed along Chelly's side, pinning Guppie's leg to the side of the mech. It would have hurt like hell, but the exosuit prototype protected him at first. A fraction of a second later, the jackhammer augmentation on the fist kicked on, sending both Guppie and his mount crashing into the wall of the rowhouses. Chelly's gyroscopic steering mechanism tried to right her, which was just as well. Guppie was lost in a haze of pain. When he fumbled at his leg, he could *feel* that the cage of the suit had been partially crushed; his hands came away bloody.

It didn't hurt, though. His head and shoulder screamed from the pain of the impact, but his legs didn't feel a damn thing.

That's probably bad, he thought, but in a way he was glad. It meant that he was able to get back in the fight sooner. He maneuvered Chelly the rest of the way through the hole in the wall just before the soldier's next hit landed. The walls of the house cracked, and the floor above him sagged, already weakened by the fact that the houses had been so badly damaged over the last few months.

At the beginning of any mission, Guppie had managed to keep all of his goals in his head at once. *Get to the Monument. Hold the hill. Back Pammy up. Protect your friends. Get your hands on a suit that'll make the whole process a hell of a lot easier.*

In the course of this fight, he'd been backed into a corner. That had only happened a couple of times during his military career. There was no thinking himself out of a fight. He couldn't rationalize with the enemy. Their toys were fancier and the stakes were higher, but in the end, this was no different than being dropped in a room with one enemy and one knife and being given the order to survive. Forget damaging the suit—he wouldn't be able to use it anyway, if he died.

Guppie bared his teeth at the hole in the wall, calculating his advantages with all the accuracy of a computer. "Come to papa," he growled.

The soldier battered through the wall a moment later, and

Guppie grinned. "Surprise," he said.

Boom.

The first stage of the explosive flare hit the suit full force, blasting the soldier back into the street and taking most of the remaining wall with it. Guppie followed, cursing a blue streak when his open wound scraped against the bricks. He hoped he'd be able to bend the metal back in order to free himself, ideally before his adrenaline wore off, but there was no time to worry about that. He made it out of the building just before the rowhouse gave one dying groan and collapsed in a cloud of plaster and cement.

The soldier was lying in the road outside. Guppie kept his distance, counting down the seconds, and he pressed his palm to his bleeding leg. *Three... two... one...*

The second stage of the explosive shattered the suit's helmet and nearly collapsed the chestplate. The soldier went slack and didn't move again.

"Sorry, Chelly," Guppie panted. "Didn't mean to let you take the hit." He navigated the mech over to the fallen soldier and stared down at the suit, trying to gauge how much, of anything, was salvageable. In a decision between a busted suit and a mech that was currently crushing his right leg, he didn't love his choices.

There were more jets overhead now, and the boom of the ThunderGens told him that the caravan was already moving south. He gripped the rough edge of one metal brace and tugged, gasping with pain as he peeled it back.

These bastards wanted a fight, did they? Well, good news. They were gonna get one.

20

LEN

EVEN BEFORE HE heard the first jet, Len was already questioning the plan. From the sky over the city, he could make out the glittering Clanker army far ahead of the human caravan.

They hadn't bothered to try to replace the Cessna's doors or the missing copilot's seat, so while Len was in the left-hand pilot's seat, Klarie was next to him on her knees holding a ThunderGen. That was the extent of their firepower in the old plane.

He had other concerns. He wasn't convinced that they should have told Pammy there was a backup detonator. On the other hand, by the time Greg had thrown open the cover of the Pelican case where the devices were housed, there hadn't been time to tell him, *Hey, this is our girl and we trust her, but maybe we shouldn't tell her everything...?* Besides, if Pammy couldn't get to the hivemind, then who among them could?

He'd spent so many years being cautious, doing his best to

prepare for every eventuality. This whole fight was happening too fast. He needed *time* to pivot and adapt.

And time was one thing they didn't have.

The capital came into view, and the Clankers kept streaming south toward the highway that crossed the Potomac.

"I'm going to loop back," Len told Klarie. "Signal to Vera and the caravan that we're still on track."

He was about to bring them around when they both lifted their heads.

"Wait," Klarie said. "Do you hear something?"

Klarie could spin around on her knees, but Len had to twist all the way around in his seat to get a decent view of their periphery with his one good eye.

Three jets were coming in hard and fast.

The Cessna would be comically outclassed by the jets. If they had any advantage, it was that they were *so* slow and low-tech that actually targeting them might be a challenge.

"That's a big problem," he said grimly.

No sooner had the words left his lips than a flare went up from ground level, and the jets looped back. One of them exploded in midair.

"Someone just bought us time. Let's move."

Len jerked on the controls and spun them around.

Klarie did the right thing and, rather than waiting for any signal, brought the ThunderGen to her shoulder and aimed right out the open, unobstructed side of the plane and fired at the nearest jet.

There's one advantage of not having doors.

As far as Len could tell, she didn't hit anything, but the jets did break off their attack; with their relative speed, just a moment of disruption was enough for them to go thundering past the Cessna and off into the distance.

"Ah, hell." Klarie gestured her left hand wildly before clamping it back on the plane's frame. "We've got company."

She was right. The first three jets were only the beginning. Half a dozen more were headed their way from the east, somewhere out over the Chesapeake Bay.

"What a homecoming," Len grumbled. "They're really rolling out the red carpet. All right, Klarie, new plan. We're gonna high-tail it across the river. See if the jets will follow us into Clanker territory, okay?"

The girl nodded understanding. She wasn't going to like the next part, though. He started to slide out of the pilot's seat. "I need you to come take the controls. Power is set. You just need to hold the heading."

Klarie's eyes bulged, but to the girl's credit, she nodded and slid into the seat. Len took the ThunderGen from her. He was a much better shot than her, and he needed to at least give their pursuers something to think about.

And it wasn't as suicidal of a move as it seemed. He'd given her some rudimentary flight instructions, and flying erratically in a general direction was basically what evasive maneuvers would look like at this point.

"If you could just give me a verbal before you change course...?"

"Right." The girl bared her teeth in a mad smile. "If I scream like a pissed-off chicken, I'm gonna change direction."

"Works for me," Len told her. He spun around and wedged

his thigh against the base of the far open side of the Cessna, and shoved his back against the closer edge. This way, he could point the ThunderGen directly behind them.

The wind whipped around him, and he was uncomfortably aware of just how long the fall would be if he fell out.

He pulled the ThunderGen up and sighted down the barrel.

Deep breaths, Len. You got this. When his next shot threw scatter without hitting a damn thing, he had to remind himself that he wasn't burning through ammo.

On the other hand, the jets were figuring out how to fire on them. The one closest on their tail fired a missile, but it was past them in the blink of an eye. He should have used his machine guns for a strafing run. Klarie screeched and veered ineffectively, but the change in course caused the second jet to pull out of its attack run and bank around them, exposing its underbelly. That gave Len a split-second view of the jet's tail as the afterburners fired.

He sighted and fired. This time, his shot hit the target. The jet didn't explode in any pleasing manner, but its thrusters instantly flamed out, and the pilot ejected as it plunged into the Potomac as they passed over the river.

They were over the heart of the city, and Clanker territory, now.

Len had another reason to stay on the Clankers' tail. At the moment, if Pammy defected or her mission failed, the rest of them were never going to know. At least if he stayed close to the wayward branch of their blended army, Len had a better chance of determining if a backup plan was needed.

An unexpected calm descended over him. He was back in the city, in the place where it had all begun. Back then, he'd been blindsided by the nightmare of losing both Carla and his sense of safety in one fell swoop. Funny to think that after half a decade of running and hiding and fighting, his whole past and future rode on *today*.

No sweat, he thought grimly, *but you're going to find out if your efforts have paid off before you sleep again... assuming you live long enough.*

21

PAMMY MAE

AS THE CLANKER army surged toward the Potomac, Pammy Mae was painfully aware that the aliens were no longer truly interested in following her instructions. The King of Parkton's dissent sat on her shoulders like a weight, carrying her down even as they moved forward.

There are no new morsels, he complained as they reached the banks of the Potomac. *The only meal here is you.*

At least their hunger seemed to have abated now that there were no new human smells. The King might have his eye on her, but the other Clankers were more interested in following their royalty. An instinctive urge to move had taken over the masses, and as they surged through the streets, the tramping of their feet became a frenetic drumbeat, joining in harmony with their song.

Pammy didn't dignify the King of Parkton's accusations with a response. Instead, she led the swarm toward the 14th

Street Bridge. She didn't need a map to guide her way. The presence of the hivemind pulled at her like a lodestone, and every time she closed her eyes she saw its raw form pulse and ripple behind her eyelids. It was waiting for her in the heart of the city. The gait of the Clanker beneath her made the little pack tap against her spine, a reminder of her mission.

I don't need to win, she told herself. *I just need to make sure that the hivemind loses.*

Her army was halfway across the bridge when she became aware of the wall that blockaded the far side. The battered husks of cars had been stacked one atop the other, barring the way between Pammy's force and the Virginia border. She pulled up short, and the rest of the army stopped behind her, muttering in confusion.

Quiet, she told them, brushing her fingers across the tymbal at her hip.

Silence descended upon the mingled mass of alien bodies. All the hives were listening to her now. Their Kings and Queens were losing their sway over the individuals. Whether it was the hivemind itself that unified the Clankers with single-mindedness, or whether the fungus had simply taken advantage of the creatures' natural instincts, there was no denying that when they gathered in such numbers, mob mentality took over.

After hours of Clanker-song, the sudden hush was breath-taking. There was no traffic, no music, no birdsong to disrupt their quietude. Pammy held her breath, waiting for something to happen, knowing full well that it would. The hivemind knew she was coming.

There was always the possibility, of course, that its power

was absolute, but she didn't believe that. She *couldn't* believe that. If it was true, then she was playing right into its plan. Whenever she'd felt it nudging at her conscious mind, it hadn't been a *command*. It was an urge. An impulse.

She could only hope that it had a similar effect on the Clankers at her back.

A long moment passed before the first glittering forelimbs appeared over the top of the barricade, wagging against the gray sky in frantic silhouette. Soon a Clanker appeared over the top of the wall, and then another, and another, standing stark against the otherwise lifeless landscape.

Pammy had been building an army, but the hivemind hadn't sat idly and waited for her to arrive.

She urged her mount forward and then turned back to face the legion of her followers. As she did, she began to play the first song she had ever used to win the Clankers to her side. It was the same one she'd played in Keystone when she'd battled with the old Queen: a song of militancy, a song of hunger. Her pageant days might as well have been a thousand years ago, but her old training was still second nature. Her role back then had been to convince the judges that she wasn't just the obvious choice, but the *only* choice.

We cannot both survive. They are trying to keep the food for themselves. Their deaths are the only means of our survival. Defend the Queen. Defend the nest. Defend the future.

This last refrain was taken up by the Clankers, and chanted again and again for the benefit of those too far away from the front lines to hear. *Defend the Queen. Defend the nest. Defend the future.*

Only the King of Parkton didn't join in. He stared at Pammy with his honeycomb eyes. *You're lying,* he said. She could only barely hear him over the rattling of her followers.

He was wrong. Pammy had floated through the hivemind's collective memories for well over a month, and she had seen just how disposable the Clankers were in the eyes of the central colony. The hivemind wouldn't think twice about abandoning whole hives to a slow death on a dying world, so long as the organism itself survived. Those like the King of Parkton, who saw themselves as clever or valuable, lived in the hope that the hivemind would choose them when it moved on; but in reality, their chances were slim. The Clankers were no more important in the grand scheme than the species that fed them.

She didn't bother trying to explain that, though. Instead, Pammy flipped the King the bird and led the charge.

Even before she reached the far bank, the Clankers had begun to overtake her. They streamed past, and their chants gave way to their battle cries, forming a plan of attack before they even breached the wall. The hivemind must have assumed that the human army would be following this route, because the blockade barely slowed the Clankers, who surged up its face. Their feet found little gaps and divots as they climbed, and within seconds they were hurtling over the far side, tackling their opponents as they went down.

Pammy had never seen Clanker warfare with her own eyes, and certainly not on this scale. It shocked her a little to realize that the aliens could be as brutal with one another as they were with their prey. Her own mount speared its first opponent with its forelimbs, driving both legs straight into the other creature's underbelly. Seconds later, it lashed its serrated proboscis across another Clanker's eyes before slipping it between the lapped plates along its back and severing its spine.

The urge to fight made Pammy's hands twitch, but as before, she had just enough of herself left to remember her mission.

She had the disruptor. She was the one who stood the best chance of making it to the hivemind. Instead of giving in to the collective drive of the Clankers, she pushed her army forward, driving the front lines of the enemy back with every step.

She wouldn't stop until she reached the metro tunnel that led down to the invasion's rotten, ravenous heart.

22

VERA

"I THINK WE LOST YOUR BOYS," Lavelle said of Cooper and Guppie, who had disappeared somewhere ahead of the group.

Vera gritted her teeth at the phrasing. "Like hell we did." She half-expected her mother to scold her for her misuse of language, but Burcu held her tongue.

"I didn't mean it like that." The older woman patted Vera's arm. "I think they've gone another route. They know where we're headed. We can meet them there, all right?"

Vera nodded, although it struck her quite suddenly that this was the first time she'd been well and truly separated from her friends since the time she'd tried to leave Little Creek on her own. Back then, she hadn't even made it out of town before she had Clankers on her heels, popping up out of the sewers and sabotaging her getaway car.

That was then. You've got a whole host of people at your back now, most of whom are looking to you for guidance. She wasn't on her own anymore, but even so, it felt like an omen. Even when Johnson had splintered their group, they hadn't *chosen* to scatter.

The caravan had left the neighborhoods behind, and the buildings were getting taller. Boroughs and bodegas gave way to museums. On an ordinary afternoon, these roads would have been lined with food trucks eagerly hawking their overpriced offerings. As a child, Vera had never been allowed to spend even her pocket money on such things, and even when she was a grown woman making a living at the hospital, she'd reveled in the secret thrill of spending seven dollars on a watery slushy before wandering through one of the museums on Constitution Avenue.

There was no time for nostalgia to sink in. Even before they reached Federal Triangle, she saw the plumes of dirt and rubble rising against the sky.

Vera had asked Lavelle before they headed out if her group knew anything about combat. It wasn't a question she'd ever imagined herself posing to a little old Jewish lady from Le Droit Park. "Not a clue, honey," Lavelle had told her.

Now, Vera stopped at the head of the caravan and turned back to face the milling crowd of men and women behind her. Her feet slid into a wider stance of their own accord, and she cupped one hand around her mouth.

"Keystone unit!" she bellowed. "I want those of you with ThunderGens on point and flank. The aim is to keep moving. We're clearing a path and heading to the monument, not engaging in combat. Understood?"

Her people were already moving. Estes fell back to the rear, shouting as he went, while the D.C. group moved inward. The moment everyone was in place, Vera waved her arm over her head and led the charge.

Right into a wall of gleaming metal.

Vera had known on an intellectual level that the dog-like combat mechs in Keystone had only been prototypes. Maddox had explained how the DARPA engineers had taken the most polished of their creations when they'd abandoned Keystone. That knowledge only made stumbling into a row of the upgraded versions more daunting. They were roughly the same size as the ones Cooper had modified, and like the originals they had no functional heads, although some creative soul had taken it upon themself to paint snarling monster faces across their front-facing panels. Instead of hand-welded bodies, however, these were sleek and shiny and walked on four limbs, each of which sported razor-sharp claws.

At the end of the day, a monster was still just a monster, though. Vera lifted the ThunderGen to her shoulder, aimed, and fired, fully expecting the creature she'd hit to land on its ass in the street.

Instead, just as her rifle shuddered, a silver-blue honeycomb pattern shimmered in the air between them. It rippled when her shot hit, but the machines beyond didn't budge.

"Energy shield?" she murmured, falling back a pace. *Crap.* How were they supposed to fight an enemy who wouldn't even take a hit?

A red eye blinked to life between the nearest mech's shoulders. The honeycomb pattern vanished.

It's going to fire, she thought dumbly, and in the split-second between when that red eye took a bead on her and fired, Vera pulled the trigger again. This time, the mech shuddered and slid back across the pavement. Its claws left deep gouges in the tarmac.

"New plan!" she bellowed. "We're taking these things out. Split up and draw their fire. They can't track us all!"

She wasn't sure that anyone would be able to follow her logic, but they didn't have time to hold a symposium on how to piss off war mechs. She was already moving.

Vera had set her eye on her original target, and she approached it at a run. When it aimed at her again, she dropped to the ground in a roll that would have made Pammy cover her eyes in horror. She felt the skin of her knee break open, and the hot pavement was going to leave her with road rash or worse, but she kept rolling until she was right under the mech. It tried to back up; apparently its systems didn't allow for it to aim at anything on the ground between its legs. Vera wedged the butt of her ThunderGen against the pavement, slammed her fist into the barrel so that it was pressed against the mech's chest, and fired.

So much for that energy shield, huh? she thought with a grin as the mech was blown skyward. It sailed back toward the sidewalk and landed on its side, where it scrabbled against the concrete in an attempt to right itself.

The caravan was already surrounding the mechs. When she'd shouted her orders, Vera had anticipated that the Keystone soldiers would be leading the charge, but she was wrong. A cloud of civilians had descended on the mechs. Evidently the creature's scanners couldn't tell one type of ammo from another, because they activated their shields for everything from sonic pulses to chunks of concrete. Lavelle's people threw anything that came to hand, and the wardogs spun in frenzied circles while their shields blinked on and off as they attempted to get off a single blast of laser fire.

Her chest swelled with pride, but there were more mechs coming from down Constitution. Even as they charged, three loud booms sounded in swift succession, and Vera looked up to see a trio of soldiers in metal suits climbing to their feet.

Someone behind her shouted, and one of the smoke bombs they'd brought from Camp Keystone whistled through the air and bounced off a mech's hunched shoulders. More followed, and within moments the street was filled with black smoke that left Vera unable to tell battle cries from screams of pain. They were fighting blind; the mechs were stronger, but they were vastly outnumbered. As the smoke rose above her head, Vera fixed her eyes on the sky, where the top of the Washington Monument was visible.

Give me a second, fellas, she thought, wishing that Cooper and Guppie could hear her. *I'll be there as soon as I can.*

23
CARLA

"THIS IS GOING to blow your mind," Merry Clark growled, "but I don't appreciate being taken hostage."

Stew leaned over the back of her seat, resting one elbow on the headrest. "I hear you," he said conversationally, "but let me say my piece. See, we've been held captive by your people for the last, *oooh*, five years? And I really don't see you helping us *without* a gun to your head, so, you know. We can agree to disagree on that."

"Stop talking, Stew," Nathan complained. "You're monologuing again."

Stew pressed one hand to his chest. "Sorry, Nutty, but if this isn't the start of my supervillain arc, I don't know what is."

Stew liked the sound of his own voice, but Carla was more worried about the pilot. She kept glancing sidelong at Nathan like she was imagining how hard it would be to elbow him in the throat. She leaned forward, bending between Nathan and Stew, to lay a hand on Merry's shoulder.

"Hey," she said in the most soothing tone she could muster, "I promise you, Miss Clark, we're not the bad guys."

"*Warrant Officer* Clark." She tensed up under Carla's palm and looked down at her hand before her gaze bounced back up to her face. "I'd like to believe that," she murmured. "Why should I?"

"Because we don't want to hurt anyone. At least, not anyone *human*." Carla pulled her hand away again and sighed. "We think some portion of our military leadership has been cooperating with the aliens." She hesitated. "Perhaps not entirely of their own free will."

"We *know* they sat on their asses while a huge number of civilians got sucked dry," Stew added.

"And we're not going to sit by and let that happen," Dr. Sharma added from behind them.

Merry's anger seemed to fade, and she frowned down at her hands. At least she wasn't glaring daggers at Nathan anymore; that was something. "Yeah," she murmured. "I think you might be right."

Nathan's eyebrows shot up. "Really? You agree with us?"

"Sit down, Nutty," Stew barked. "She's trying to act friendly and throw us off our guard."

"No, I'm not." Merry's eyes searched the ground below them. They were leaving the bay behind, although from this height and in the wake of the fires that had ravaged the coast, Carla couldn't tell exactly where they were. "A few days ago, I went on a run into the city with this guy who..." She shook her head and fell silent.

"You think he was one of the bad guys?" Nathan pressed.

To Carla's surprise, the pilot let out a bark of laughter. "Listen, we're not exactly overrun with heroes lately, are we? I've seen people in the city. I knew there were survivors. I left them. So *bad guys* is a relative term, no matter how *good* you claim to be." She shook her head. "But this guy? He was weird at first, but he gave me the creeps. Walked right into the mouth of the nest, and he came back *smiling* with a case of bottles, all of them filled with... hell if I know what, but something *weird.* Something he took out of the nest. I've been keeping tabs on that place since day one, and I'm telling you, it's no good." She drummed her fingers on the pitch control. "He was a walking red flag, as my mom would have said."

Carla crouched down beside Merry. "Can you take us where you took him?"

"To the *nest?*" Nathan clutched his rifle. "Carla, we've got two guns and a tablet that makes a loud noise! What good do you think that's going to do against an alien horde?"

"Probably not much," Carla admitted. "But where else are we supposed to go?"

"We might have a bigger problem," Merry said. She squinted down at the radar. "We've got planes on our tail."

Stew spun around. "Are you still good on the guns, Mr. Sharma?"

At least he's calling the man by his proper name, Carla thought.

"I am." Mr. Sharma's voice wavered, but he was already swiveling around in his gun turret.

"Hold your fire," Merry said. "We're outnumbered, and if they hit us, we're *all* screwed."

"How many are there?" Carla asked.

"Not sure." Merry glowered at the readings. "A handful, at least, and I should warn you that the fuel gauge isn't looking great. Not your guys' brightest idea, stealing a chopper that wasn't refueled. My Black Hawk was running on fumes, but these UH-1Y Venoms burn through a tank like nobody's business."

"Noted," Stew said flatly. "We will *definitely* keep that in mind for next time."

Merry gave him the finger.

"I think this is a long shot," Carla said, "but can you please take us where the last guy went? If you do, we'll leave, and you can go back without us. Explain what happened. Tell 'em where we went, for all I care. We don't want to get anyone else hurt, but if we don't do something, we might as well lie down and give up."

Merry turned her head to meet her eye. She seemed to be sizing her up, and Carla held her gaze, hoping that she would believe her. After a long moment, the woman sighed.

"I've had a perfectly functional mic this whole time," she said, tapping her headset. "If I wanted to sell you morons out, I could have turned this on and let my boys hear exactly where we were heading. They could keep their distance until we reached our drop point, and you'd be dead before your feet hit the tarmac."

Carla's stomach lurched.

"But I didn't," she added. "Because here's the thing. I used to be one of the good guys. You're damn lucky you got me and not somebody who would tip your asses right out the side doors." She raised her voice, and when she spoke next, she'd shifted into battle mode. "Dr. Sharma, is it? You may fire at will."

When the first shot went off, Carla *felt* it rather than heard it. The blast of the firing mechanism thrummed through her bones.

"I can't see anything." Stew swiveled his head toward the open doors of the cockpit. "What's happening?"

"Stick your head out if you want to find out," Merry said.

She was obviously being facetious, but Carla was tired of waiting around and letting other people decide what would happen to her. She grabbed her laser rifle and approached the open door.

"Still have that strap?" she bellowed to Dr. Sharma. Her voice was almost carried away by the wind, but apparently Dr. Sharma heard, because she produced the strap from her right and passed it along. Carla looped the strap around the bottom of the post holding the seats in place, praying that it was a sufficiently reinforced hard point, then planted her boots against the ground, and leaned.

If she'd been facing into the wind, she doubted that she could have kept her eyes open. Even pointing forward, she was buffeted about so badly that she almost lost her footing. At least she was able to get enough of a view behind them that she could take aim. She didn't want to risk running the laser rifle so hot that she lost her grip, so when she fired the first time, she only kept her finger on the trigger for a second. Her shot went wide, and when Merry changed course, she almost fell.

This isn't going to work. She pulled herself back inside and reconsidered the setup. After a moment, she tried looping one leg around the lip of the opening and hooking her knee over the top of the bar that supported the landing skid. It wasn't comfortable, and it was far from elegant, but it beat flapping around in the wind like a pennant.

When she fired again, she was able to control her shot. On the third try, she hit one of them head-on, clipping a wing. The laser wasn't powerful enough to sever it clean off, but the air resistance was able to finish what Carla had started. The wing peeled away from the body of the fighter, and the jet spun sideways into its neighbor. Sharma's shots hit a third.

Carla couldn't hear the jets firing, but she assumed they must be. Why else would they follow the Venom? *Unless they're just tracking us to see where we go. Does Greene have the resources to run drones?*

If so, he's an idiot for wasting them on us. The minute we touch down, we're walking into the lion's den.

Merry bellowed something, but from her position, Carla couldn't hear a word. Her leg was cramping up, and her shoulder was starting to ache. Once she pulled herself back inside, she wasn't sure she could manage another round of this. She might as well try for one more shot before giving up.

Her finger was on the trigger when a white-hot bolt of pain sheared through her shoulder. She screamed into the wind, not even realizing that her grip on the laser rifle had slackened until it was already slipping out of her fingers and tumbling away through the sky. In her shock, she almost let go of the strap, and if Stew hadn't grabbed her in time, that would have been the end of Carla Bonaparte.

She was still dangling out the door when a plane flew by. Only it wasn't a military jet; it was a small private plane, one of the noisy little ones with a propeller in front, which made no sense at all. *What is that doing here?*

It must have been the pain. That was the only explanation. Time seemed to stop as Carla stared out at the plane. She could have sworn that she knew the face on the man who was staring back at her open-mouthed, leaning out the side of the plane much as she was the chopper.

It wasn't him. Of course it wasn't. But for one sweet, agonizing moment, she let herself believe that it was.

Len.

Then Stew was yanking on her, and she was tumbling face-first into the cockpit again.

"—go and get yourself shot doing *stupid friggin' stunts!*" Stew yelled.

"Sorry," Carla mumbled. "Dropped the gun."

"Almost dropped yourself, too," Stew said. He yanked on Carla's shirt, then sighed with relief. "Looks like they only took a chunk out of you. Honestly, it's no better than you deserve."

"Good news," Merry said, flicking through the controls with a steady hand, although her voice belied her nerves. "Our new friend somehow took out the last two jets on our tail. Bad news? We're low on fuel."

"There's more back here," Sharma's daughter called from the rear of the ship.

"Yes, and when you figure out how to refuel a chopper in the air, you can take responsibility for doing exactly that," Merry said.

"Why carry the extra payload?" Stew asked. "Why not just fill the tank to begin with?"

"She *would* have a full tank, only some dipshit decided to steal her before she could refuel, so the backup is all we've got!" Merry said. "In the meantime, like it or not, I'm putting her down. I'll try to keep us to the roofline, but—"

"Oh, no," Nathan moaned. "Oh my *God*."

"—but it'll be better if you don't look down," Merry finished drily.

Stew and Carla exchanged a look, and then in unison rolled toward the door again. The city was rising up fast beneath them, and the streets appeared to be flooded, as if the Potomac had overspilled its banks and sent dark water boiling over the George Washington Parkway.

It's not water. Carla gripped her arm and stared down at the land in horror. *It's* invadendae.

She'd understood how ruthless they were, but not how numerous. And now it seemed like every alien in the world was waiting below them, poised to attack the moment the helicopter reached land.

They wouldn't have to wait long.

24

COOPER

COOPER'S JACKAL was navigating the rooftops of the Federal Triangle when his headache started. It began with a pressure behind his eyelids, so intense that it turned his stomach and left him dizzy. He squeezed his eyes shut in an attempt to block it out, but that only made it worse. It was as if someone was standing just over his shoulder, whispering *Attack, attack, attack,* except that it came to him in images rather than words. The urge to descend to the street and turn against the civilians fighting there dragged at him like an undertow.

"What the hell?" he whispered aloud, gripping his forehead. He slumped against the back of the Jackal. "No way." Hearing his own voice helped clear his head a little, but the pressure was still there, pushing and pulling his mind out of shape. The impulse came from somewhere else.

From someone else, he thought, and sat up straight again.

His little experiment with the jelly had done more than made it possible to talk to the Clankers. It had given the hivemind a way in.

Knowing that the thoughts weren't his own made it easier to push them aside. Whatever compounds Pammy had ingested when she ate Clanker-flesh must have been much more potent than what Cooper had swallowed. She was able to talk to the Clankers that much more clearly, which probably also meant that the hivemind would have a much easier time getting into her head.

Cooper looked down at the street below, where soldiers in exosuits were converging on the caravan even as it forced its way along the street. Given the pressure in his head, he'd expected to see Clankers following them.

Unless the hivemind wasn't only giving orders to Clankers now.

Oh. He steered his ride to the edge of the rooftop. What if he wasn't the only person other than Pammy to have made that connection? If the alien hivemind could benefit from having all of its soldiers on the same wavelength, another army could do the same. And if the human soldiers had agreed to drink the alien Kool-Aid...

Then I just hacked their command system.

He surveyed the streets around him in search of Guppie's Jackal, and spotted it a block behind the caravan. It was walking alongside a man in a damaged exosuit. For a moment, his heart dropped, until he spotted a familiar head of thinning white hair poking out the top of the suit. Cooper headed his way, noting the man's lumbering trajectory.

Guppie must have switched his mech onto autopilot, because when Cooper found him on street-level, Chelly was following the man in the suit like a faithful dog.

"Guppie!" Cooper headed closer, wondering how he was going to explain the fact that he'd suddenly developed the ability to not only speak to the Clankers but listen in on the hivemind's commands, and that he'd conveniently forgotten to mention it to anyone until now. Before he could sort that out, he realized how awkwardly Guppie was moving.

Guppie lifted a massive mechanical hand in greeting. "Hey, kid."

"Damn, gramps, how did you damage your suit that badly?" he asked. "I wouldn't think you'd need to be able to walk to keep that thing running."

"I don't." Guppie smiled thinly, although his gray hair was matted with sweat. "The suit's got that covered."

Cooper slid off the back of the Jackal, giving Chelly a cursory glance as he passed. When he did so, he froze; a broad smear of blood covered the side of the mech, and one of the metal braces had been twisted beyond recognition. The blood was drying black, but Cooper was pretty sure that wasn't Clanker-blood.

"Hey," he said slowly, "you all right, Guppie?"

His friend waved him away, although his face had gone pale. "I took a hit, but I'm still going, kiddo. Where's the fight?"

"You're almost there. But I think we should pick another route."

Guppie groaned and waved his armored fists. "I can handle it!"

"I didn't mean to protect you," Cooper said. Guppie looked like he could use a medic, but even if Cooper had been able to wrangle him into agreement, the only medics around were in the middle of a firefight at the moment. "Right now there's one force coming at the caravan from the front. It means our whole group is bunched together, which, uh, *probably* means that the others are, too. If we spread out a little, we'll stretch their resources thinner." He spread his hands invitingly. "We can draw some of their fire and make it easier for the caravan to get through, you know? Open up the map a little."

"Spread 'em out," Guppie agreed thickly. "Yeah, all right." He didn't even comment on Cooper's video game analogy, which was more worrying than anything else. He would have liked to ask Guppie what was wrong, but the older man was already moving, headed toward the peak of the obelisk in the distance.

He's not okay, Cooper thought, but there wasn't much he could do other than scramble onto the back of his Jackal and try to steer Guppie in the right direction.

THE CARAVAN HAD ALREADY PUSHED the fight down the road in an attempt to close in on their target. The goal of getting the fight out into the open made sense, as it would make their group harder to flank. On the downside, it also meant that it was harder for them to flank the enemy. By the time Cooper and Guppie were able to get behind the enemy line, there weren't a lot of places to hide.

They went in anyway. Guppie led the charge, fists swinging, and caught one of the mechanical wardogs off-guard. It only just managed to get its power shield up in time, and when it did, the fist's hydraulic backup hit the shield with such force that the mech slid backward.

Damn. How did he manage to snag a suit that powerful off somebody who was already wearing it? One look at Guppie's face answered the question: he was hurting. All that firepower had come at a cost.

The wardog was so focused on fending off Guppie that when Cooper's mech slid around to one side, it took no notice of him, even when he fired a flare. It hit the ground at the wardog's feet and exploded; the first blast was contained by the shield, and by the time the damaged machine was finished off by the second-stage detonation, Guppie had managed to back away.

A hydraulic groan brought Cooper around to face his next target. It was a soldier wearing a suit like the one Guppie had nabbed, but with an intact helmet. It stumped along on thick legs, with one arm raised toward its shoulder to help balance the massive piece of equipment it carried. For one disorienting moment, Cooper couldn't tell if it was holding a boombox or a massive box fan. Then the soldier activated the weapon, and the whole world stopped.

When Cooper came to, he was lying face-up on the tarmac several feet from his mech. He blinked a few times, trying to understand why had happened, and why his head felt like someone had slammed his skull repeatedly against the road.

Guppie hadn't been hit by the blast radius of the soldier's

weapon. He was charging, fists raised and teeth bared. When the soldier tried to fire on him, Guppie feinted left so fast that he became nothing more than a blur. The muted *pop* of the weapon going off was familiar enough. The soldier was carrying a ThunderGen, only in cannon form.

I wonder if it could take out a fighter jet, Cooper mused as he hauled himself to his feet and back onto his ride. He had barely slid into place before he fired the electrical charge.

His shot was mistimed. One of Guppie's fists crashed into the soldier's torso, throwing him off balance. The soldier staggered, and Cooper's charge missed it, hitting the thunder cannon instead.

"Move!" he bellowed to Guppie, but the old man stuck around to deliver a second blow, giving his enemy time to aim again. Cooper bit back a cry as the soldier fired point-blank on his friend.

Guppie went sprawling, but the soldier wasn't in much better shape. The thunder cannon was evidently at less than half-power, and it fizzled and sparked as he aimed at Guppie's fallen form. When he fired again, the cannon burst apart, blowing most of its tech out the back and onto the road.

"Guppie!" Cooper bellowed. The hivemind's commands were still pushing him forward. It wanted him to attack the soldier. *Its commands must be confused,* he thought, until he realized that it didn't matter. The hivemind didn't care what the humans did to one another, not really, so long as it got what it wanted in the end. To a mind that could ride along with numberless consciousnesses across uncountable worlds, no life truly mattered.

Cooper didn't see things the same way. He fired the electrical pulse again, and when the soldier in the exosuit fell to his knees, he let Chelly take care of the rest. He went to Guppie, sliding off of his mech's back to land on his knees next to the older man. "Can you get up?" he asked.

Guppie was already thrashing around like an overturned turtle. "I'm fine," he gasped.

"You don't *look* fine," Cooper insisted.

Guppie glared at him. "Listen, kiddo, you know I care about you, right? Know that I think you're smart and all that? Well, do the math. Our medic's in combat, there's no place or time to recover, and this is it. The last battle. Nobody gets to sit this one out, okay? So help me up and stop bitching about a little blood loss. The suit can pick up my slack." He rolled onto his knees at last and stopped to catch his breath.

A round metal object struck the ground and Cooper's side, and both men glanced up to find Guppie's damaged mech standing over the fallen soldier, whose helmet had been pulled away and now lay on the ground beside them. The mech's AI, still intact from before Cooper had gotten his hands on it, appeared to be working just fine.

"Good girl, Chelly," Guppie grunted as he scooped up the helmet. "That's what I'm talking about." He mashed the helmet on his head and got to his feet. When he spoke again, his voice was warbly and distorted from the helmet's speaker. "You coming, kid?"

The sounds of battle were moving closer; pretty soon the caravan would reach them, and there would be one last push to the open green of the monument. After that would be a waiting game. Waiting for Pammy to strike the final blow. Waiting for the hivemind to collapse.

And I might be the only person on our side who'll know for sure when it does... or if it doesn't.

"Yeah," Cooper muttered thickly. "I'm coming."

Not like he had a choice.

BEYOND WASHINGTON

The Hi'aiti'ihi People
Humaitá National Forest, Brazil

———————

There were eight of them now. They didn't speak of the dead; those who remained slept less than usual, and never at the same time. Even in their sleep, they were always listening for the sound of approaching *abaisi*.

The shaman didn't measure time. Her language had no way to trap it, because there was only ever the *now* and the *not-now*, just as there were *humans* and *not-humans*. Any moment other than the one the tribe currently inhabited was unimportant, because there was nothing to be done about it. For the first time in her life, a sense of constant unease rode on the shaman's shoulders like a hungry spirit. It fed on her.

The *abaisi* didn't follow the rules of any other living thing that the tribe had encountered before. Nonetheless, the prior elder had begun to understand them before he was taken. The current elder often deferred to the shaman on matters pertaining to the *abaisi*.

It had been her idea to come to the open place between the trees and stand with her back to the water. She had watched the creatures carefully, memorizing the patterns of their noises and the rhythms of their days. Their language was different from that of the Upright People, but there was still a rhythm to it. There were still rules. The shaman had tried to whistle it, but her mouth couldn't recreate the sounds. It had taken her day upon day upon day to fashion an instrument from wood and reeds, and to find the curved jaguar bone that brought the right tone and the necessary spiritual power to its player.

It had been her idea, too, to play the simple song that she had taught herself while watching the *abaisi* go about their work. It went against the shaman's instincts to will the death of any living thing, but the new creatures were unnatural. Two times, the Igagai had visited her on the banks of the river and warned her that the war against the *abaisi* was a spiritual war, one that followed different rules than an ordinary hunt.

The shaman adjusted her grip in the instrument and dragged the rib-bone across its surface, sending up a sharp thrum. She mirrored its sound deep in her throat so that it filled the open place, resonating through the trees. She'd been forced to guess what the sounds meant, precisely, but this was the noise the *abaisi* had made when they fed on the ninth member of the tribe as she lay dying on the forest floor. It was a sating-hunger song, a celebration of abundance and easy gathering.

Come to me, the shaman thought as she rode out an emotion that walked the knife's edge between fear and anger. *Come eat me, if you can manage it.*

Even when she heard the answering thrum, she kept playing. She stood with her back to the muddy waters of the lake and waited, repeating the refrain until it echoed in her chest. The *abaisi* weren't as plentiful as other species, but a small group of them had settled by the still water. If left unchecked they would soon grow as plentiful as Brazil nuts or howler monkeys, and they would destroy the forests, leaving nothing in their wake.

The *abaisi* answered her song. She heard them moving through the undergrowth, shuddering between the trees, wreathing the princess flowers and cupuacu and hanging moss in shifting shadows cast by their serpentine bodies. And all the while, she played.

Until she heard the whistle.

At the elder's signal, the tribe released their arrows. Every one of them flew true, and three of the great beasts collapsed into the soil, stirring up the bracken and moss as they died. The remaining handful of *abaisi* drew into a protective circle as the members of the tribe dropped from the trees to land on bare feet. They had fashioned long spears that would reach farther than the limbs of the beasts and knotted flaked knifepoints to the ends, bound with cords made of gut and sinew. As the members of her tribe surrounded the *abaisi*, the shaman began a new song, one composed of whistles and deep humming.

The shaman hadn't written this song. It was a gift of the Igagai, one that had blossomed in her mind like a dream. The tribe had practiced it with care, each learning their part, whispering it to one another in the late hours of the night when the call of the tree frogs grew so loud that it drowned out their efforts.

The shaman's visions had been correct. As the tribe's voice joined in a discordant cacophony of shrill whistles and deep throat-song, the *abaisi* shuddered with a sort of madness. They ran in every direction, desperate to escape the song, only to impale themselves one by one on the tribe's long ironwood spears. The few who almost escaped were chased down on foot. The shaman herself leapt onto the back of one of the beasts and drove a wooden blade into the weak joints of its carapace with such force that her hand sank wrist-deep into the flesh beneath.

When the last of the beasts was dead, the tribe gathered by the shore of the lake. Even their youngest member, the child who had hidden during the slaughter, joined them.

The elder examined the water, then nodded to the women. "Make us a net," he said. "We will sift out the eggs and the young from the water, and we will destroy them. The *abaisi* will not have a chance to put down roots here."

They crushed the eggs and speared the young until every last one of the *abaisi* was scoured from the lake. As she washed their blood from her hands in the shallows, the gnawing ache in the shaman's belly eased. In that moment, the *abaisi* were gone. Whether or not they would return wasn't a concern in the now. There were more pressing considerations: what to eat for dinner, where to camp for the night, how much distance to put between themselves and the lake. Her stomach was empty and her tongue was dry. That was more pressing than any concern for the future.

There would be other *abaisi*. Other lakes. The shaman didn't let them trouble her. She left her little instrument beside the shore. If necessary, she could always make another. She would confront them in the not-now if and when it came.

25
LEN

LEN WAS BACK at the controls of the plane, relegating Klarie to watching the skies with the ThunderGen at the ready.

"We're following the helicopter," Len said hoarsely.

"Are we bringing them down?" Klarie's hands were steadier. Either the adrenaline had her system humming, or she was getting more comfortable with their situation.

"Just ... we're just following them," Len said. Unlike Klarie, he was more on edge than ever. When they'd passed the chopper, he could have sworn that the woman dangling out of the door was—

No. Don't get your hopes up, you'll only feel that much worse when they're dashed all to hell. All the same, he couldn't shake the feeling that it was Carla. And wouldn't it be fitting for the two of them to meet like this, in the place around which the fate of the world now revolved?

Maybe it wasn't so crazy after all.

Klarie glanced over at him. "Are you okay, Len?"

"I think I'm losing my mind," he whispered. "And no, we're not shooting them. Not yet. Not until I know for sure that I'm wrong." He passed his hand over his eye and shuddered.

In the streets below them, two armies of Clankers broke over each other in a wave. There was no sign of Pammy, although at this point, that could have meant anything. Len's head was out of the game, and until he had proof one way or another, he wasn't going to be of any use to anyone.

Something was apparently wrong with the helicopter. Len didn't have to know much about their flight patterns to know that it was dropping fast. Did it mean something that they hadn't tried to take aim at his plane? The more he thought about it, the more the selfish, illogical parts of his brain tried to make the pieces fit. It was a military helicopter, but they'd definitely been fighting off the jets. He'd run into Lavelle Steward only hours ago. Once all the soft, squishy parts of his brain got to hoping, he knew he was in trouble.

"Are you going to land with them?" Klarie asked warily.

"Not yet. But we'll stay close." Len never took his eye off the chopper. It landed on the roof of a beige building that looked as though it had once been a hotel. Len had driven on the George Washington Parkway more times than he could count, but his trips rarely brought him to this part of the city.

Len pressed his face to the window. *Please, please, please,* he thought, and practically held his breath. When the woman he'd seen before stepped out of the chopper and stared up, he swore his heart was going to stop.

"I'm taking us in," he said. "I'm taking us in, I'm taking us in

—" He had to press his hand to his mouth and bite down on his palm to stop himself from chanting the same words forever.

The Clankers must have heard them coming in for a landing, but whatever Pammy had done to get them to turn on one another evidently held their attention. At that exact moment, Len couldn't have cared less about the battle raging below them.

It was all he could do to stop himself from launching himself out the side of the plane and onto the rooftop below, because with each passing second, he was more certain that it was her.

It seemed to take an eternity to circle around and land on the parkway near the helo. As the plane touched down, he could see figures emerging from the building where the helicopter had landed.

He'd barely killed the Cessna's engines before he was tumbling out of the cockpit.

He spread his arms wide, and Carla launched herself into his arms.

"Len?" She sounded as incredulous as he felt. "Baby, *how?* What happened to you? How are you—?"

She kept talking and talking, asking questions he couldn't answer, and all the while she was holding him so tight he thought that he might split apart and shatter into pieces.

Screw the city. Screw the war. If a bomb dropped on them from above, he wouldn't have cared. He'd kept his promises to both of them.

He'd survived.

And he'd found his way back to her.

. . .

AFTER LEN LEARNED of all the others with Carla, they'd all returned to the rooftop to refuel the helicopter. From their escape from Little Creek, Len knew only too well how limited the Cessna's ability to haul cargo was, and he'd be damned if he was letting Carla out of his sight.

"So let me get this straight." Stew peered out at the aliens he could make out from the rooftop. "Right now, one of your friends is down there speaking alien to these suckers, while even as we speak, my *mom* is leading an all-out attack on the city?"

"Co-leading," Klarie corrected. "But the rest sounds right."

"Hot damn." Stew stood up. "Merry, are you about done with refueling?"

The pilot gave Stew the finger over her shoulder.

The sound of their banter washed over Len like a wave and kept going. He wasn't listening. The only thing he cared about was the steady thump of Carla's heart beneath his hand.

"Is that too tight?" he asked as he pulled on the bandage. She'd taken a hit in the air, and although she insisted she was fine, Len had been equally stubborn about dressing it. He couldn't stop thinking about the shape Guppie had been in when he first crossed paths with him and Vera. He'd pulled through, but he'd looked pretty rough there for a few weeks. Len wasn't going to let Carla suffer for a second longer than necessary. Besides, who knew how many seconds any of them had left?

Nathan Nolte was staring out at the Clankers with wide eyes, while Dr. Sharma hovered nearby with her family.

Sharma's arm tightened around her daughter's waist. "Are there any safe places left?"

When Len didn't respond, Klarie said, "Hard to know. Keystone wasn't exactly *safe*, but we pulled through. And we found a new enclave only hours ago. There might be other people out there who made it."

"That's nice in theory." The pilot stowed the empty canisters, then turned back to them. "But we don't have an infinite fuel supply, and we can't very well go frolicking around the countryside in search of other survivors. We need a plan. We've got maybe an hour of fuel and then this baby's going to be land-bound, like it or not."

"Our people should have reached the Washington Monument by now," Klarie said. "If Len and I lead you in, they'll let you land safely. It shouldn't be an issue."

Carla's hand lifted to catch Len's wrist as he tied off the bandage. When he glanced up, her eyes were fixed on his face. Back in the day, they'd been good at reading one another. Judging by the way she was looking at him now, they hadn't lost that talent. He knew exactly what she was thinking, and he already agreed.

"That's a great plan." Stew nodded emphatically. "We can meet up with Mom, tell her everything we know, and join the last stand against enemies both foreign and domestic." His face lit up. "Hey, that's pretty good, don't you think? What do you say? Steward's last stand!" He struck a heroic pose out over the city.

"I say you're delusional." Sharma adjusted her glasses with the arm that wasn't clinging to her daughter. "But I *do* think we should go to our allies. We might be able to provide them with information."

"And they might be able to provide us with weapons," her daughter added.

"Either way, this is how we're going to be useful." Mr. Sharma lifted his chin defiantly. "Very well, let us head into the thick of battle."

Nathan lifted his rifle. "I'm not much of a soldier, but I'll do what I can."

Klarie slapped one palm against her thigh. "Are we ready, then? Len?"

Len's hand had lingered on the fresh bandage over his wife's shoulder.

"Actually..." He cleared his throat.

"We're not coming," Carla said.

Everyone turned to stare at them. Stew's head bobbled back and forth emphatically. "Oh, no. Hell, no. You're already planning some sort of crazy suicide mission, aren't you?"

"I've got a recording of the sound wave," Carla said. "And I'm not walking away from this until I know for sure that thing is dead."

"You barely have *weapons!*" Sharma cried.

"But Pammy has one of the disruptors," Len said. "I was already planning on following her to make sure she finished the job. Now I can do that without dragging Klarie into it with me."

"Len, screw that." The girl advanced a pace and shook her head. Her eyes were bloodshot, and her lips quivered, pulling down at the edges. "No way. You're not pulling some sort of suicide mission now."

"Of course not. Quite the opposite." Len took Carla's hand. "We were always supposed to do this. I don't know how to explain it, but... Look, I spent years in the woods waiting for the world to end, and when it did, I'm the only reason the Little Creek Five wasn't the Little Creek One. I went out that night because I was *supposed* to." He slapped his palm over his heart twice. "We needed all of us to get this far, and none of us would have made it if I hadn't followed my gut. And my gut's telling me that I need to see this through." He forced a smile and pointed at his face. "Besides, I want to look that alien sono-fabitch in the eye when it goes down. I want it to know that it picked the wrong planet to mess with."

"By all accounts, it's a fungus," Stew mumbled. "Pretty sure it doesn't have eyeballs."

"Not true." Nathan hooked his thumb over the ledge of the roof. "It's got a metric *shitton* of eyeballs, if you count every-thing it's infected."

Stew waved a hand in acknowledgment.

"Do you at least want me to get you closer?" Merry asked. She was the only one who didn't seem surprised by their plan. "The Crystal City metro stop is a few blocks away."

Carla shook her head. "We'll go underground. There's a stop nearby. I'd rather not walk through the front door."

"If that's where Pammy Mae is headed, then the fighting is going to be the most intense there," Len added. "We wouldn't stand a chance."

"So you're just going to waltz in with a phone that plays a screechy noise?" Klarie demanded.

"There's a ThunderGen in the plane," Len said. "We'll take that, too."

Nathan got up and approached them, then held out the weapon he was clutching. "You can take this one, too."

Carla accepted it with one arm and threw the other around her labmate. "Thanks, Nutty."

Len left them to say their goodbyes while he retrieved his ThunderGen from the plane. Klarie hovered over his shoulder, and when Len straightened up, Klarie grabbed him in a bear hug. She was a little thing, but she was strong. "Be careful," she whispered in Len's ear. "If you get killed out there, I'll have to kick your ass, you know? And it's going to involve a Ouija board and a whole production, so maybe just spare me the effort."

"I'll try." Len patted the girl's back stiffly. "And say hi to the rest of the crew for me, all right? *Hi.* Not *bye.* Got it?"

Soon enough the helicopter was airborne. Len and Carla stood on the roof, watching as it headed toward the silhouette of an obelisk in the distance. Clouds of dust and smoke were rising from the ground in that direction, a sure sign that a battle was unfolding out there, and that his friends were putting up a fight.

"You ready, baby?" Carla asked.

Len took a deep breath and clutched the ThunderGen to his chest.

"Yeah," he said. "Born ready. Been waiting my whole life for this."

26
VERA

VERA'S STRENGTH was flagging by the time they reached the grass. She had almost forgotten their purpose in heading south. All she could think was that she needed to keep moving, keep fighting, keep breathing, keep pushing. They'd left a few of the wardogs in their wake, and even a couple of soldiers in ravaged exosuits, but they'd left plenty of their own, too. At some point, she would have to take stock of their damages and count their dead.

Soon, but not yet. They only had a little further to go.

"Vera?" Estes popped up at her elbow. "One of the trucks got hit."

"Right." She fired on one of the wardogs just as it dropped its shield to aim at one of Lavelle's people. "Let me just snap my fingers and fix it." She lowered her ThunderGen and turned to follow him, more exhausted and battered than she had ever been in her life.

Estes led her back to the supply truck. Deimos and Phobos were howling inside, and when Vera stuck her head inside, the bloodhound licked her face in greeting.

"The tire we patched the other day is shredded," Estes said. "And I think one of the axles is broken, but either way, she won't move." He looked at Vera, waiting for an answer. For a solution.

A bubble of mad laughter rose in her throat. *You think this matters?* she almost asked. *You think one truck's worth of supplies is going to be enough to keep us going, even if we do somehow survive?* She swallowed it down. Even if the supplies wouldn't be enough to last any longer, they'd be enough for a day, at least. That was all people needed, really: the assurance that planning for the future wasn't an exercise in futility.

"Move what you can to the ambulance." Vera waved to the vehicle that carried the Pelican case and their backup disruptor. "Prioritize medical supplies." Following her own advice, she hoisted a crate of Peachey's supplies into one arm, balancing the ThunderGen in the other.

The dogs tried to follow, and it wasn't as if she could just leave them there. Len had trained them well, but they wouldn't be any use against the mechs and the exosuits. After a moment of waffling, Vera whistled to them. "Heel." Both dogs stuck to her as she hurried back to the ambulance and threw the doors open. She heaved her crate to the back of the truck and whirled back to the road, only to find herself face-to-face with her father's soot-smudged countenance. Harun offered her a thin smile before following her lead with a crate of his own.

Vera pulled him aside, and Burcu arrived a moment later, Vera gathered them each in a tight embrace.

"Wait a moment," she said, before kneeling down in front of the dogs. She patted their heads, then pointed to her parents. "This is my family," she told them. "I need you to protect them, okay?"

Deimos's tongue lolled, and Phobos's eyes darted suspiciously to the older couple.

"They look a bit wild, şekerim," Burcu murmured, wringing her hands.

"No wilder than the aliens," Harun pointed out.

Vera ignored them, pointing an emphatic finger at her parents' faces. "*Protect.* Got it?"

Deimos moved toward Burcu, and even when she flinched away, he nudged her hand with a wet nose. Phobos followed the bloodhound's lead, then glanced back at Vera as if to make sure he'd understood.

"Good boys," Vera said as she got back to her feet. She patted her mother's arm once before setting off back into the fray.

The truck was nearly empty, so Vera left Estes to finish the task. Instead, she turned her attention to the civilians who were milling about in glassy-eyed shock, firing their weapons almost at random.

"We're holding this position," she barked, indicating the monument. "If anything comes at us, do whatever it takes to stop it or drive it back."

"Vera?" Peachey appeared at her side. "Are we going to establish a medical station?"

Shit. Of course. She'd just filled the ambulance with supplies, which would likely mean that their medic wouldn't have any cover while he worked. Not that an ambulance wall would provide much cover from the wardogs and the exosuits, never mind the aircraft. Vera spun in a quick circle, trying to determine which position would be best. The constant boom of artificial thunder wasn't doing anything to help her think.

"Set up on the west side," she said. "Tell whoever's over there to set up around you so that you can get as much cover from the monument as possible." There wouldn't be much, but she was working with what they had. Peachey nodded and bolted away to get started.

One of Lavelle's people had managed to set up a small cannon on a tripod, and was keeping the wardogs at bay with a constant barrage of artillery. Even so, the mechs were creeping forward, gaining ground inch by inch. They advanced in a row, like Roman soldiers in tortoise formation, using their energy shields to form an impassable wall. Many of the soldiers in exosuits had moved behind them, taking advantage of their cover and timing the blasts of their thunder cannons to coincide with the moments when the wardogs dropped their cover.

Vera dipped behind one of the vehicles and took a deep breath, doing her best to clear her head. The thunder cannons had already damaged the monument's white surface. At some point, the whole thing might very well collapse. Their enemy was better organized and better armed.

Think, Vera. How do you retaliate against a force like this? If only Guppie were there, he'd no doubt have some suggestions.

She was still struggling to formulate a plan when Lavelle's

hand landed on her shoulder. "We have a situation," the older woman said. Somewhere along the line she must have taken a blow to the head; her white hair was stained pink at the temple.

"Yeah?" Vera stood up. "Worse than before?"

Lavelle pointed west toward the river, and Vera swore. A host of Clankers was headed their way, marching through the shallow waters of the World War II Memorial. They must have taken a different path than Pammy's army and slipped through.

Either that, or Pammy's dead. Or worse, she's gone full Clanker. The pessimistic little voice in Vera's head made her squirm, but she refused to let her imagination get the better of her. For now, all that mattered was that they were under attack.

"There's got to be a way to use this," Vera muttered aloud.

Lavelle snorted. "Really? Your Clanker-talking girl took off already. I don't think that you're going to be able to steer them so easily without her."

"Maybe not, but—"

Vera's reply was interrupted by a massive *boom*, and the precise line of wardogs scattered. At first, she thought that one of the exosuits must have malfunctioned and turned on its fellows, but then she saw the Jackals following in the suit's wake. Cooper was riding one of them, and whatever he'd just detonated had left some of the wardogs limping.

"Focus on the Clankers!" Vera cried to Lavelle. "Keep them back. Don't let them come any closer than the walkways, but don't target them beyond that. Let's see if we can drive them around the verge and get them to target the soldiers. At the very least, they might make it hard for the wardogs to hold a line."

"I'll see what we can do," Lavelle promised.

Vera's weary fugue had lifted. It had always been easier to support the people she cared about than to keep going on her own account, and now that she could see for herself that Cooper and Guppie were still alive and well, her sense of urgency returned tenfold.

"ESTES!" she bellowed. "*Where are you? I need backup!*" She scooped up a ThunderGen and ran across the grass toward her friends without waiting for an answer, firing as she went, taking advantage of the unshielded back of every wardog and every dent in the armor of the exosuits.

Hopefully Lavelle would run the base of operations for the time being. Vera's shoulder ached from the constant jolt of the ThunderGen's kickback, but at least she didn't have to think as she aimed.

Think of it as a game, she told herself. *A game where you don't have to worry about who you hurt, so long as your friends stay alive.*

27

GUPPIE

THE WORLD HAD BECOME something that happened *to* Guppie, not a space that he moved through. The suit's design made it easy to pilot; he barely had to twitch his muscles to get it to respond, and its internal calibration meant that even when his legs couldn't support him, the suit's reflexes made up the difference.

The trouble was all in his head. Every planned attack took a few seconds to move from his brain to his muscles, and without the structural support of the suit, he would have toppled face-first onto the concrete. Fortunately, he was able to keep fighting, but he was lacking any meaningful edge. The other soldiers in their exosuits were younger and faster and fitter than he was, even on a good day, and today was anything but.

His next punch barely clipped the suit of the nearest soldier, and the hydraulic enhancement to his fist sent him off-balance. Guppie stumbled and crashed into the other man, and they both toppled, with Guppie landing on top. In the scuffle that followed, his opponent managed to land two solid hits to his shoulder and chest. The damaged breastplate collapsed inward until the twisted metal scraped against his collarbone. At last, Guppie managed to get one arm under the other man's chin and pin him to the pavement, then brought his fist down with such force that when the hydraulics kicked in, the glove's knuckles scraped the tarmac.

Guppie stared down at the cracked helmet beneath him and gasped for breath. *Get up,* he told himself, but his body wouldn't obey. Without the signals from his muscles, the suit didn't know what was expected of it. All he really wanted was to rip off the damned helmet and send it flying so that he could catch a full breath.

Get up.

Movement from up ahead caught his eye, and he lifted his chin to watch as a wardog galloped toward him. Its shield dropped and its laser flickered on, but Guppie could barely bring himself to move.

"Come on, you sonofabitch," he muttered, bracing his fists against the road on either side of the fallen soldier before him. "Give me what you've got."

The wardog was only a few yards away when a weight hit Guppie's back, and Cooper's Jackal vaulted over him. It landed on the wardog from above and carried it to the ground. The two of them tore at one another like living things, until Cooper fired a bolt of silver-blue lightning and the unmanned mech short-circuited.

"Guppie!" Cooper called.

From farther away, another voice called his name, too.

Guppie finally dragged himself upright. "Vera?" he mumbled.

She was striding toward him, firing blast after blast from her ThunderGen with the pinpoint accuracy of a surgeon. Estes was behind her, leading a group of Keystone soldiers in her wake.

The mechs were falling back, but they hadn't gone far, and only then did Guppie register the host of Clankers closing in from his left.

He forced himself to his feet at last and immediately listed to his left. He would have fallen if Chelly hadn't appeared at his side. She was running the AI, of course, it wasn't like she *cared* about him, but all the same Guppie felt a wave of affection for the mech.

"Good girl, Chelly," he slurred.

Cooper was shouting something and waving to him, and Estes was doing the same, so Guppie lumbered toward them. His soldier-brain took over. He needed someone to tell him what to do.

He made it a few steps before Vera dipped beneath his elbow, propping him up from one direction. "Guppie?" she asked. Her voice was watery and faraway. "Talk to me."

"I'm sorry," he said. "I'm sorry I couldn't..." But the weight of all the things he'd *failed* to do built up on his tongue and dragged him back into silence.

"Don't talk," she said. Even through the helmet, she could obviously tell that something was wrong. "Just come with me."

She led him toward the monument, balancing him from one

side while he rested one hand against Chelly's back. Cooper and the Keystone soldiers covered them, but the white obelisk felt impossibly far away, while the rattling forms of the Clankers drew ever nearer.

"Not gonna make it," he muttered.

And then he heard the whine of the thrum of the rotors from above.

He stopped and lifted his face skyward, shading his eyes with his hand to block the glare across his visor. He was braced for another squadron of jets, but it was a single chopper, dipping low above them.

"Cooper!" Vera hollered, waving toward the heavens. "Take 'em out!"

Cooper, too, had stopped to stare. He shook his head, then pointed mutely at the clouds. Vera's expression brightened as the chopper's mounted gun took aim at the wardogs.

"Keep moving!" Estes called, and their little band retreated. At long last, Guppie made his way into the shadow of the Washington Monument.

Peachey's medical station was already flooded with injured civilians, but Vera pushed past them and helped Guppie into a sitting position at the base of the monument. The moment she removed his helmet, her face turned ashen.

"You're hurt," she said. It wasn't a question.

"It's fine." He forced a smile that evidently did little to convince her. "I just need some water."

She narrowed her eyes and reached for the latches on the side of his suit. On instinct, he batted her hand away. "Leave it. Without the suit, I'm dead weight."

Vera's lips narrowed to a thin line, but she got to her feet. "Water, huh? I'll grab you some."

He had the feeling she knew what he was thinking. If the suit came off, she'd never let him back into the fray. He'd have to sit this one out, just like he had when the situation in Keystone deteriorated around them. He wouldn't let that happen. "Thanks, I owe you one."

Vera shook her head. "I'll be back."

"Sure." He went limp against the wall, but he kept his eyes open. One more push. That was all he needed.

He wasn't leaving the others to fight this last battle alone.

28

CARLA

THE LONG DESCENT through the unlit stairwell of the abandoned hotel left Carla lightheaded. It had been a minute since her last meal, and while the shot she'd taken to her arm had been little more than a laceration, the blood loss was still clearly getting to her.

It wasn't just her injuries throwing her for a loop, either. Over the years, she'd imagined finding Len in a hundred different scenarios, each more romantic than the last, and yet she'd never pictured him like *this*. He was a different person altogether. Harder, colder, and beat to hell and back. It broke her heart to think what he'd been through in her absence.

At the same time, it made her hopeful. He'd been through the mill and come out stronger for it. The new Carla would have been no good for the old Len, but maybe they could find a way to fit back together.

She had to hope so, anyway.

For the time being, she followed him to the ground floor, then out to the front of the building. A few of the windows remained intact, offering a view of the street while still making it possible for them to lie low. The *invadendae* were still streaming past, although their numbers appeared to be thinning. They crouched just below the windows so that only the tops of their heads would be visible from the outside, and watched the procession.

"Where are they *going?*" she asked.

"To the metro," Len said at once, dropping fully out of sight. "I'm telling you, Pammy Mae's the Pied Piper of Clankers."

"Clankers?" she repeated, bemused.

He pointed to the aliens. "Clankers. What do you call them?"

"*Homoptera invadendae.*"

His face broke out in a grin that was heartbreakingly familiar, even with the eyepatch that barely covered the scars on the right side of his face. "Honey," he said, "you know I love you, but that's a damn mouthful. I'm going to stick with Clankers, thanks."

She grinned back at him, and a weight she hadn't realized she was carrying lifted off her shoulders. "Fine, if you'd rather be speedy than accurate. What happens now?"

He lifted himself up again to peer over the window frame. "Right across the street. It's not far, but…"

"But it's like rush hour traffic with flesh-eating aliens," she said flatly. "Yeah, I see the issue. So how do we—"

"*Get down!*" Len bellowed. He tackled her so that she fell back along the wall just as the window above them exploded.

She could see why he called them Clankers, now that she thought about it. The rattling had alarmed her when she was dealing with one alien in a controlled environment, but now that there were thousands upon thousands of them marching rank and file toward ground zero, the sound was deafening. Without the window to muffle it, the whine grew louder still, until it seemed to take up physical space inside her head. She lay on her back, rendered dumb by the sound and the shower of glass and the shock of watching not one but *three* of the aliens plow through the window.

Len suffered no such shock. By the time Carla realized what was happening, he was already on one knee, blasting their assailants to kingdom come. The aliens were blown back by the clap of his weapon, and the next set of windows blew out. One of the aliens was thrown against the side of the window frame with such force that it was severed nearly in two. It thrashed and rattled, soaking the wall with a spray of greasy blood before finally going limp.

"That's right!" Len screamed, pulling himself to his feet. He rotated so that he faced out the window and fired again. "If you're not with her, you're against us, and I'm *not*"—*Boom!*— "taking any more" —*Boom!*—"of your shit!" *Boom!* He was breathing hard, his mouth open in a ruthless snarl, and when he glanced down at her, Carla flinched. "Get up," he ordered. "I need backup."

She scrambled to her feet and lifted the rifle onto her shoulder, aiming out into the street. The Clankers outside had stopped their relentless march and turned toward them, and she caught her breath. Seeing them had been one thing.

Knowing that they saw her? It was enough to make her knees tremble.

Len lowered the angle of his rifle, aiming at the wall this time, and it disintegrated under the force of the blast, leaving only the metal studs beneath. He slipped between them and stepped out into the street, leaving her no choice but to follow him.

One brazen Clanker tried to approach, but Len sent it tumbling away, knocking it into its fellows. When one moved to their left, it was Carla who fired. One shot from the laser was enough to melt its exoskeleton into a bubbly mess, and the alien let out a blood-curdling noise that echoed back across the walls of the buildings around them. The others became quieter, and more than a few of them backed away, clearing a path for the two humans as they watched their ally writhe and scream.

"You can tell your hivemind there's more where that came from. You hear that, bastards?" Len jabbed one finger at his temple and waved the gun toward them at random as he stalked across the street.

"Do they understand you?" Carla hissed. She still wasn't clear on how this Pammy Mae person had managed to talk to the aliens.

"Oh, I think they get the point."

It didn't take a genius to do the math, however: there were only two of them, and the aliens were numerous. With each pace, they closed ranks, and their low hum grew louder. Their standoff could only last so long.

A long black tongue shot toward Len's back, and he rolled forward to duck. Carla wasn't even sure how he'd known it was coming, but that was beside the point. The moment his focus broke, the aliens descended *en masse*. They would be buried under an avalanche of bodies unless she acted fast.

"Stay down!" she hollered, and pulled the trigger. This time, she didn't let go; she just kept spinning, first for one full rotation, then two. The barrel of the laser rifle grew so hot that she could feel her palms blistering, but that was only pain. She could handle pain, if it meant she and Len would still be there when she stopped hurting. The smell of her own flesh mingled with the meaty stench of burning Clanker, and she let herself scream as she finally released the trigger. The string of curses she flung at the wall of injured monsters seemed to come right from the center of her chest, from the hollow place left by everything she'd lost.

She staggered, and Len caught her elbow.

"Come on," he said.

She shook her head, already fighting him, but when he tugged on her arm she did as he asked, stumbling away across the road. He used his own weapon to blast a path through the barricade of dead and dying Clankers, and he kept firing until their feet hit the top step of the metro stop. He let her sink down on the top step, then tried to wrench the laser rifle away from her.

"No," she groaned.

"Give me the gun, Carla," he said.

"You'll get hurt—"

He swore and yanked his eyepatch away, giving her a good look at the place where his eye had been. "I've been hurt plenty," he bellowed. "Give me the damn gun!"

She let him pull it away from her, and he exchanged it for his. She let her head rest against the concrete beside her, lost in the throbbing pain that radiated out from her palms. *He's stronger than you,* she thought dimly. *He was always stronger than you. He carried so much of your baggage and asked so little in exchange.*

Carla was drifting when Len tugged her arm again.

"Okay, baby," he said. "Come on."

She swayed to her feet and almost tumbled down the steps. In an instant, he had dipped under her armpit and wrapped one arm around her waist to steady her.

"Shouldn't be this hard," she mumbled. "Just some burns..."

He snorted. "Yeah, and blood loss. Come on, Carla, one step at a time."

When she glanced at her arm, she saw that he was right. Her blood had soaked through the bandages. Either it had never clotted properly, or she'd managed to reopen it in the fray.

I didn't survive the Floating Fortress and the lab and the general just to die here, in a hole in the ground, she thought. The anger helped clear her head. She might be hurt, but dammit, she wasn't going down. She took the steps carefully, hanging on to the gun Len had given her so that she wouldn't lose a second one.

"You're doing great," Len assured her. "If I hear them coming after us, I'm going to have to let go, okay? If that happens, just hold on. You don't have to keep going without me."

"Yeah," she grunted. The pain was a little more bearable

now, although her head was still spinning. "I'll wait right here for you. Of course I will."

They had to stop twice before they made it to the bottom of the steps. Both times, she leaned against the wall until he started leading her again. At the bottom of the steps, he sat her down against one wall, then disappeared into the darkness. He returned a moment later with two bottles of Gatorade and a pair of candy bars.

"I melted the vending machine," he said matter-of-factly. "How are you feeling?"

She shrugged as he sank down beside her. "Not great, but not the worst. Are you all right?"

"I'm doin' great, baby." It was too dark to see if he was lying.

They sat there, chugging their drinks and breathing heavily into the unexpected stillness of the station. The only sounds they could hear now were the distant noises from the street level, and a deep rumble from somewhere down the tracks, like the sound of an incoming train streaking toward the station.

"You know," Len said after a long moment, "this is how it started for me. Underground, feeling so small I wasn't even sure I mattered anymore, wondering if the world I'd woken up in was the same one I'd go to sleep in that night." He snorted. "Covered in bugs, too. I guess it's inevitable that it would end the same way, huh?"

Carla peeled back the wrapper of her candy bar and bit into it. The sweetness of the sugar on her tongue almost brought her to tears. "Why aren't they following us?"

Len waved one hand toward the steps. "Same reason as ever. Because they don't think we're worth the trouble. Idiots."

They finished eating in silence. Carla set her wrapper aside and placed the empty bottle inside it. She felt oddly guilty for littering; never mind that even if she'd bothered to hunt down a trash can, nobody was coming around to empty them anymore.

"All right." She pushed herself to her feet. She could feel that it was too soon, but the world wasn't going to wait around for her to feel better. "Time to find your friend. Where do you think she is?"

"If I know Pammy, all you have to do is follow the sound of trouble, and that's where you'll find her." Len nodded toward the dark tunnel and hefted his gun. "Maybe we should play that alien-repelling sound while we stumble around blindly in the dark."

The tablet in Carla's pocket didn't connect to any signal. When she powered on the screen, the battery was at ninety-five percent. "Keeping it going could run down the battery," she pointed out.

Even in the dim light, she could tell that Len was on the brink of laughing at her. "Baby, what are you saving it for? Either this is a one-way ticket to the underworld, or by the time we come back out, the Clankers will just be a bunch of scared bugs lost on an alien world without their overlord to guide them. Either way, I'm pretty sure now's the time to go for it."

"Planning to burn all our resources and go out with a bang, huh?" She hit play, and that awful nails-on-a-chalkboard whine started up again. It was bad, but no worse than burning her hands to cinders, or being trapped in a bunker against her will.

The two of them lowered themselves onto the tracks and set out toward the Crystal City stop.

29

COOPER

COOPER WAS STANDING on the lawn when the chopper touched down, and he lifted his hand in greeting. The soldiers in their exosuits had withdrawn back toward the road, and the Clankers had taken up a silent watch from the distant buildings.

"Nice to have a breather," Estes said. He rolled his shoulder so that the joint popped, and sighed with relief when it did. "I bet they'll hold off until nightfall."

"Yeah," Cooper said vaguely. The stillness didn't feel like a reprieve to him. If anything, it made him nervous that something bigger was coming. Another group of soldiers, maybe? A tank? Some new weapon they hadn't faced yet? His nerves were frayed, and the hivemind had gone quiet for the time being.

Still, he slid off the Jackal's back and jogged over to the helicopter. He didn't recognize any of the people who stepped out, save Klarie. Len wasn't with her. Instead, she was now accompanied by a tall, skinny, wild-haired man in fatigues, whose glasses sat askew on his face.

"*Jeremy!*" Lavelle Steward almost tripped over herself in her haste to reach him. When he spotted her, his face lit up, and he opened his arms wide. They collided, and she almost knocked him clean off his feet in her excitement.

The rest of the group hung back to exchange uncertain glances. Cooper recognized their wary expressions from the days after the fall of Camp Keystone, when the Little Creek Five had sought to make sense of everything they'd done. By now, he no longer questioned the implications of fighting other humans, but he had no doubt that he'd pay for it later when the guilt seeped into his dreams.

While Lavelle and the man approached the crew of the chopper, Klarie jogged over to where Cooper and Estes stood. She raised one hand in a high-five. "You're not dead," she said brightly.

"Not yet," Cooper agreed. "Where's Len?"

Klarie scratched the back of her neck. "Uh, it's kind of complicated. We kind of got in a firefight with his wife's team, and then the two of them took off toward a metro stop, and—" Klarie lifted one shoulder in a little shrug. "I told you, it's complicated."

Lavelle led the rest of the group over to them. She had one arm wrapped around the skinny man, and was staring up at him with open adoration. "Cooper, Mr. Estes, I'd like you to meet my *zeeskeit*, Jeremy. His big brain is the reason our little enclave survived."

"Aw, stop it." The man glowed under her praise. "And you

can call me Stew. Only *Mamme* gets to use my given name. So, I hear you've got some sort of disruptor?"

"Not us." Cooper nodded back toward the caravan. In the unexpected cease-fire, the soldiers and civilians had begun to erect something that resembled an encampment. "Vera will know where it is."

They moved up the slope as a group, while Stew made introductions. Cooper tried to keep track of the new arrivals, but he kept glancing over to the Clankers and the mechs in turn. While Stew waxed poetic about their escape from whatever facility had kept them prisoner, Klarie caught Cooper's elbow.

"Hey," she murmured, nodding toward the museum. "Does it seem kind of... weird, how they're all being so quiet? It's almost like they're both waiting for orders." She lifted her eyebrows significantly. "Maybe from the same source?"

"Maybe," Cooper admitted. "I just wish I could hear what they're up to."

Klarie's brows pulled together, but he didn't elaborate. He was too busy trying to work out what they were waiting for.

He would have bet his life that it had something to do with Pammy Mae.

GREG HAD TAKEN a hit somewhere along their route. They found him under Peachey's care, with one arm wrapped in a sling. He explained the theory of the disruptor again, and the group of scientists peppered him with questions that, to Cooper's ear, sounded like the science portion of the expanded SATs. Vera and Guppie had come over to listen in, and of the members of the Keystone caravan, only she and Peachey seemed to be able to follow the conversation.

"I have to admit, it's a sound theory." Dr. Sharma folded her arms over her chest and frowned up at the monument. "It's too bad nobody *else* thought of it." She rolled her eyes toward Stew and the diminutive man who'd been introduced as Nutty.

"Even if we had, Greene wouldn't have implemented it," Stew shot back.

Sharma pursed her lips. "You could have found a way to leak it to the wider public before the aliens arrived."

Lavelle waved her away. "All this is beside the point. My little Jer Bear was able to leak the original message, which is the only reason we have a weapon *now*."

"Which raises another question." Dr. Sharma glanced sidelong at her husband. "How will we know if your agent is able to detonate it successfully?"

I'll know if Pammy manages to kill it. The words were on the tip of Cooper's tongue, but he bit them back.

Instead, Greg spoke up. "If she succeeds, we should see an immediate change in the behavior of any aliens we encounter. As for how we tell if she tried but failed?" He shook his head. "Without a network or a grid, there's no good way to communicate with her long-distance. We'll just have to play it by ear."

"She's still alive." The soft voice caught them all off guard, and every head in the group swiveled toward the pale, drawn countenance of Emma Jean Johnson. Pammy's mother was leaning against the side of a van that the D.C. contingent had brought with them, which was currently being used as a makeshift shield on one side of the med station. She was clutching the lightning rod to her like a beloved memento. "I would know if she had died. Kevin didn't believe me when I said that, but she's my girl. My baby. I would *know* if she was gone." She ran an absent hand over her temple, as if to imply that her connection to Pammy Mae went beyond mere maternal intuition.

"When you say that the *invadendae*'s behavior would change," Stew interjected, "do you mean something like this, where they back off and watch for no good reason?"

Greg shook his head. "Honestly, your guess is as good as mine. We're talking alien biology here, so even if everything else was up and running, I'm not convinced that we could say anything with absolute certainty."

"Either way, we're not going to be able to do much more tonight," Vera said. "It'll be dark in a few hours, our troops are exhausted, and we need to regroup. Let's post a watch tonight, hold our position as best we can, and see what we're dealing with in the morn—"

A head-splitting surge of pain roiled between Cooper's ears, so urgent and all-consuming that it brought him to his knees. He could *feel* the scream leave his throat, but he couldn't hear himself. It was as if a cherry bomb had been detonated inside his skull. It was a hundred times worse than getting hit with a pulse from the ThunderGens. Pressing his hands to his ears didn't help, even when his ears popped from the pressure. His vision went completely dark for a few seconds.

When his eyes were able to refocus, he saw Klarie and Vera before him, backed by a group of concerned strangers. Vera's mouth was moving, but no sound emerged.

"It's Pammy," he gasped. "Something's happened with Pammy."

Vera frowned and shook her head. Her lips moved again.

"Just trust me." Another throb of agony left him doubled over. "Something's wrong with Pammy." His knees dug into his ribcage, and his forehead scraped the earth, but every other sensation paled in comparison to the pounding between his ears.

"The hivemind found her," he said into the darkness that now shrouded his senses. "It found her, and it caught her, and it won't let her go."

30

PAMMY MAE

AS THE KEYSTONE Hive and its followers drove their enemy back into the Crystal City metro entrance, Pammy Mae began to shiver. Her stomach lurched with every movement of the Clanker beneath her, and her vision became blurred and murky. When she closed her eyes, strange visions danced across the insides of her eyelids. Opening her eyes didn't guarantee that they'd disappear.

Her mount reached the top step of the metro entrance, and Pammy glanced sideways to find the King of Parkton standing only feet away, chattering in mistrust and irritation. She could have sworn that there was a man sitting on the Clanker's back: her uncle, Captain Kevin Johnson, smiling at her with the same lost, disbelieving wonder he'd shown right before Len and Vera and Cooper fired their guns.

You're sick, Pammy, he said. She heard the words not in her ears, but in her own head. *Something's wrong with you, kid. Looks like madness runs in the family.*

"Leave me alone," she snarled, and turned her face away.

Do you really think it's that easy, Pammy? Her uncle's voice was almost sympathetic. *Do you think you can avert your eyes and plug your ears and casually walk away?*

"Stop," she snapped. "Just... stop."

It didn't work for me. What makes you think you're so special?

Pammy shot him a bitter glare, then slapped her hand over her mouth at the sight of him. Three holes in his chest sent little rivulets of blood streaming down his chest. He dragged his fingertips through the mess, still watching her. Still smiling.

"You're not real," she told him as her Clanker advanced into the darkness below.

In the mouth of the metro tunnel, the Crystal City Hive formed a wall that blocked the invaders from pushing forward. There wasn't enough room for the Clankers to engage in regular combat. Instead, they jostled one another ineffectually. The dead only served to reinforce the wall.

The first junction emerged from the darkness below. At first she couldn't make out what the Crystal City Clankers were saying, as their voices lapped and overlapped off the concrete walls around her until they finally gained meaning: *Send the queen.*

The King of Parkton was the first of her army to join in. *Send the Queen,* he rattled. *Send the Queen, defend the nest, defend the future.*

Having her own battle cry thrown back at her came as little

surprise. She had known that her sway over her Clankers could only last so long, and that one way or another the hivemind would turn them against her. It could have them kill her, if it wanted to.

But maybe it didn't need to. It might very well have other plans for her.

Send the Queen. The rattling came from all directions, and the Clankers on the street pushed forward. If she didn't move, she would be crushed between two armies. Their song was deafening—she was trapped in the midst of a swarm of hundreds, if not thousands, of the surging creatures, each of whom was striking its oversized tymbal with the raw emphasis of a human scream.

"All right!" She bellowed the words as she swung to the ground, balling her hands into fists and holding them in front of her. As if that would make any difference. "If you want me so badly, I'll come to you."

There was no way that the Clankers could have understood her, even if they could have heard her over their demands. That was how she knew that the Crystal City Clankers were under the hivemind's control: because *it* understood her, and *it* was the reason they fell silent the instant the words were uttered. Behind her, the commingled hives that had followed her to D.C. were still chanting, with the King of Parkton's measured thrum echoing the loudest of all.

Send the Queen.

Pammy turned back to her army and struck her thumb across the tymbal in a single note of agreement.

Her army fell back, bristling with anticipation. They were

still independent enough to make their own choices and follow their own desires, unlike their counterparts. Still, if the two hosts had been facing off in battle, she wouldn't have been able to tell them apart. She was the outsider. The weakling.

It should have frightened her, but mostly it just made her tired.

Pammy took one step deeper into the metro. Without having to communicate aloud, the wall of Clankers shifted in unison, creating a passage between them just wide and tall enough for Pammy to fit through alone.

She swallowed and hooked her thumbs through the loops of her bag. If she refused to go, the King of Parkton would decry her as a liar and a coward, and no doubt kill her to make an example to the rest of her army. If she went forward, the hive-mind could turn the other Clankers against her the instant she was surrounded. There would be nothing left of her but empty skin and drying bones.

That's right. Pammy glanced over her shoulder to find Sean Hawes standing just behind her. His eyes were milky and pale, and his chest and stomach had been split down the middle, just as they had been when she last saw him back in Little Creek. The puncture marks in his shoulders were crusted in dried blood. He grinned at her, exposing blackened teeth. *Step into the belly of the beast, Miss Butter. You've swallowed Clanker, after all. Only seems fair to close the circle.*

They weren't real. Of course they weren't. They were ghosts, or memories, or some other figment of her imagination. If only she would touch him, he would be nothing more than smoke. She could wave her hand through him and prove that he was nothing more than empty air.

She believed it. She knew it. And yet, Pammy couldn't quite bring herself to try, just in case she was wrong.

Pammy had never stopped to wonder if the voices of the Clankers were all in her head. If the hivemind could manipulate her into seeing something that wasn't really there, perhaps it could manipulate her into hearing things, too.

Aww, Miss Butter. Sean pursed his lips in mock sympathy. *Doubting yourself? First place never doubts herself. You've already lost.*

"You've got him all wrong," Pammy spat. "He wasn't a *dick.*" She made a rude gesture at the figment of her imagination and walked away, slipping through the crevice between the aliens' shells. Sean's laughter followed her into the darkness until the Clankers behind her closed ranks, and Pammy Mae was left alone amidst the shifting mass of hostile monsters.

DOWN SHE WENT, and down, following the path the Clankers laid out for her. Pammy could hear them moving over the walls and ceilings of the tunnel, but she couldn't begin to guess how many there were. Surely without a steady supply of food, the tunnels couldn't support enough aliens to pack the space. They must be streaming downward, intent on guiding her toward her end goal.

And why, she wondered? Why steer her through the underground passageways rather than simply killing her?

She didn't need a light to see by. Instead, she guided herself by touch. When she closed her eyes and let herself drift, the passage became even easier to navigate, for she could see through the eyes of every Clanker that surrounded her. Even so, she couldn't understand the intent of the hivemind, or what it wanted with her.

Pammy could only hope that she, too, was holding something back from the hub of alien consciousness.

A dim light appeared in the distance, and her heart pounded against her ribs. She knew what was waiting down there, and that she would have only one chance to unmake it. Pammy gripped the rope handles of her sports pack tight, painfully aware of the smooth curve of the disruptor pressing against the base of her spine.

Almost there. She shivered as the voice that spoke behind her, soft and gentle, almost loving. *So close, Pammy Mae. You've got this.*

"Nate's dead," she said aloud.

No I'm not. I'm right here.

She squeezed her eyes shut and pulled her shoulders up to her ears. "He isn't. I'm alone."

Oy, Pammy. How can you say that when you can feel the Akrido all around you? They're hungry, *baby. Almost as hungry as you were.*

The Clankers were indeed closing in. The passageway grew so narrow that she had to shrug off the pack and turn sideways, with the disruptor clutched to her chest. Her arms and back scraped against the brittle shells, and she had to stoop to keep moving. With her legs bent at an awkward angle and her head bowed, she crab-walked along the tunnel.

You always hated losing, didn't you, baby? Nate's voice lilted behind her in a cruel parody of the way he used to talk. She was glad that she couldn't see him. Her last memories of his life were bad enough; never mind how he'd looked when she carried him out of the tunnel under the road to burn what was left of him.

You loved the rush of flying, but you hated the fall, he whispered.

Pammy's lip curled in disgust. "I never fell."

Not back then, baby. But you've fallen more than once since then, haven't you, sweetheart?

The ceiling of Clankers lowered. She was almost there, but to keep moving forward, she had to sink to her hands and knees and crawl along the dirty floor. When her Clanker-armor got stuck, Pammy yanked it free with a grunt and left it there. The tymbal got stuck, too, and she paused for a moment. How was she supposed to talk to the Clankers without it?

What do you need to tell them? Nate's voice taunted. *Do you think it's going to be a pageant? A popularity contest? That you'll win them over with debate or a pageant interview?*

Pammy took a deep breath and let one hand rest on the tymbal. She hadn't let herself dwell on the days leading up to the invasion. The memory of everything she'd lost made her sick to her stomach. In that moment, though, she let herself remember the thrill of driving her old ATV through familiar terrain. She thought of Logan's scream when she reached the lip of the gorge, and Nate and Pike's shock when she didn't hit the brakes. Other people doubted her, but that younger version of herself had known her limits... and her strengths.

She gritted her teeth and yanked the tymbal away from her

side. All she had left were her dirty, blood-stained clothes, the ones she'd borrowed from her mother back in Camp Keystone. Pammy kept her grip on the handles of the sports bag as she crawled through the narrow gap.

The press of Clankers came to a sudden end, and Pammy found herself crawling on all fours into a room illuminated with a shifting, watery golden light. She sat back on her heels and lifted her head.

She had seen the hivemind before, but never in person, and the size of it both sickened and amused her. Its heavy gelatinous form sagged under its own weight, and it rippled as its thick membrane puckered and relaxed, evidently at random.

Pammy opened the top of the drawstring bag and lifted the disruptor free.

Aren't you forgetting something? Nate asked.

She glanced back just in time to feel a fist connect with her temple, and she went sprawling. As she fell, she wrapped herself around the disruptor to protect it from harm.

It didn't work. The man standing over her knelt down beside her and batted the disruptor away. When she tried to scramble after it, he placed one knee on her back and forced her chest to the floor.

"We're pleased to meet you," he said as he pressed the barrel of a gun to her spine. "We've been waiting for you, and here you are."

Pammy flinched as he pulled the trigger, but the gun in the stranger's hand wasn't a pistol or ThunderGen. It felt less like a bullet than a needle, one that slipped between her vertebrae and scraped the bone.

"Relax," the man cooed. "You've been fighting so hard. You've earned a rest."

Pammy Mae bared her teeth and whipped one arm up, elbowing the man in the side of his kneecap with as much force as she could muster. Back in Little Creek, that effort might have broken the cartilage in his kneecap, but she'd been growing weaker ever since the day King Clanker had carried her away to the school. Whatever he'd injected her with sapped the last of her strength.

"Your effort is impressive," he said, "but we think you'll find that the paralytic hampers your ability to resist. We know what you're afraid of, Pammy Mae Johnson."

Her name was poison in his mouth, and when he said it, other voices reverberated through the inside of her skull, the voices of people who were long gone: friends and classmates, neighbors and acquaintances and even familiar strangers whose faces she knew but whose names she'd never bothered to learn, all of whom had been claimed by the hivemind and swallowed by the Clankers.

"'M not afraid of *you*," she mumbled. Her tongue was thick and leaden in her mouth.

"Not us." The man got up and dug one toe beneath her shoulder, then kicked her limp body onto her back. His eyes were blue as a summer sky, but there was no warmth in them. It had been the start of summer when the world ended, when the ships rained down from above carrying the invaders within.

He made a sharp gesture to the Clankers, and they spilled through the door. Pammy tried to move, but to no avail. The first Clanker that reached her speared its forelimbs through her shoulders and pushed her back against the wall, then higher, until she was eye-level with the stranger who stood silhouetted against the warm glow of the alien horror. At least whatever formula had rendered her inert also dulled the pain.

The man knelt down to retrieve the disruptor. He held it above his head, examining it from all angles. "So close," he said. "But proximity doesn't matter, *Miss Butter*. You are outnumbered. Outclassed. You're a speck of dust in a vast and swirling nebula. You were nothing. You are nothing. You always have been."

Her mouth didn't work, but she didn't need to speak for it to hear her. Instead, she glared past the man at the monumental, shapeless mass. *Then why are you afraid of me?*

The man whipped his head toward her. He tucked the disruptor under his arm and strode to where she lay slack against the piercing limbs of the Clanker that held her. Without a hint of fear, he dipped between the beast's legs and stood with his face inches from hers, his lips curled in a snarl, his free hand braced against her chin to ensure that she met his eye.

"We are not afraid of livestock."

She met his blue eyes without flinching and saw the motes of the nebulas he'd mentioned dancing there. *Then kill me.*

"Too simple." His sneer sharpened to a smile. "We want you to suffer. We want you to pay. When this little uprising of yours ends for good, we want you to see it." He backed away and waved to the Clankers. "Bury her."

"What—?" Pammy began.

She had claimed that she wasn't afraid of the hivemind or the Clankers. If the alien had extended his proboscis, she would have done her best to spit in its eyes before it split her in two. She wasn't prepared for the burbling of the swarm, or the rush of foam that came from all directions.

No, she thought, flopping her limbs useless against her captor. *Not this. Not the slow decay of corrosive spit. Kill me, you cowards!*

The stranger turned his back on her. In the space behind him, Nate's ghost appeared, twisted and corrupted by the hive-mind's vision of him. He grinned at her and waggled his fingers as she tried and failed to scream.

The Clankers covered her in foam and then withdrew, hurrying back out into the tunnels to execute the hivemind's next orders. The first time, in the natatorium of the Heartland County High School, they'd covered her entirely. This time, they left a gap around her eyes, so that she couldn't see anything but the bioluminescent monstrosity.

Nate's ghost blew her a kiss. *Welcome,* he crowed, *to Earth's next great extinction event.*

BEYOND WASHINGTON

Three Eons
The Throng

THE FIRST THING the throng knew was hunger. It had no sense of time, very little sense of place, and no hint of ambition. It had adapted to fit a niche in the food chain of its homeworld. That which died decayed, and the throng fed on the remains. For an era, the throng found satisfaction in consumption. Vertebrates and invertebrates alike became its meal, and that early iteration of the throng grew in size and weight as it formed a colony, weaving its fibers through the soil of that long-abandoned world.

It was the spore that changed everything. In an attempt to spread beyond the confines of its habitat, that ancestral throng sent up a cloud of spores that floated away on the thin wind of that Mesozoic world. Of the millions of spores that wafted across that world's ever-evolving crust, many landed on places where there was nothing to consume, and subsequently perished. Others, as was intended, found new habitats that suited their needs. And one?

One was consumed by one of the apex predators of that world, an amphibious creature of admirable size and incessant hunger known to its descendants as a Widemouth.

Within days of its consumption, that first host was gradually rendered too weak to move. Its webbed, triple-jointed limbs went still. Its brain functions became isolated from its limb mobility. The throng fed on its living tissue, breaking it down while the Widemouth decayed from within, until it became ribbed with the thick white fibers of the throng's roots. In time, the Widemouth died. The offspring of that spore would have died, too, if the Widemouth hadn't used its last strength to return itself to its birthplace, where dozens of members of the new generation were feeding and growing. Their curious mouths roamed over the paralyzed, near-dead Widemouth in the hopes of finding sustenance. Instead, they found infection.

The Widemouths evolved quickly, and the throng evolved alongside them in an evolutionary arms race that the throng could never win. If the Widemouths perished, the new strain of the fungus would die along with them. The less virulent strains of the throng left their hosts alive for months, even years. Within a millennium, the Widemouths and their offspring could live into old age before succumbing to a secondary infection caused by the throng's subtle adjustments to its hosts' biology, and its hosts forgot that it had ever been a danger.

THREE HUNDRED MILLION years passed. The throng's adaptations had brought it some measure of independent intelligence. Instead of paralyzing the body of its host, it now took root in their brainstems and spinal columns. Instead of eating its hosts alive, it had developed into a non-pathogenic fungal parasite. The descendants of the Widemouths had long since begun to call themselves the Sinsin, which in one of their languages meant *the upright ones,* and wherever they went, the throng went with them. They populated their world and built cities that defied gravity. At last, the Sinsin turned their eyes to the stars.

They visited their moons first. The throng went with them, but it was trapped in the cycle of the rebreathers; even if there had been anything to occupy, it had no way out into the atmosphere. The Sinsin moved outward, settling other worlds and altering their biomes to be hospitable, much as the throng had colonized them.

It was then that they reached the first inhabited world. The Sinsin were small and sturdy, with clever brains and deadly weapons that, when tested, proved to be no match for the black-shelled residents of that new world. All eighteen of the Sinsin crew were slaughtered and devoured, and in the wake of that nightmare, the Sinsin sent no more ships to that planet.

They didn't have to. Their throng-infested fed the bestial hunters of that world. Where their hosts failed, the throng became that world's foremost pioneer. The Sinsin had been complicated and clever; its new hosts were not. The organism that had settled into its role as a benign parasite evolved again. The Sinsin were dead, but they had left their ship behind, and the throng had taken root in billions of brains. It could pick and choose knowledge at its leisure, and began to do so in earnest.

It was no longer content to feed on whatever happened to come its way. Why settle for passive dominion of one world, when it could have them all?

THE DESTRUCTION of Limpid Hydraxa Planetoid P-Q42 was enough to slake the thirst of the Akrido for a time. Their unique biology allowed them to go months or even years without feeding, which made their long voyages beneath the stars possible. Some of them died along the way, and the throng gathered them together before their bodies gave out, feeding on their bodies so that it might survive the journey, rendering their biomass into smooth liquid that became the central hub of its intelligence from which it controlled all its disparate hosts. The Akrido were strong-willed, but their natural instinct was to gather and migrate, and those instincts made them easier to bend.

A new world lay ahead, and in the ships they'd stolen from other conquered worlds, the Akrido entered their dormant state. This was the only time that the throng ever dreamed, and it spent its days reaching from mind to mind to see what all its other parts had managed. Even when it occupied billions upon billions of organisms—the Akrido, the Sinsin, and the survivors of other species that it had infected on its journey through the void—the throng was lonely. No other strain of its species had managed such a conquest. Nothing had.

It was considering the nature of its voracious isolation when the message came through. A coded song, written to mimic the language of the Akrido, sent from the planet that it had selected as its next quarry.

It was not a threat, but an overture of partnership.

While the Akrido slept, the throng considered this offer. Its current hosts had been biologically receptive to conquest, and their brutal hunting methods were effective, but their limitations were evident. What would it be like to take up residence in a host as clever as the Sinsin, whose technology was already sufficiently advanced to allow them access to the skies beyond their world?

With the help of the Akrido, the throng could only conquer.

With the help of humanity, it could *build*, until it had settled every corner of the universe and devoured everything in its path. The hunger it had felt since the days of its inception might finally be sated.

31

COOPER

"COOPER?" Vera gripped his shoulder with one hand and pressed her other palm to his forehead. "What happened? Are you okay?"

"No." He sat on the edge of Peachey's bench while the others crowded around him. "I'm telling you, Pammy's in trouble. She lost the disruptor, and she's trapped."

Vera and Guppie exchanged a skeptical glance.

"I'm serious!" he exclaimed, slapping his palm against the table. "It let her walk right in. It's got her right now. She's alive, but—"

"And you know all of this how, exactly?" Klarie folded her arms and squinted at him.

"Uh." Cooper winced. "So, you know how Pammy figured out how to speak Clanker? Turns out, whatever connects them to the hivemind isn't just in their meat. I *may* have ingested some of it last night—"

Vera recoiled. "And you didn't say anything until now?"

"What the hell did you eat?" Guppie demanded.

"I've definitely missed something." Stew scratched his head. "So you can interface with the *ophiocordyceps?* Can you teach me how?"

Cooper hooked one thumb toward the cluster of Clankers watching them from the trees and sighed wearily. "Sure. Just go chow down on some Clanker tartare, or slurp on the stuff in one of the honeycomb things they carry around. If there was some big Clanker battle on the far side of the bridge, I bet they dropped plenty."

"I'm not even going to ask what possessed you to try that," Vera snapped. "Why didn't you mention anything until now? What makes you think your connection only goes one way?"

"Listen." Cooper held up both hands. "I *don't* know that. So if you need to make a plan without me where I can't hear, fine. Do it. I'll stick my fingers in my ears and sing the Stars and Stripes backward, but I need you to believe me. She's in trouble, and this all ends if we don't save her *now.*"

Vera pursed her lips.

"You're that sure?" Guppie asked.

"Hang on." Sharma made a time-out T with her hands. "Are we really trusting this intel? From someone who's been hiding the truth until now? What if he's being controlled, and this is a trap?"

Vera licked her lips. "The possibility occurred to me."

"Vera." Cooper leaned forward to grab her arm. "Remember when you wanted to get out of Little Creek, and I went back for Pammy instead? I told you that she was alive, and you didn't believe me then, and we all got split up. I'm not being puppeted by some alien mushroom. I'm going to try to find her again, got it? And if you decide that you're staying, or that I'm not allowed to touch the disruptor, fine. But I'm still going."

She wrinkled her nose. "You're going to charge into the Clanker nest all on your own. Without us. Without backup. With thousands of aliens waiting for you to walk right into their hive. That's the plan?"

He set his jaw. "If I'm right, we're dead either way. I'd rather die doing the right thing, if it's all the same to you."

Vera pinched the bridge of her nose and closed her eyes. Everyone was looking at her, even the helicopter pilot who had just arrived.

"Let's pretend," she said, "that I make a plan. And I tell you *only* what you need to know. Will you do exactly what I tell you?"

"Yes," he said without a moment's hesitation. "I will. I promise."

"Come on." Vera waved to the rest of them. "I have an idea." She shot him a furious glare before turning away, and the rest of them followed her, all but Guppie.

"Don't you want to see what she has in mind?" Cooper asked.

"Nah." The older man leaned against the makeshift table. "She'll tell me later. I'm not going to be much use for anything other than smackin' stuff, you know?" He mimed punching invisible enemies with his hydraulic fists. "I figure you need a friend right now, kid."

Cooper clasped his hands in his lap. "Hey, gramps?"

"Screw you, kid." Guppie made a halfhearted attempt to get him in a chokehold. Cooper played along, and let the older man ruffle his hair with his robotic knuckles.

"All right, all right, you win." Cooper shrugged him off. "But seriously, I wanted to ask... did you ever get sent on a mission that you didn't think you'd come back from?"

"Aw, hell, Cooper." Guppie slumped against him. "You're too damn young to be thinking that way."

Cooper quirked an eyebrow at him. "How old were you when *you* enlisted?"

Guppie snorted. "Too damn young."

"Fair enough."

"No one's making you do this," Guppie said.

The sun was sinking toward the horizon. They had another hour or two before twilight, and one way or another the sun was going to rise on a different world.

"Maybe nobody else is," Cooper told him. "But I am."

The group returned. A stone-faced Vera held up a bag similar to the one Pammy had taken with her. Inside, a smooth, round object heavy against the synthetic fabric.

"We took a vote," she told them. "Merry is going to fly you to the drop point. Estes and Klarie are coming with you. The rest of us are going to hold the fort." She sighed heavily. "I'm sorry, Cooper, but I'm not sure how I'm supposed to trust you now. Len's still out there, and we've got too many people to look out for."

Lavelle Steward nodded in agreement. "We've survived this long. If things go wrong in the night, we can always retreat. I owe it to these people to protect their lives. I'm sorry, but we don't owe your girl jack squat."

"Then I'm going with him," Guppie said.

Vera shook her head. "You'd only slow him down."

Guppie recoiled, and the expression on his face just about broke Cooper's heart.

Vera took a deep breath, and her frown softened. "I *know* you're bleeding, even if you won't let me see. Cooper's going to need to move fast if he has any hope of finding Pammy before— well, before whatever he thinks is going to happen actually does. You'll be more useful here with me." She laid a hand on his arm. "Please? Estes is dead-set on going. I need someone I can trust here with me to hold down the fort."

Guppie's jaw worked as his gaze slid from Vera to Cooper and then back.

"It's okay, Guppie. She's right... you'll be the one here with the most tactical experience. They'll need you." Cooper reached for the bag.

"Nope." Vera passed the pack to Klarie instead. "You lead the way. I'm not taking any chances in handing this over, just in case I'm not being totally paranoid. You can lead the way, and they'll follow."

"Sorry, Cooper." Klarie tucked a curl of black hair behind one ear and stared down at her combat boots. "I agree with Vera."

"Nothing to apologize for." Cooper lifted both hands and forced a smile. "I get where everyone's coming from. I should have spoken up earlier."

"Don't get killed, you little brat." Guppie pulled him into a tight hug and squeezed him a fraction too hard. "And if you find Pammy, take care of her, all right?"

"I will." Cooper patted his friend's back twice before pulling away.

Vera hesitated for a moment before reaching for him and drawing him into a hug that was almost as rib-crushing as Guppie's. "Be careful," she whispered. "We're counting on you making it out in one piece, okay?"

Cooper stepped back and squeezed her arm. "Take care, Vera. No hard feelings."

Estes clapped him on the shoulder and turned him toward the supply truck. "Come on. We're burning daylight."

"I'M afraid this might be a one-way ticket," Merry Clark shouted over the whirr of the rotor. "We're running low on gas."

"You sure you want to do this?" Cooper asked.

The pilot nodded. "I know where I'm going, and I gotta admit, I'm worried I made things worse." She shook her head. "I guess I figure I gotta balance my karma out."

Cooper sat back in his chair and turned to Klarie. "You could still go back, you know."

She jabbed a finger in his face and scowled. "And spend the rest of my sorry existence wondering if I sent you to your death alone? Screw that."

Cooper clicked his tongue and rolled his eyes toward Estes. "So what's *your* excuse?"

Estes was mostly upbeat and jovial, but his usually smiling face was perfectly blank. "You and Maddox went into the woods trying to protect this crazy girl," he said. "I don't know if she's going to save us or ruin us, but either way, letting you go alone this time would be a bit like spitting on his grave, don't you think?"

"Yeah." Cooper swallowed past the lump in his throat. "I guess."

"If he was here, he would have volunteered for this suicide mission," Estes said. "But since he isn't, I reckoned I ought to come in his place."

Merry flew them over the river to an empty plaza. The pilot frowned at the ground below as she brought them in for a landing. "This place was crawling with aliens less than an hour again," she muttered. "I don't like this."

If there had been a way to safely transport his Jackal in the chopper, Cooper would have done it. He felt painfully exposed as they stepped out into the open with only a few ThunderGens and a handful of smoke bombs for self-defense.

"What happens now?" Cooper hissed. "Do we just... go in?"

Estes scoffed. "Hell, no. Are you crazy? First we have to draw them out of the tunnels. Otherwise we'll be fighting blind on their home turf."

Cooper glanced at the overcast sky. "If we wait much longer, we'll be fighting blind, anyway."

"Cooper." Estes met his gaze. "I *need* you to trust me. Got it? I know what I'm doing. I'll take point, you and Klarie can back me up, and Merry's on rear guard. Are we clear?"

The women nodded, and Cooper clung tight to his weapon. He didn't like that Klarie was carrying the disruptor. What if the hivemind *could* see into his head and would know to send all the Clankers right toward her?

And how much longer could Pammy survive on her own underground?

Nothing you can do about that now, he told himself. Klarie and Estes were the only people who had trusted him enough to follow him on a suicide mission. He owed them the same respect.

"All right," he whispered. "I trust you."

Estes winked, and his old bravado returned. "Then let's *do* this, son!" He spun toward the mouth of the metro stop and let out an echoing whoop, firing the ThunderGen toward the sky so that the blast reverberated off the crumbling walls of the buildings around him. "*Hey, you big ugly Buggers! We got the goods, so come and get us!*"

The darkness below them stirred. Shadows gave way to waving limbs, and the rattle of the Clankers began. The first to fully emerge was one of the largest Cooper had ever seen, with more legs than usual, all of which were much too long.

"Hello, your highness," he muttered, lowering his eye to the scope of his weapon. He didn't need to speak Clanker to recognize the King of Parkton when he saw him.

The alien advanced a step, singling Cooper out of the group. Because he recognized him from the day before? Or because the hivemind could peer into his head with its all-seeing eye? The king's many-eyed head swung back and forth like a bobblehead, then fixed on Klarie.

That one, he said.

Cooper's heart dropped to his boots. "They know," he said.

"Estes, they know Klarie has it!" *Which means that Vera was right. My connection to the hivemind goes both ways.*

Even as he thought it, the ache in his head started up again. As Clankers swarmed up the steps, he fired into the crowd of aliens, but he had to squint his eyes against the stabbing pain.

"Ready, Klarie?" Estes bellowed.

The girl nodded even as she hoisted one of the smoke bomb canisters off of her belt. She reeled back like a baseball pitcher and threw it with all her might. It landed midway between where Estes and the first of the Clankers stood. The King of Parkton stared down at it in confusion for a moment as he was enveloped in a cloud of blinding smoke.

"Get ready to run!" Estes hissed.

"Run?" Cooper demanded. "Run where? Not into the metro?"

"Don't worry." Klarie winked at him and rolled her shoulders. "I was great at track. I made nationals last year." Before Cooper could protest, she turned on her heels and sprinted away in the direction of the George Washington Parkway.

"Klarie!" Cooper screamed, but she was already gone, leaping and dodging with all the agility she'd shown in Keystone when she was evading Johnson's soldiers.

"Hold your position!" Estes snarled as he backed a pace toward the building behind them. "We'll hold them off. Give her time to move. If you know where she is, then the hivemind will, too."

The King of Parkton broke through the smoke, running at full speed, its elongated limbs moving so fast that they became a blur. Estes let out a wordless scream of fury and started firing, but the Clankers were spilling out into the road.

Cooper let out a whine of dismay. He'd been trying to play hero, and he might have cost them their last shot at victory. Vera had been right not to trust him.

Estes' blasts were precise and accurate, but even with Merry's backup, he couldn't hit them all. While a few of the Clanker soldiers were flung backward into the crowd, the King of Parkton banked to the left and scuttled past them. Cooper's blast managed to knock the King sideways, but his attention was still fixed in the direction Klarie had gone. He shouldn't have been able to see her through the smoke, which meant that he knew what path the girl had taken because *Cooper* knew.

For a few seconds, Cooper raged against himself, but one glance at the King of Parkton was enough to turn the tide of his anger. Yeah, he'd made a mistake. And yeah, he should never have drunk the Kool-Aid, figuratively speaking. But he'd gained a little trust with the Keystone Hive, and he firmly believed that its members would have backed Pammy Mae to the death. The King was somehow to blame for all this.

"I'll be back," Cooper called, and he began to run.

When the invasion started, he hadn't been much of an athlete, but he'd gotten used to mounting and dismounting his Jackal. He vaulted onto the back of a nearby Clanker and clamped his knees over its glittering carapace.

"Cooper!" Estes called, but his voice was already fading. The Clanker didn't take kindly to its new rider, but there wasn't enough room for it to stop and wrestle with it; its fellows formed such a tight-knit wave of bodies that its only choice was to bear

Cooper along, however unwillingly, or else be crushed in the surging tide of its kin.

That gave him an idea. Cooper clamped his knees tight and tried to feel the rhythm of its movements, calculating his next shot as he took aim. The first blast sent a spray of rubble flying off the corner of a building behind the King of Parkton, but it didn't harm him. Cooper was almost dislodged by the kickback, and he had to brace one arm against the back of his mount's head to stay upright. The King of Parkton was ahead of them and gaining ground. Before long, he would be out of range.

Come on, Cooper, do one thing. One useful thing, to make up for all the stuff you've gotten wrong.

He drew a deep breath, closed his eyes, and found his balance again. Once, when his biggest problem was a hangover and a series of nervous DMs, Kat had implied that he was brave. He hadn't felt brave at the time.

Oddly enough, he felt just the tiniest bit brave now.

Cooper opened his eyes and took aim. His finger twitched on the trigger, but he held his aim a fraction of a second longer, just to be sure.

The blast from his ThunderGen hit the King of Parkton just behind his head and sent him sprawling on the pavement. He lay there, stunned, but he wasn't badly wounded. He would have gotten up again.

He wasn't fast enough. Hundreds of thousands of surging legs beat down on him, each sharp enough to pierce his exoskeleton. He was trampled beneath the masses, and didn't rise again.

Cooper's relief was only momentary. There was no sign of

Klarie, and there was no way that one ThunderGen in his hands would be enough to protect her even if he found her. If she got lucky, she might be able to find some safe hidey-hole where the Clankers wouldn't spot her. She was good at things like that. But what use was the disruptor if it couldn't be deployed?

32

GUPPIE

GUPPIE WATCHED in frosty silence as the helicopter lifted off the lawn. He was surrounded by strangers, including Vera. *Especially* Vera. The way she'd spoken to him and to Cooper wasn't like her at all.

The moment the chopper took off, Vera's shoulders relaxed. She sighed heavily and turned to the group.

"All right, folks," she said. "You know what to do."

The Stewards, the scientists, and Emma Jean broke away, heading toward the supply truck with all the confidence of people who had a plan.

Vera laid her palm against the metal brace of Guppie's arm. "I'm sorry," she said. Her weariness had returned with interest, and dark shadows stood out stark beneath her eyes. "I shouldn't have spoken to you like that. I'm just scared."

Guppie shook his head. "I just can't believe we sent Cooper out there. Telling it like it is, that's one thing. I know I'm a liability at this point, but Cooper's just a kid, and Pammy risked her life to save everyone. We were supposed to stick together."

She swallowed hard and pulled her hand away. "Cooper volunteered to go, and the others knew the plan. I know that there are risks, but I'm not asking them to do anything I wouldn't do myself."

"Vera?" Lavelle Steward came trotting back over with a ThunderGen, two canisters of Devil's Piss, and a child's backpack with a Tinkerbell print. "I put a medical kit in there for you, too, just in case."

"Thanks." Vera shrugged the backpack on, tucked the canisters into the mesh pockets intended for water bottles, and accepted the gun. "You'll look out for everyone, right? Especially my parents." She swallowed hard. "I can't say goodbye, so maybe you can say it for me? And look out for the dogs."

"Just so long as you look out for my Jeremy." Lavelle gave Vera an awkward one-armed hug. "Felix has agreed to come with you, too. He'll show you the way."

Vera nodded. "We'll be there in a minute."

Lavelle nodded and left them there in the shadow of the monument. Guppie examined the backpack. "What's that?"

"It's the second disruptor." Vera shuffled her feet. "We're pretty sure the hivemind can get into Cooper's head. Klarie, Estes, and the pilot volunteered to take a decoy. Cooper doesn't know, so if we're right, Estes will focus on drawing the Clankers out through the metro. That should leave the tunnels relatively clear. Cooper doesn't know the details, but he was dead-set on helping Pammy... so yeah, I didn't tell him the whole truth, but I didn't turn my back on him, either."

"You want them to empty the tunnels," Guppie repeated. "Because you plan to use them?"

Vera nodded. "There's an entrance north of the White House, away from where the Clankers and the soldiers are currently stationed." She indicated the two groups of enemies to the east and southeast. "Lavelle's people are going to draw their fire, so hopefully they'll be too busy to notice us slipping away."

"Us?" Guppie repeated.

Her lips curled into a hopeful smile. "Assuming you're still offering to help."

He snorted. "And I won't slow you down?"

"Please, Guppie. You're the reason I even made it out of the gas station that first night. I was counting on you coming with us."

There had been a time when Guppie had regularly visited her garden center without bothering to ask her name. If the world hadn't ended, she might still be calling him Mr. Martin in her old derisive tone while he bought birdseed to fill his feeder, just to make the time pass.

He missed a lot of things about the days before the invasion, but life without Vera wasn't one of them.

"Of course I'm coming," he told her. "I wouldn't miss it."

GUPPIE HAD STARTED to feel better while they rested, but once they got moving again, he felt the scabs open up as the wounds on his leg started bleeding again. The exosuit did all the work of moving him forward, but his legs still had to bend along with the suit's joints.

Felix and Stew led them to the edge of the new encampment, and the four of them crouched down out of sight. The movement made the tendons in Guppie's leg scream, but he bit back any complaint. Vera was counting on him, and this was her grand plan. He wasn't going to let her down.

Stew lifted his hand to signal to his mother and the other scientists. They nodded, and Lavelle shouted something. This was soon followed by a burst of gunfire and ThunderGen bursts. One of the scientists, Nathan, had taken it upon himself to borrow Cooper's abandoned Jackal.

"Now," Stew hissed, and the four of them hustled away across the grass, running toward the distant trees that lined Constitution Avenue.

They were almost to the road when Guppie glanced back and saw a shadow giving chase. At first, he thought it was an enemy soldier, but when he turned and raised his fists, he realized that it was Emma Jean Johnson, her pale hair brushing her shoulders and her teal glasses askew. She was carrying the lightning rod with her.

"What are you doing?" Vera hissed as she caught up with them.

"I'm going to protect my girl." Emma Jean adjusted her glasses. She looked more alive than Guppie had ever seen her. There was even color in her sunken cheeks, brought on by the exertion of sneaking after them.

Vera's eye twitched, but she seemed to decide that there was no point in arguing. Instead, she only hissed, "Stay close."

Emma Jean was a narrow thing, more reminiscent of a scarecrow than a woman. Guppie had known her a little before the invasion. Not that they'd been close, but he knew her reputation: she was confident, self-assured, and poised. It must be difficult, he reckoned, to think yourself in total control of your life, only to discover that the universe has other plans. Still, she had no trouble keeping up with them. It was Guppie who struggled. Vera stayed back with him as the other three pulled ahead.

"Sorry," he grunted.

"Take your time," she said. "Cooper was right, everyone else is scattered all over the place. I'm not leaving you, too."

Maybe you should, he thought, but he couldn't bring himself to encourage her.

The sounds of battle raged behind them, but they were entering an empty stretch of city, one where no soldiers and no Clankers lay in wait to ambush them.

"We're getting close," Felix hissed when the others let them catch up. "Farragut West is only two blocks away. We'll follow the blue line."

"We should hurry," Stew added. "Even if your friend does manage to draw them out of the tunnels, how long can four people keep a few thousand *invadendae* occupied?"

"Hey." Guppie panted for breath as he glared at the scientist. "The next time you want to imply that our people are gonna get eaten, maybe don't."

"Your mother is in danger," Emma Jean said. "As is my daughter. Let's try to remain optimistic." She pushed past the two men, and the rest of them hurried to follow her.

The metro stop was easy to spot on the empty street, and the five of them descended into the darkness one after another. Felix and Stew had flashlights, and Felix led the way while

Stew brought up the rear. Entering the silent underground was like stepping into a tomb or a mausoleum, and Guppie couldn't help but take that as an omen. Even in that still, stagnant air, he was sure that he could hear a distant sound like an erratic heartbeat, although that might have been his own pulse pounding in his ears.

"Getting there," Vera assured him. "We're close. And who knows, maybe we'll run into Len down here?"

"Yeah," he croaked. "We could have a big reunion down here." *Or the Clankers could pick us off one by one and finally get around to finishing what they started.*

HE WASN'T sure how long they'd been moving through the tunnels. His focus had narrowed to a pinpoint that centered only around the pain in his leg.

Guppie nearly trampled Stew when the scientist stopped abruptly. "Do you hear that?" he hissed. Instead of pointing his flashlight ahead of them, he swung the beam back.

There was nothing to see, but now that he wasn't moving, Guppie could hear it, too: the mechanical clang of metal on concrete, steady as the measured tread of boots.

Vera cursed under her breath and backed away. "Someone must have seen us come this way. We need to move faster."

"No, we don't." Guppie dug in his heels. "You do."

"I'm not leaving you!" Vera hissed.

"Yeah, you are, because if the hivemind finds out what you're really up to, it's over. If something catches up with me, all they'll see is an injured old man stumbling around in the dark. Let me hold the line. I'll buy you as much time as I can."

Emma Jean was already running, and Felix was right behind her. Stew stayed long enough to push the flashlight into Guppie's hand. "In case they saw the beam," he hissed as he gave a sloppy two-fingered salute.

Vera hesitated, but the noise was getting louder.

"Go," Guppie insisted. "It's a good plan. You'll make it work."

Vera's lip wobbled, but she nodded. When Stew set off in pursuit of the others, she followed, although she kept looking back until the tunnel curved and she was gone.

Stupid old man, Guppie thought wearily. *You spent so much of your life trying not to care, and now that you do, you're too stuck in your ways to do anything about it. You've let so much slip by you.*

At least you're always good at holding the line.

He gripped the flashlight in his immense metal fist and let himself stumble toward the wall for support. If whoever was behind him saw him as weak and helpless, so much the better. Any edge he could gain, however small, would buy him that much leeway in the fight that was sure to follow.

The figure that rounded the corner was even bulkier than the standard exosuits. The man inside was seated in a central cockpit with controls that allowed him to power the upright machine, reminiscent of how Guppie had powered Chelly as opposed to the way he wore his stolen suit. The new arrival was easily twice the height of a man, and it had to keep to the middle of the tunnel to avoid scraping the concrete ceiling. A visor mostly obscured the pilot's face.

"Hey," Guppie panted, noting the man's stars and bars. "I got banged up pretty bad, General. Lost the rest of the platoon in the process, too." *There's no way he knows all the folks under his command, right? Maybe I can act like one of his men and catch him off-guard.* He shone the beam of Stew's flashlight in the officer's face, hoping to blind the man to his overabundance of white hairs.

"Is that so?" The man's voice ricocheted unnaturally off the curved walls. "What happened?"

"We got beaten back by the monument. The civilians took out a couple of the wardogs, and the line fell apart." That, at least was true, even if he was fudging exactly which side he'd been on during that particular skirmish.

"Pity," the general said. The shadows cast by the flashlight lent his visage a lurid air. "What's your name?"

"Bleeker." The name popped out of Guppie's mouth automatically, borrowed from one of the dead at Keystone. He stood upright and swayed on his feet. "Thomas Bleeker."

The general laughed. "Is that so? Because we've heard otherwise, Mr. Martin."

Guppie's breath snagged in his lungs.

"General Greene has been kind enough to let us in." The man licked his lips and dragged his thumb across the corner of his mouth, as if savoring something he'd eaten hours ago but could still taste. "This is a new experience for us. Your nervous systems are so complex, and yet you're still so easy to command." The general's smile dropped away abruptly. "Well, most of you. That little girl of yours has a stubborn streak."

Oh, no. Cooper was right. Guppie braced his boots against the floor. *And he's not the only one that tasted the special sauce.*

"Pammy. Mae. Johnson." The general shook his head, spitting out each part of her name with unabashed disgust. "It is *so* satisfying to feel her distress. She had been a thorn in our side—is that what you say? A stone in our shoe."

"So you finally caught her, huh?" Guppie glowered at the general. "Took you long enough." The man sure liked to hear the sound of his own voice, and as much as Guppie hated having to listen to him yammer about his triumphs, every second he stood there bought Vera that much more time.

"We most certainly have," Greene said. "Oh, and how satisfying it is to pick you off at last. Please forgive our earlier incompetence. We have every intention of making up for it." He toggled a joystick on his controls, and the right arm of his suit lifted. It pointed toward Guppie and let out a low whirr as it began to glow.

He had just enough time to hit the ground and roll before a blast like a small supernova illuminated the tunnel. Guppie grunted as he hit the floor in an ungainly somersault before landing on one knee in the corner. Chunks of rocky debris and a cloud of gray concrete dust rose from the wall. He wasn't sure how well the suit could have taken a hit like that, but Guppie was pretty sure his skull wouldn't have fared well.

"So many toys," Greene said. "Your species does so *love* its toys. Just think how quickly we could spread with toys like these..." He laughed with childlike delight and spun toward Guppie again.

Vera had a good head start, but in a long, straight tunnel, there wouldn't be many places for her to hide if the general got past him. Her mention of his pathetic attempt to weaponize gas station snacks brought a bitter smile to his face. He'd been injured then, too, but in the process he'd bought Vera enough time to save them both.

I don't need to be strong to stop this guy. I just need to be smart enough to distract him until I can land a hit.

His adrenaline was going haywire. He could think more clearly than he'd been able to in hours. There was no point in rationing his strength anymore. No more running. This was it.

"Make way," he murmured, and he charged.

The general's next supernova blast hit the corner where Guppie had been crouched a moment before. The hydraulic fist of his exosuit hit Greene's mech in the knee from the side, and the joint exploded in a shower of sparks and steel shrapnel.

The general screamed a curse and tried to spin toward him, but Guppie had already driven his armored elbow into the back of the other knee. With one knee already blown out, the mech stumbled backward and tripped over Guppie, landing on its back between the rails.

Blood was pooling in his metal boot, hot and slick. Even with his adrenaline up, Guppie didn't have much strength left. He jumped onto the mech's chestplate and wrapped his left arm around the mech's elbow, forcing the cannon toward the ceiling.

"Stop!" the general snapped. "This won't save you."

Guppie couldn't say for sure if it was the hivemind talking

or the man himself, and frankly he didn't give a damn either way. "Probably not," he rumbled. "But if I'm going, you can be damned sure you're coming with me."

His free hand lashed out at the general's controls, activating every command at once just to make sure he didn't miss the firing mechanism. Greene screamed as the mech lurched and the cannon shuddered, glowed, and finally fired. Blocks and tiles showered down from above them in a cascade of masonry as the archway collapsed on them both.

33

CARLA

CARLA HAD KILLED the sound some time ago in the hopes of preserving her battery. They had heard the *invadendae* some time before, but the tunnels were ruled by stillness now. They had yet to encounter a single alien since entering the metro stop.

"Are you sure the hive is down here?" she asked.

"Pammy was certain." Len's voice belied a few doubts of his own.

"So why haven't we stumbled across any? Judging by how many were on the street, this place should be *teeming* with them."

"Maybe she succeeded," Len suggested. "Or the hivemind is so focused on fighting off the army she amassed along the way, it's had to throw all of its resources at stopping her. How are your hands?"

"Fine," Carla grunted. When she ran the pad of her thumb over her palm, she could feel the blisters forming there. It would make it hard to fire even the weapon that Len had given her, never mind the laser gun, but she wouldn't worry about that now. She couldn't. All she could do was put one foot in front of the other to catch herself in a state of perpetual falling.

"Any idea how we'll know when we're close?" Len asked. His left arm was around her, which put Carla on the side of his missing eye. It had been a calculated decision on his part, no doubt, to account for his blind spot, but it made her sad. All she could think about was time: how much they'd lost, how much they'd wasted, how much had been stolen from them.

"Let me draw on my experience with battling alien hordes," she deadpanned. "Good thing my graduate program covered that topic in detail. I wish I'd taken better notes."

"You must be feeling better," Len said drily.

"Or I'm losing my mind." Carla sucked in a breath. "Wait. What is that? I thought I saw a light."

Len tensed against her shoulder. "Start the recording again."

She fished the phone out of her pocket and hit play again, wincing at the high-pitched noise. "Of course, if any of our people are after us, this sound will bring them down on us in a heartbeat."

"Then we'll shoot them. Speaking of which, can you walk without me? I'd like my hands free on the off chance I need to fire up the laser rifle."

Carla hadn't truly needed to lean on him for some time. She stood upright and slipped her phone back into her coat pocket, fumbling with the stock of her borrowed ThunderGen. The weight of it against her blistered palms stung, but pain and patience had become relative in the last few years. She'd learned to dissociate from the moment. Probably not a healthy response, mentally speaking, but a necessary one for survival.

The two of them crept down the tunnel. The light that Carla had spotted before came and went like reflections dancing off the surface of a pond. They rounded a bend, and the light became steadier, a beacon guiding their way off the main tracks and into one of the service tunnels.

"What is that?" Len demanded.

Carla gulped. "According to my freshman notes, it's how we figure out we're close."

He slipped ahead of her, and to her chagrin Carla didn't try to stop him. Even with only one eye, he was a better shot than her. He was bolder, too. Carla had the advanced degree, but ever since she'd known him, Len was the one who invariably knew what to do in a crisis. Her policy had always been to stay out of his way and let him do his thing, and she was happy to implement it again.

A far-off rumble shook the tunnels, and they both froze, looking back over their shoulders in the direction from which they'd come.

"I don't like this," Len hissed. "I wish I knew what was going on."

Carla had been making that same wish for approximately the last sixty-three months. "Keep going," she whispered. "If it's aliens, the sound should keep them away from us. If it's not..."

"Then we're two sitting ducks," Len muttered.

Carla tried to force a smile. "Armed ducks."

He rolled his eye at her and soldiered on.

The light grew brighter, until she finally saw a shifting mass ahead of her. Her jaw went slack, and she caught Len's shoulder, drawing him to a halt.

"Is that it?" she whispered. "The thing we're looking for?"

He trembled beneath her palm; his heart was pounding so hard that she could feel his pulse under her fingertips. "Yeah," he croaked. "I guess it must be."

"Let me go first."

Len shrugged her off. "No way. I've been on the outside preparing for this for months. *Years.* You don't know what you're doing."

"Len." Carla turned him toward her and laid one blistered hand on the side of his face. Being able to drag her thumb across his cheek was worth the pain. "Please, let me go first. If something happens to me, you'll figure it out. If something happens to you, though..." She tried to laugh, but it came out as a wheeze. "The world's in trouble, because I won't know what to do."

"Don't get sappy on me," he complained, but his eye was suspiciously bright in the glimmer cast ahead.

"Wouldn't dream of it, baby." She patted his cheek and slid past him, taking point as she went. The wail of the Steward Message still sounded from her pocket, and she prayed to whatever higher powers might be listening that it would keep the aliens at bay. Hell, it might put the hivemind itself at a disadvantage. They'd never had the opportunity to test whether it was the *invadendae* or the invasive strain of cordyceps that reacted to the soundwaves.

Carla shuffled forward into the room at the junction of the tunnels, and her jaw dropped. The life form that lived there was like nothing she'd ever seen: vast and terrible and somehow beautiful, as if every star in the night sky had been suspended in liquid amber and wrapped in a moon-dappled skin. Her grip on the ThunderGen loosened as she approached.

"Amazing," she murmured, mesmerized by the phosphorescence ripples that floated within. "Lovely."

She was startled by a soft noise from the wall behind her, as if someone was trying to scream but couldn't open their mouth. Carla turned her head. She had just enough time to make out the outline of a human swathed in what looked like soap suds.

Then something struck her in the side of the head, and she dropped like a stone.

34

VERA

VERA WASN'T sure what caused the explosion, only that the blasts behind her made her flinch every time, and that the final detonation sent a plume of concrete dust billowing out behind them. *Guppie, what happened?* She closed her eyes tight in an attempt to stop herself from crying.

"Don't think about it," Emma Jean told her. "If you can't do anything about it, don't think about it."

As far as Emma Jean went, that seemed like reasonable advice. She was good at burying her head in the sand and pretending that the world had vanished. That wasn't something that Vera wanted to do, as a rule, but for the moment she had few other choices.

She couldn't go back for Guppie. All she could do was keep running.

In the warren beneath the city, Vera lost track of time. They had only Stew's light to see by, and for a beanpole, the man could run. Her attempts to calculate how long it had been since Cooper had panicked, since the helicopter had lifted off, since she and Guppie had parted ways all failed, and she was left with only forward momentum.

"Any idea where we are?" Stew panted.

Felix shook his head. "I *think* the last platform we passed was Arlington, so we're almost there. But we haven't hit a Clanker blockade yet, so..." He let the words trail off, leaving the air thick with the implication that they *would* eventually. Three ThunderGens and a lightning rod weren't going to stave off a whole Clanker army.

It came as a shock to her when the tunnel opened up again to reveal another platform. They'd passed a few, and despite the near-blackness that shrouded them, she'd felt exposed. In those open spaces, they could no longer rely on the walls of the tunnel for some degree of protection.

This time, they were halfway past the platform when floodlights hummed to life. Vera raised one arm to block the glow, and uttered an oath as silvery spots danced across her vision.

"Damn," muttered Stew. "I don't like that."

Vera squinted beneath her arm to find a row of silent soldiers in exosuits like Guppie's descending upon them.

Emma Jean didn't hesitate. She lifted her lightning rod as though it were a lacrosse pole and swung. At the height of the weapon's arc, she jerked it to a stop, and a spiderweb of blue bolts leapt between the rod and the nearest soldier. Even as he collapsed to the ground, Emma Jean moved so that her back was pressed against the pack Vera wore, so that they could cover one another. Next to them, Stew and Felix did the same.

"Keep moving!" Vera yelled. "If we get back into the tunnel, we can hold them off!" One of the floodlights blinded her, and she cursed, turning her weapon on it. The sonic discharge of the ThunderGen reduced the bulb to little more than brilliant dust.

One of the soldiers dropped onto the tracks next to her and swung his fist at her torso. With a snarl of rage, Vera fired point-blank at his moving fist and nearly took his arm off in the process. Before he could recover, she dug the barrel of her rifle beneath his chin and fired. The helmet flew off, and it took a good chunk of the man with it.

Stew and Felix crab-walked toward the tunnel, driving the soldiers back with the blasts from their guns. One of their opponents dropped to the ground and rolled across the platform right over the edge, evading the shot that Felix had aimed at his head. The soldier drove his metal fist into Felix's chest with such force that Vera *heard* his bones break. As the hydraulic extension of the arm expanded, Felix was thrown against the far wall lining the train tracks, taking Stew with him.

Emma Jean lost no time in driving the rod directly against the metal structure of the exosuit. She activated it, and the resulting stench of seared hair and sizzling flesh turned Vera's stomach. Her gaze was fixed on Felix and Stew's limp forms. She'd taken oaths, dammit. She couldn't just leave them.

"Keep your head in the game!" Emma Jean bellowed. A ribbon of lightning struck another soldier in Vera's peripherals, and then a hand clamped down on the back of her collar. "You don't have to be perfect. You just have to be better than everyone else, and right now, that means *reaching the target.*"

"Y-yeah," Vera panted. As Emma Jean dragged her onward,

however, she couldn't help but worry that she was doing the wrong thing. What would Lavelle say if Stew was dead? Given the hit Felix had taken, she wasn't sure *either* of them was still alive. Would she really have to tell both Lavelle and Nazarena, *I'm sorry, but you trusted your sons to me, and I left them behind?*

"Don't think about it," Emma Jean said. "They need you to be strong, Vera, don't *think* about it!"

She glanced back over her shoulder as two more of the soldiers dropped down into the gap beside the tracks and approached Stew and Felix.

Back in Little Creek, she'd gotten good at running away. She'd tried to convince Cooper that Pammy Mae couldn't be saved. She'd abandoned Len and Guppie in the bunker so that she could chase after her family. She'd left Sean Hawes to die. Now she'd abandoned Guppie all over again.

Vera was sick to death of running.

"I can't *do* this," she snapped, yanking away from Emma Jean's grip. "I'm a doctor. I don't give up on people."

"Eyes on the prize!" Emma Jean wailed, but Vera couldn't control the outcome of the war. She couldn't guarantee that she'd succeed, even if she turned her back on these men the way she'd abandoned the others. She *did* know, however, that if she left now, she'd spend whatever was left of her life regretting it.

Vera pelted toward the soldiers, screaming so loudly that her vocal cords burned as she fired again and again. One of the soldiers had raised his armored foot to stomp on the fallen men. Vera knocked him backward on the tracks with a blast. She stood above him with the ThunderGen pointed at his chest and fired point-blank. The kickback dislodged something in her shoulder, but the soldier got the worst of it: his chestplate collapsed in the front and was driven against the rails from behind, crushing him inside the metal structure.

His fellow sneered and batted Vera's gun away. It hit the rails behind her with a clatter.

"That's enough," the soldier snapped. "We're tired of you, Vera Khan. All of you. You are a waste of resources—"

"Save the spiel." Vera pulled the canisters of pepper spray out of the pockets of her fairy princess backpack, one in each hand, and sprayed them both directly into the soldier's face.

The helmet offered some protection from more direct attacks, but they still had some sort of air intake filter, and it was far from perfect, judging by how quickly the soldier began to cough and hack. He waved his hand in front of his face as he fell back, in an attempt to clear the air.

"That's what I thought," Vera sneered. The soldier fell to his knees and clawed at his helmet. Before he could free himself from the helmet, Emma Jean's lightning rod went off again, and the soldier went down for good.

Vera scrambled over to where the two men lay. "Are there more?" she asked, even as she felt for a pulse. Stew's head was bleeding from where it had hit the concrete, but his pulse and breathing seemed normal. She was more worried about Felix.

"I don't see any." Emma Jean shuffled closer to her. "What are you going to do with them? You can't *carry* them, Vera."

Vera bit her lip. "I guess not. But we could move them into the tunnel."

Emma Jean's brows pulled together. "My daughter is in

trouble, Vera. If you're going to waste time, give me the pack and I'll go ahead."

"No," Vera said. "Just give me a moment to look at them, and then we'll go." She peeled Felix's shirt open and grimaced when she felt his broken ribs through the already bruising skin. She needed to move him, but—

"I'm sorry about this, Vera," Emma Jean Johnson said.

Something dug into Vera's spine, and the world turned incandescent. Vera screamed and slumped forward, but couldn't escape the pain or the silvery fireworks that danced across her vision.

After that came a sea of endless and merciful darkness.

35

LEN

"CARLA!" he screamed, lunging forward as the man knelt over his wife and pressed a silver-barreled gun to the back of her neck. He swung the laser rifle into position, but the man was too quick; he twisted back toward him and fired the weapon in his other hand. It was a strange-looking pistol with a squat rectangular barrel.

Unlike the ThunderGen, it emitted no noise at all. Instead, it delivered a silent punch to his solar plexus that inflamed his airways. He tried to breathe in and found that he couldn't. Len clawed uselessly at his throat until the sensation eased slightly and he was able to suck a thin stream of oxygen in through his open mouth.

"Bet you don't like that," the man said conversationally. He was done with Carla and was already tucking the silver gun into his belt. "The Akrido feel the same way about that sound of hers. It's very inconsiderate of you to subject them to such unpleasantness. It doesn't bother *us*, but we can't have that." He nudged Carla onto her back and reached for the phone in her pocket.

If he stops that sound loop, the hivemind will have every Clanker in the city down here in a matter of minutes. Len still couldn't breathe right, but he'd been training to shoot with one handicap. He could manage another.

The man's fingers dipped into Carla's pocket a fraction of a second before Len fired. He was sure he had him, but even in its eyeless body, the hivemind must have been capable of sight, because he flung himself aside just as Len fired.

"Oh," he purred, "look at you. Still fighting, even when you can't speak." His brow wrinkled, and when he spoke again, his cadence was different from before. "I remember you. Len Bonaparte. The nobody who's still making trouble."

He's only talking to buy himself time, he thought. *The hivemind is used to relying on the Clankers to do its dirty work, and they won't come in here until the sound on Carla's phone stops. There might be other humans coming, though. I need to take him out as soon as possible.*

He fired again, leaving a clean line charred in the wall behind where the man had been standing moments before. "So close," he taunted as he slipped around the back of the hivemind's juddering mass.

Len stepped over Carla's prone form, so that one foot was on either side of her. She was still breathing, but she hadn't moved since the man had struck her.

"Who are you?" he asked as he scanned the room. He twisted around to make sure that he didn't leave his blind spot open. That was when he spotted the foamy mass stuck to the wall. It looked like a person, but it was suspended two feet off the floor. The bubbles where its shoulders would have been were stained pink.

On the floor at its feet lay the broken remains of the disruptor.

Len swallowed, which only irritated his still-inflamed throat. In a voice so hoarse it sounded like a stranger's, he asked again, "Who are you?"

"*I* am Agent Dante," he said. "And *we* are the throng."

Len could roughly pinpoint his location on the far side of the alien mass. There was no way he could get a clean shot from this angle.

But who needed a clean shot when the only thing blocking his line of sight was the enemy?

The beam of the laser rifle wasn't powerful enough to cleave all the way through the hivemind's mucilaginous body, but it *was* enough to damage its dermal layer and cook a three-foot-deep core of the jelly beneath.

"*No!*" Dante snarled. He rolled sideways and landed on his knees to aim the square-barrelled pistol. Len dropped to his knees, still guarding Carla, and aimed at the gun. His aim was slightly off, so instead of clipping the pistol, he clipped the man's hand.

"*Asshole,*" Dante hissed, cradling his charred thumb to his chest. The pistol hit the floor with a clatter.

Len ignored him, aiming instead at the rope-like anchors that helped suspend the hivemind from the ceiling. A regular gun wouldn't have been much use, but the laser was powerful enough to sever the thick cables. The resulting smell reminded him of spoiled meat left too long in the sun, and his gorge rose.

Dante scrambled to his feet with a snarl. "You can't hurt us." His voice rose in a strained cacophony, as if tongues other than his were joined in the effort of speech. The skin of the injured hivemind puckered and throbbed with each word. "We are a colony. We are a *strain*. We have inoculated every member of our collective consciousness. Long after your species is gone, we will remain."

"Maybe," Len grunted. He swung his laser rifle back toward Dante. "But guess what? Nobody's going to miss you."

Dante tried to dodge, but Len was ready for him this time. He aimed slightly to his left so that when Dante threw himself in that direction, he entered the beam of the rifle. He screamed as his ribcage passed through the scope; by the time he hit the floor in two pieces, however, he was silent. Dante's injured hand reached for Len, and his eyes rolled to meet his gaze. His lips parted, but no sound emerged.

Len got to his feet and strode over to him. Greg's disruptor hadn't survived the attempt to end the hivemind, but he'd made a good point topside. The double-tap was always the right choice.

He aimed the laser rifle right between Dante's cold blue eyes. "I'll see you in hell, you miserable sonofabitch," he croaked.

And then he pulled the trigger.

. . .

CARLA SHIVERED when he laid his fingers against her pulse. Len's own heart throbbed in his ears so loudly that he almost didn't feel her slow, answering pulse beneath his fingertips. But there it was, soft and steady, a blessed reassurance that there was still something left worth fighting for.

The foam outline of Pammy made a muffled squeak, and Len hurried over to her. He could just make out Pammy's eyes in the mess.

"Hold on," Len said. Between the voice jammer Dante had used on him and the high whine of the phone in Carla's pocket, he wasn't sure the girl would even be able to hear him. He began to scrape at the bubbles with his bare hands. It was slow going. Each scoop of the bubbling material stuck to his fingers and palms as he worked, so that even when he'd managed to remove it from Pammy's body, it built up on Len's own arms.

When he finally cleared the foam around Pammy's mouth, the girl sucked in a breath so greedily that she choked.

"I'm sorry, Len," she blubbered. "I walked right into it. I failed. And it hurts, it burns... And I failed..."

"You're doing just fine," Len assured her. A preternatural calm had come over him. He'd done everything that he'd sworn to do for the last five years. True, they hadn't saved the world, but that had never been Len's goal. He was alive, Carla was alive, and those who had separated them were dead.

Pammy slumped further forward until her own weight peeled her away from the wall and she collapsed into Len's arms. Beneath the soapy residue that still clung to her skin, Len could make out the perfectly circular holes on either side of the girl's chest. The skin there was already turning green and black as the corrosive lather worked its way into her open wounds and hastened the spread of infection.

"I'm sorry," Pammy murmured. "He got me, Len. I didn't hand it over, I swear." She pressed one palm to her temple and shuddered. "Oh, God, it hurts. Why won't he stop?"

Len pushed a wet, sticky curl of blond hair out of Pammy's eyes. "Who won't stop?"

"Nate." Pammy pointed to a patch of empty air over Len's shoulder. "He keeps talking, but he was never like that, not before. Although I guess I didn't know him as well as I thought."

"Hush now, you're okay." Len rocked back and forth on his heels and hugged his friend tight. A fierce surge of love rose in his chest for all the rest of the Little Creek Five. He'd doubted the wisdom of taking in stragglers more than once, but they'd saved him time and again—not just his life, but his humanity. He owed them the same.

How am I supposed to get them both out of here? he wondered. Carla was comatose, and Pammy wasn't much better.

The pounding of footsteps sounded in the hall outside, and Len turned his eye to one of the doorways that converged on the room. A pale figure hurtled toward them and collapsed on the floor beside Pammy.

"Oh, sweetheart!" Emma Jean sobbed. Her face was smudged with dirt, and her lightning rod was still clutched in one hand. A grimy child's backpack hung from her shoulders.

"Emma Jean?" Len blinked. "How did you get down here? Did anyone else come with you?"

"Oh, my poor baby girl." Emma Jean pried Pammy out of Len's arms and held her close. "What did they do to you?"

"Vera?" Len shouted to be heard over the sounds that filled the room. He got no answer.

At least he had help now. He could carry Carla out. If Emma Jean carried Pammy, they might be able to get back to the caravan, as long as no more soldiers attacked them and the wail of the phone's speakers kept the Clankers at bay.

"Get up," he told Emma Jean. "We need to get moving before—"

Even as he spoke, the screech of the phone died.

The silence was abrupt and startling. Len left the Johnsons to their tearful reunion and crawled over to where Carla lay. He tugged the phone out of her pocket, praying that all he would need to do was press play again and restart the loop.

He hit the power button, but the screen stayed dark.

"No." He pressed his thumb to the button again and again, but to no avail.

From the darkness outside their little room came the rough rattle of Clanker-song. The hivemind wriggled, and the stars floating inside danced faster, as if it was laughing at how close they'd come to surviving, only to be trapped in the heart of the subway system in the midst of a feeding frenzy.

36
PAMMY MAE

"MOM?" Pammy clung to Emma Jean's arm. "How did you get here?"

From behind them, Len called, "Up! Now! We need to get out of here."

Lights rippled across the walls, pale yellow and deep gold. She was lying at the bottom of a lake, looking up through a swarm of Clanker-fry that danced between her and the sunlight. Nate's ghost stood over her, laughing in delight as her rebellious army approached.

"I don't feel good," she said.

"I know, sweetheart." Emma Jean kissed her fevered, sticky forehead. "But I brought you something."

"Now!" Len was struggling to lift the body of the woman who he'd arrived with. Her head lolled against one shoulder, looking for all the world like a marionette with its strings cut.

Instead of lifting Pammy in her arms, Emma Jean shrugged

off her backpack and set it on the ground beside her. The pink plastic zipper opened to reveal a metallic sphere.

Nate's ghost snapped his mouth shut, and his eyes gleamed like two black pinholes through which a starless sky peered back.

"The disruptor." Pammy struggled to sit up. "Ma, you brought it."

Len's eyes widened.

"It's our last shot." Emma Jean lifted her chin. Pammy had seen that expression on her mother's face before. It was the one she wore when her only child was about to get a little tough love. "Pammy, you know what to do, don't you?"

Pammy accepted the sphere and cradled it to her chest, turning it over and over in her trembling palms. "I remember how to set it off. But I can't just set it off here."

The Clankers were so close now that Pammy could make out their commands and replies. She reached instinctively for the tymbal, forgetting that she'd tossed it away hours before. Even if she could have spoken to the aliens, she doubted they would listen.

"I'll hold them off." Len lay the woman back down and reached for the laser rifle he'd used earlier, then ran to where the dead man lay and retrieved the boxy pistol he'd dropped. "Do whatever you've gotta do, but *hurry*." He bolted toward the tunnel entrance. The sounds of battle began immediately, but Pammy didn't have the strength to turn her head.

"Focus, Pammy." Emma Jean patted her cheek. "Tell me the plan."

How many conversations around the kitchen table had

begun just like that? They'd discussed debate topics and home-
work assignments and how Pammy was going to pay Jerry
Peterson back the time she'd accidentally damaged one of his
prized rosebushes. The night before the Butter Queen pageant
began, they'd sat down to discuss Pammy's interview questions.
What's the plan?

She licked her lips, trying not to think about how bitter the
foam had left them. "We can't just set it off outside. We need to
—*I* need to—figure out how to get it inside."

No, you don't. Nate glowered at her. *You can sit right there
and wait for the end. You can join us, you know. We'll need a
new Ambassador, now that Dante is gone. We could spare you
and your family and your friends, if only you'll join us...*

Pammy kept talking. "I can't walk there, Mom. Can you
carry me?"

Emma Jean pressed her forehead to Pammy's. "Of course,
sweetpea." With that, she struggled to her feet, clutching her
daughter tight.

We forbid it. Nate had vanished, only to be replaced with
her old Self-Defense teacher, Ms. Pennington. She placed her
hands on her hips and blocked Emma Jean's path. *Don't try to
win.* It was advice that she had given the girls all summer long,
but this wasn't Ms. Pennington. This shade was simply a
weapon plucked from the depths of Pammy's memory, an
authority figure she'd once respected. The hivemind hoped to
capitalize on that, but it wouldn't work.

Pammy turned away and pressed her face into her mother's
shoulder. "Keep moving," she whispered. "Don't let me change
my mind." The hivemind was clawing at her, raking its way

through her psychology in a desperate attempt to find some-thing, *anything*, it could use to destroy her.

None of it was real. The only solid thing in the world was Emma Jean. Before the Little Creek five, before her friendship with Nate and the other boys, before she understood the differ-ence between the present and the future, Emma Jean had been there for her.

"I won't," her mother said.

They reached the side of the enormous alien body. Emma Jean knelt to the ground again, oblivious to the dozens of phantom limbs that clawed at her. They were all there, everyone that the invasion had taken: Pike and Logan; the sophomore girls whose heels had broken as they fled the crash site; Sam, who'd been the first victim that night in the woods; Mr. Cassidy, the music teacher; Walker and Jenny, who had holed up with Sean in his basement... she knew them all, and recognized each and every one of their voices among the screams that echoed through her head. Rising above them all came Len's roar, although Pammy couldn't discern whether it was a battle cry or an acknowledgment of pain.

Emma Jean ignored them all and reached into her boot to produce a thin, serrated knife. She drove it into the cell wall of the hivemind. Golden liquid bubbled up around the blade and spilled down over the malleable skin. The ghosts around her screamed in pain.

It's not enough! It won't be enough! You can't kill us from out here!

"You know what you remind me of?" she whispered. "All

those other girls who showed up to the pageant and told me that they were so sure they would take the crown."

Emma Jean couldn't possibly know who Pammy was speaking to, but lips still curled into a smile. "But not *my* girl. You didn't think you were going to win."

"Nope." Pammy clutched the disruptor. "I *knew*."

Emma Jean yanked on the knife, and it tore a jagged line through the skin. A slow-moving gel, like winter molasses or aged honey, sagged from the opening.

"I can take it from here," Pammy said.

"Oh, honey." Emma Jean pressed one palm against the slow-moving jelly. "I know you can. But I'm not leaving you now." She leaned forward, oblivious to the frenetic wailing of a hundred angry ghosts.

The syrupy innards of the hivemind's structure pressed tight over Pammy's nose and mouth, blocking her airways at once. It was so thick that she could barely open her eyes, and when she did, they burned.

Emma Jean carried her a little way, but they were moving much too slowly. It wouldn't be enough to damage this part of the organism. She needed to get to the middle.

I love you, Mom, she thought, and pushed away from her mother's grasp. This time, Emma Jean let her go.

It took an agonizing stretch of time to paddle through the honey-sweet decay. The closer Pammy got to the center of the mass, the more she understood. This part of the hivemind was comprised of the remnants of old meals that it had fully colonized and consumed.

Her lungs ached and the edges of her vision darkened, but

Pammy pressed on. She would gladly lose, if that was what it took to make sure that her opponent didn't win. One hand clutched the disruptor to her belly, while the other groped blindly in search of the main colony.

She was slowing down when her fingertips brushed against a hairlike web of roots. Pammy knotted her fingers in them and pulled, dragging herself forward with the mycelial threads that formed the base of the central hivemind. Her palm brushed against a smooth and spongy bulb.

She could go no further. This would have to do.

Pammy tucked herself against the core of the hivemind and ran her fingers over its surface. Even as she did so, visions popped through her mind like a fireworks show, telling her the story of hundreds before her who'd tried to resist annexation by the throng.

Sean Hawes' voice whispered in her ear. *What makes you think that you'll be any different, Miss Butter? You're dying. Hell, girl, you're as good as dead.*

He was right. She couldn't fight her body's reflexes any longer. Pammy opened her mouth to take a deep breath and sucked the decay of the *cordyceps* deep into her lungs. At the same time, her finger found the button that would activate the disruptor.

There was no pain, because she was beyond suffering. The body she had inhabited was lost to her as the *cordyceps* took root and devoured her from the inside out. The main colony consumed her, and in so doing magnified her connection to every sub-colony in the universe.

For one brief, magnificent moment, Pammy Mae Johnson

existed in the mind of every living thing that the throng occupied. She witnessed dozens of worlds, some ravaged by a Clanker-fueled apocalypse, some built into green-swathed utopias that blended nature and modernization into one seamless loop. Her body smiled as her consciousness scattered across innumerable individuals and dozens of galaxies. What she'd done wouldn't be enough to kill the species, but the strain that had controlled the Clankers would be eradicated in one fell swoop.

The hivemind rearranged around her as every cell shuddered and bloated and burst. Her body, already shot through with mycelium threads, was no exception.

She was everywhere and nowhere, until at last her wish of the last few months came true, and the burden of existence was lifted from her shoulders.

Pammy Mae Johnson was set free.

BEYOND WASHINGTON

Coalsun Settlement
The Jacc-Dodson Object

Pri-Nell crouched behind one of the metal pillars that supported the roof of the Panaudicon. He could hear the rattling of his enemies from the far side of the room. He held his breath and closed all three of his eyes, adjusting his grip on the raygun.

The defense contractors on P-A and P-A1 had effectively neutralized the threat of the invasion that had destroyed the MASS. It wouldn't bring back the dead, however. In honor of Agg-Garr's memory, Pri-Nell had volunteered to serve on one of the outgoing missions to the other impacted worlds. The

Thrummers were always two steps ahead, and their collective consciousness made it difficult to get the jump on them.

Difficult, but not impossible.

Pri-Nell lifted his wrist to his mouth and spoke into his armband. "Bildrax?" he whispered. "Let me know when they take the bait."

The armband briefly flashed blue, Bildrax's signal that the message had been heard and understood. Pri-Nell turned his head to meet the eyes of the Dodsonite rebel leader. Sanna was watching him intently. He nodded to her, and she lifted her chin sharply, waiting for his signal.

On the far side of the Panaudicon, the Thrummers' melody grew louder. Any moment... any moment...

The armband flashed green.

Pri-Nell made a sharp gesture with two fingers extended before rolling to his feet on the far side of the pillar. The twenty-six members of the local rebel branch came with him, firing on the cluster of Thrummers gathered against the far wall.

Bildrax's mechanical voice spoke over the sounds of rayfire. *"Please be advised, Pri-Nell, that although we baited this group, the Thrummers have you outnumbered. There are more outside the building, and the limitations of my monitors don't allow me to account for them all."*

"Heard and understood," Pri-Nell replied. One of the Thrummers tried to catch his ankle with its long, malleable tongue, and Pri-Nell hopped sideways, gripped the pillar with his many-jointed toes, and flipped upside-down to continue firing, dispatching his attacker efficiently as he had now done hundreds of times.

Sanna's people weren't so lucky. The Thrummers outside heard the battle, and three threes of them rushed in to offer assistance to their hivemates. One of the rebels screamed when a Thrummer tongue curled around her sturdy neck and dragged her onto her back across the venerable anthracite pavers. She tried to claw her way free, but the Thummer's proboscis descended and split her in two so abruptly that her screams didn't end for some time.

Sanna charged at the Thrummer whose feeding tube was now buried in the belly of her comrade. Pri-Nell had seen that expression on other faces before—no matter the species or their relative features, he could always tell when someone had finally had enough. Sanna folded back her ears, bared her needle teeth, and swiped at the Thrummer's eyes. Her claws came away stained black, and the Thrummer staggered even as it tried to spear her.

Pri-Nell hissed a curse and flipped black to the floor. He leapt after Sanna, landing only a few spans behind her. The claw marks across the Thrummer's face were brutal but shallow. He fired into the midst of the glittering mass and finished what his ally had started.

Unfortunately, they were now separated from the main unit. While Sanna scrambled to her dead friend's side, Pri-Nell spun in a circle, wondering which of the present Thrummers presented the greatest threat.

It's Sanna's fault for being emotional, he thought. *She should have followed the plan.* Then again, he'd been the one to chase after her, so how was he any better? The anti-Thrummer effort was driven from a place of emotion by necessity. That was the whole point of standing together: because every life mattered, and every individual was worth protecting.

"Bildrax?" he barked. "A little help?"

The armband began to play the screeching, high-pitched noise that they used to deter Clanker attacks. It was only a temporary solution, but given that the Thrummers had a much more permanent action in mind, he'd take it.

The beasts fell back, but the sound coming from the armband was too soft to be particularly effective.

"Speakers!" Pri-Nell croaked.

"*I'm sorry, Pri-Nell,*" Bildrax said in that eternally emotionless voice, "*the speaker system has been compromised. The Thrummers appear to have damaged one of our outer lines.*"

Pri-Nell cursed. He had proof of the infectious hivemind that compelled the Thrummers, but he'd never figured out how to counteract it. His research contacts back in the colonies had posited that there was one central hub of intellect, and that so long as it was intact, the organism would always have the advantage.

The rest of the rebels were still fighting for their lives, and the nearby Thrummers were still watching them intently. The sound might be enough to keep them away from Pri-Nell, but it wouldn't do his allies a lick of good.

One of the Thrummers' tongues caught Sanna around her middle and yanked her back. Pri-Nell dove for her and tried to catch her hands in his, dropping his raygun in the process. *As long as we're close enough, I should be able to protect her,* he thought. In his haste, he rolled sideways, and his arm scraped the floor.

The armband was torn away, and Bildrax's sound went with it, falling several spans away from where Sanna and Pri-Nell landed.

The Thrummers closed in, and Pri-Nell braced for the end. It was inevitable, he supposed. He'd spent the last seven years defending worlds against the Thrummer invasion and, when that failed, helping them clean up the mess afterward. If he had to die in service to a cause, of course it would be this one.

The Thrummers rattled and clanked, rising up to their full heights, with limbs extended.

And then they simply stopped.

Sanna panted with terror as the long tongue uncoiled from her waist and the Thrummer that had attacked her swayed back.

Around them, the sounds of battle died as the other invaders did the same. Sanna's people fired on Thrummers that seemed to have lost their will to fight.

Not that Pri-Nell was complaining.

He pushed himself to his knees and watched in astonishment as the surviving Thrummers streamed out the door of the Panaudicon and into the streets beyond.

"What's happening?" Sanna asked as she, too, got up and brushed the black dust off of her clothes.

"I wish I knew." Pri-Nell strode over to retrieve his gun and his armband. The strap had snapped, so he held it in his palm instead. "Bildrax, do you have any data on the Thrummers' behavior?"

"*Only that it seems unpredictable. I am seeing a change in some minor biomarkers, but nothing significant. It may be worth noting that this behavior is recurring in every settlement with a Bildrax system, however."*

Pri-Nell stumbled to the door of the ancient building and squinted out into the street. Lines of Thrummers were making their way single-file in the direction of Coalsun Lake, their sleek bodies stained red by the rising twin suns.

"Is it possible," he murmured, "that the hivemind itself has been conquered?"

"That would not be an irrational conclusion," Bildrax said.

Pri-Nell slumped against the quartz wall. "Bildrax, did you just call me *rational?* That might be the nicest thing you've ever said to me."

"Let's not get ahead of ourselves, Pri-Nell," the AI said crisply. *"We will have to gather a surfeit of data before we can leap to any conclusions."*

Bildrax was right, of course. There were truths that could only be quantified with data and tangible proof, but the one thing the AI could never quite seem to grasp was the other kind of truth. The one that *felt* real. Sanna and her people clustered at the door, watching the procession of Thrummers disperse, and Pri-Nell experienced the second kind of truth.

The worlds had changed again, and Pri-Nell would have to change with them. This time, instead of a threat, that softer brand of truth felt like a promise of better days to come.

37
CARLA

CARLA GROANED as she opened her eyes. Her head throbbed, and her body wouldn't obey her. She rolled her head to one side and tried to see what was happening, but it was pitch-black all around her. The rancid stench of decay filled her nostrils.

"Len?" she groaned. Her mouth was so dry that it hurt to move her tongue.

"Carla?" His voice was close, and a moment later his hand settled over hers. "You're awake! How do you feel?"

"Like I got stung in the neck by the biggest damn bee you've ever seen in your life." She shuddered with a dry cough and tried to lift herself onto her elbows. "What happened? Where are we?"

"I don't know how to answer either of those questions." Len settled against her. "I was fighting the Clankers, and then the lights went out, and they all left. I think... I think we won?" His voice rose to a whine at the end of his sentence.

Carla croaked a laugh. "Try not to sound so confident."

"Pammy must have set off the disruptor, but I don't understand how. I don't know where the smell's coming from, either. At first I thought the Clankers got my other eye or something, but it *feels* fine, so..." She felt him shrug. "I was so tired that I just sat down and waited for something to happen, and here we are."

"We should get moving," she said.

He snorted. "And do what? You can barely move, I might have a concussion, and neither of us has the slightest clue what's going on. What are we supposed to do?"

Carla didn't have an answer to that. She'd spent so long feeling that she needed to do *something* that the idea of sitting still was foreign to her. Then again, she didn't have much of a choice at the moment.

"What happened to your head?" she asked.

"Hell if I know," he said lightly. "But you should see the other guy."

They sat there in silence for a while, just breathing, as Carla tried to stir her fingers against the cold floor.

"Hold on." Len sat up. "Did you hear that?"

She held her breath and listened for the song of an *invadenda* or the clap of gunfire. Instead, a distant woman's voice yelled, "Pammy? Emma Jean? Hello, Pammy?"

"Vera?" Len whispered. His clothes rustled as he got to his feet, then bellowed, *"Vera! In here!"*

"Len? Where are you?"

"In here." Len's triumphant laugh ricocheted off the walls. "No idea where here is, but I'll just keep talking. Who else is with you? Is everyone okay?"

The other woman hesitated. "I'll tell you when I find you. Have you seen Emma Jean?"

"She and Pammy were in here, but they're gone now. I'm not sure what happened, we don't have a light... oh, but *you* do!" Sure enough, the beam of a flashlight bounced along the walls as whoever carried it came into view. Carla lifted her hands and squinted between her fingers as a woman in fatigues stepped into the room.

Len ran to her and pulled her into a hug, then waved one hand toward Carla. "Carla, this is Vera. Vera, this is my wife."

"Nice to meet you." Vera's voice was clipped. "Listen, we have a problem. Emma Jean stole the disruptor, and I have no idea where she... where... *oh.*" She aimed her flashlight toward the center of the room and pressed her palm to her mouth.

Carla followed her line of sight. The bright white circle of light revealed the same sack-like object that had first drawn her attention to the room. It was dark now, and the golden liquid inside had hardened to a rancid gunmetal-gray ooze. The flashlight beam picked out the slim figure of what had once been a woman and was now little more than bare bones.

The beam flicked down to pick out a bright pink-and-purple backpack lying open on the floor.

"She did it." Vera knelt down next to the pack and opened the top to peer inside. "She used the disruptor. And it *worked.*" She lifted her light back to where the woman's body hung suspended. "I can't be mad at her now, I suppose. But where's Pammy?"

"She was here," Len said. "Emma Jean was holding her."

Vera twisted toward them. "No. Do you think—?"

Len nodded.

Vera curled in on herself and began to tremble. "I doubted her," she whimpered. "And I sent Cooper away, and Guppie..." She choked off into a sob.

Len went to her and wrapped the other woman in his arms. He rubbed slow circles on her back, with all the patient acceptance that he'd shown Carla back when the world still made sense. "We all did our best," he murmured. "And it worked, right? Even if they can't be here to see it, they'd agree that it was worth it. You know that, Vera."

The woman only sobbed harder.

Len let her cry for a while before holding her out at arm's length. "Are you here alone?"

"No." Vera wiped her palms under her eyes and sniffed hard. "Jeremy Steward is out on the tracks looking after Felix. They're both hurt, and Felix is..." She gulped. "It's not good."

"Then we should go back to them," Len said reasonably. "Don't you think?"

"Y-yeah." Vera took a deep breath and stood upright. "Carla, are you okay?"

"I could use a hand," she admitted.

Len retrieved their weapons and shoved them in the Tinkerbell pack, zipping up from both sides so that the rifles wouldn't fall out. He caught Carla watching him and shrugged. "We don't know where the Clankers went, and I bet you anything that there are more soldiers out there who'd be happy to kill us, hivemind or no."

"No bet," Vera said flatly.

The two of them helped Carla to her feet, one under each elbow. They left that place behind, although Carla caught them both looking back sadly at the stinking ruin of the alien carcass.

None of them spoke again for a long time.

STEW WAS WAITING for them at the platform when they arrived, swinging his feet back and forth as he cast a long shadow against the single floodlight that rested on the platform. His bangs were stuck to his head and matted with dried blood, and an enormous bruise was spreading across one cheekbone. His gaze swept over Carla, and he shook his head. "Wow, Bone. You look like crap."

"Same to you," Carla retorted, with a bit less annoyance than she usually reserved for her longtime colleague.

The other man had taken the worst beating of all, but he was still breathing. Vera gulped and squeezed her eyes shut as they approached the edge of the tracks. "I don't think we should try to move him yet. I'm going to find the exit and see if I can track anyone down. We should have people on this side of the river... assuming the Clankers didn't get them."

She pulled herself up over the lip of the tracks, then worked with Len to help Carla up to their level. There were other bodies along the tracks, but none of them acknowledged them, choosing instead to avert their eyes and focus on the task at hand.

Once the three of them were on the platform, Vera turned to them. "I can go up alone," she offered.

"Like hell you are," Len said, but with more kindness than his words suggested. "I'm going with you."

"You can sit with me," Stew offered. "Keep an eye on Felix with me."

Carla hated the idea of being separated from Len again, but her head was killing her, and her limbs felt about as sturdy as al dente spaghetti. "Go on, baby." She kissed Len's temple. "We'll be right here."

He swung his pack off and tried to hand her the laser rifle, but she took the ThunderGen instead.

"Less painful," she explained, holding out her blistered palms as evidence.

"Stay safe," he told her before he and Vera set off toward the stairs.

Would there come a time, she wondered, that having him out of her sight didn't fill her with a tremor of blind terror? She almost ran after him, but she could barely put one foot in front of the other. Instead, she lowered herself to the ground beside Stew.

"Sorry for what I said about your husband," Stew said.

Carla glanced over at him. "When?"

"When I said that he'd have moved on in the meantime." Stew drummed his heels against the concrete wall. "I thought I was making things easier."

"It's fine," Carla said. "I already knew you were a dick."

Stew elbowed her. "Keep in mind that this dick saved the damn planet."

Carla clicked her tongue. "What have we said about phrasing, Stew?"

"I'm serious. If it wasn't for me getting the Steward Message out, the disruptor wouldn't have been developed."

"We don't actually know what's going on," Carla pointed out. "For all we know, there's a whole platoon of soldiers up there just waiting to jump us the minute we leave."

Stew patted her knee. "All right, tell you what. You dwell on your pessimistic worldview, and I'll be over here thinking about the first thing I'm going to do with my newfound freedom."

"Do I even want to know?"

"The current plan is to start a cult of personality in which I, the savior of mankind, surround myself with canned goods and beautiful women, and become the supreme ruler of humanity." Stew grinned crookedly. "And there's nothing Dr. Sharma can do to stop me."

Carla lay back against the concrete platform. "Creepy," she intoned. "Why am I not surprised?"

"Nah, but seriously." Stew's smile faded. "I'm gonna see what I can do to help Nutty figure out what happened to his family. If Greene made it out in one piece, I'm going to kick his ass to kingdom come. Then I'm going to get Mom settled and make my way up to NYC. See if anyone up there survived."

"Like your daughter," Carla murmured.

Stew sniffed and rubbed his nose on his sleeve. "For example. There's gonna be a lot to do. This isn't over, so I guess I'll just figure out what battles I think we can win and just... do that for a while. What about you?"

"We'll help with Nutty. And your mom, too. After that?"

She smiled at the ceiling. "I guess it's up to Len. Besides, who knows what the *invadendae* will do now that the hivemind is dead. Maybe we'll still be fighting them. Maybe not. It all depends."

"You really think we can make friends with the Clankers?" Stew asked skeptically.

Rationally speaking, it seemed impossible, but there were a lot of things that she'd once thought would never occur that already had.

"I guess we'll see," she said.

38

COOPER

AS THE SUN set over Washington, Cooper sat on the Memorial Avenue bridge, watching as the Clankers roamed about in confusion. He wasn't sure exactly what had happened. One minute, they'd been spreading in every direction, desperate to find Klarie. The next, they had scattered in confusion, as if their purpose was no longer clear.

It was strange to think that the creatures had once been the stuff of his nightmares. He felt almost sorry for them as they wandered aimlessly through the streets.

Gradually, the hives began to peel away as the hive Kings and Queens decided to return home. Even without their King, the Parkton Hive regrouped to retreat across the bridge toward the Lincoln Memorial, and then northward until they were lost to sight.

The first of the Keystone Hive approached Cooper as the other Clankers dispersed. *Queen?* it asked. *Queen where?*

"I dunno, buddy." Cooper massaged his temples. His headache was getting better, and when he tried to tap into the hivemind he got nothing at all, but there was no telling what that meant. It hadn't affected him as much as it had Pammy. For all he knew, it had cut him off.

Or Klarie was actually able to get down there and kill it, no thanks to me.

As he sat there, more of the Keystone Clankers approached him, forming a semi-circle on the bridge. *Queen where? Queen where?*

He tried to make the sound that would have meant, *I don't know*, but it was so bad that the Clankers didn't acknowledge his response.

"Cooper?"

He jumped to his feet and hurried to the Arlington side of the bridge. "Klarie?" he called.

She waved her arm above her head. "Thought that was you. Look who I found!" Klarie pointed over her shoulder to where Len and Vera walked side by side, every inch the worse for wear.

He hurried toward them, but stopped cold when Vera snarled and lifted her ThunderGen. "Sorry," he said, raising his hands above his head. "You were right about me, I'm sorry, I'll stay back..."

"Not you. You've got company." She nodded to the Clankers.

"Oh, no, they're..." He glanced over his shoulder at the stragglers. "They're fine. They're just looking for Pammy, and I guess they thought I'd know where to find her, so they've kinda gravitated toward me."

Len laid a hand on the barrel of the ThunderGen and whispered something to Vera, who reluctantly lowered her weapon.

Klarie wasn't as skeptical. She jogged over, arms outstretched, and grabbed him tight around the middle. "We won!" she cried. "And if the Clankers are playing nice now, even better."

"We won?" Cooper squeezed her in return. "You mean you did it?" He frowned when he realized that the bag was still on her back, with the round object still inside. "How did you manage that?"

"We were the decoys, dummy." Klarie socked him in the shoulder. "God, you're dense. Come on, we gotta find Estes and Merry."

"Decoys?" he repeated stupidly, wandering after her as she led all three of them back toward the Crystal City metro stop.

"Yeah." Klarie hooked her thumb toward Vera. "She had the real disruptor the whole time, but see, if the hivemind thought we had it..."

"Then it wouldn't target her." The tension that had been tearing him apart from the inside finally eased. "So you did believe me, but you used me, too."

"I'm sorry, Cooper," Vera said.

He held both hands up in surrender as they walked. "Hey, it worked. I respect the move. Where's everyone else? Did you find Pammy? What about Guppie?"

Len and Vera exchanged a glance, and he realized in that moment how puffy Vera's eyes were.

"We had to leave everyone else in the tunnel," Len explained. "They're hurt. Let's focus on getting them out first, and we'll explain the rest."

To Cooper's relief, Estes and Merry were waiting by the chopper, splitting a granola bar and a bottle of water. When he spotted their little group, Estes jumped to his feet.

"Did it work?" he asked.

"Sure did!" Klarie practically skipped over to him. "I hope you've got more of those. Running away from an army of killer bugs has got me pretty dehydrated."

Estes waved a hand toward them. "Speaking of killer bugs, what's going on here?"

The Keystone Hive had followed them from the bridge, milling nervously in Cooper's wake. Some of them still carried their young with them; the Clanker-fry crawled over the lapped plates of their guardians like so many spiderlings clinging to their mothers.

This could be our chance to wipe out the Clankers, Cooper thought. He could still understand them, but he couldn't read their minds, which meant that they wouldn't see attacks coming. If they got a few tanks and enough ammo and fuel, they could head cross-country and take out the invaders for good.

There wasn't much heat in his heart for them now, though. If anything, he felt sorry for them. If they needed human flesh to survive, that would settle the matter, but if he was going to learn more, he'd have to find a way to talk to them. Pammy could help him get some answers when she was feeling better.

"They're coming with us for now," Cooper said. "I don't

think they'll hurt us. These are the members of the Keystone Hive. Pammy's Hive."

Estes looked to Vera, who nodded.

"Right on, then," the soldier said. "What now?"

There were supplies at the back of the chopper. Estes and Vera gathered the medical bag, flashlights and flares, and an emergency sling, while Merry Clark climbed back into the cockpit.

"I don't have enough fuel to get us back," she said, "but Reagan National is just across the Parkway. I'm gonna try and track down some fuel. I'll meet you by the Arlington metro when I'm done."

They waved her off, and then the five humans, accompanied by the survivors of the Keystone Hive, made their way on foot across the city.

"If you're tired, we could ride the Clankers," Cooper suggested.

Vera glanced at the swarm. "No offense, Cooper, but I still don't trust them. And I can't see that changing anytime soon."

IT WAS FULLY dark by the time they reached the entrance to the Arlington metro stop. Cooper could only guess where the local Clankers had disappeared to. Perhaps even then they were fighting each other to see who would become the new ruler, and tomorrow the war would start all over again, albeit on a smaller scale.

They descended the steps into the station, and with each step, Cooper felt lighter. The reality of what had happened was finally starting to sink in. He hadn't destroyed their last chance at victory. Instead, he'd bought his friends enough time to finish the job.

Stew was snoring on the platform when they approached, while a woman watched over him. The moment she saw Len, she leapt to her feet and ran to him. Len scooped her up in a hug.

"Your friend is still alive," the stranger told Vera. "We got a plan for getting out of here?"

"A chopper should be on the way any minute." Len leaned over to give the much shorter woman a kiss.

Vera and Estes crawled down onto the tracks to lift Felix into the sling. While they worked, Cooper rotated on the spot. "Where's Pammy?" he asked. "And Guppie?"

Vera choked, and Len peeled himself away from the woman who was presumably his wife. "Pammy's not here," he said gently.

Cooper nodded. "Yeah, I can see that. So where is she?"

"Cooper." Len laid one hand lightly on his shoulder. "She's gone."

He shook his head incredulously. "Gone where?"

His brain understood what Len was saying, but his heart couldn't let him believe it, not even when Len bit his lip and squeezed his arm. "I'm sorry, Coop," he said.

"No. No way." He backed up, shaking his head. Klarie had both hands pressed to her mouth, and Cooper felt as if Len had driven the heel of his boot right into his solar plexus. "This is Pammy we're talking about. Invincible Pammy. We've both seen her *literally kill Clankers with her fists.* She isn't dead. That's crazy."

The pity in Len's eyes made him want to scream. Instead, he raked his hands across his scalp, knotted his fingers in his hair, and pulled. The pain of it helped ground him in the moment, but he was still in full-blown denial.

"*No,*" he insisted.

"Cooper." Klarie wrapped her arms around him and squeezed.

He sank into a crouch near Stew, who had sat up at some point when Cooper wasn't paying attention. The guy had the gall to look sorry for him, which was absurd. He didn't know Pammy. He didn't know what she was like, or that she could get through anything, or that she was the last person binding Cooper to his old life in Little Creek. The only other person who had ever sat down to a meal at the Lutzs' dinner table. The only one who loved his arrogant, pain-in-the-ass little brother.

Cooper needed her. And now she was *gone.*

"And Guppie?" he asked. "What about Guppie?"

Vera stood up. "He was with us. But he got... separated." She pointed north down the tunnel with the same pained expression that she'd worn at the mention of Pammy. "Can the rest of you get Felix out of here? Peachey should be able to treat him, and I can't leave, not until I know what happened."

Cooper shrugged Klarie away. "I'm coming, too."

"Are you sure?" Klarie asked. "Maybe you could take a rest."

"I'm sure," he said, hopping over the edge of the rails.

The Keystone Hive had hung back, but when Cooper

forged ahead, they emerged from the shadows into the beam of the floodlight.

"*Jesus, Mary, and Joseph!*" Carla screeched, trying to put herself between the Clankers and Len.

"They're with me," Cooper explained.

The woman shot him a look that clearly said that she thought Cooper was a damn fool, but when Len laid a hand on her back, she relaxed. "It's been a long-ass day," she sighed. "I'll ask questions tomorrow. Let me help with Felix and we can get out of here." She crab-walked toward the edge of the tracks, never once taking her eyes off the aliens.

Vera took one of the flashlights and the medical pack with her. She waited for Cooper to catch up with her before setting out in the direction where she'd last seen Guppie.

Cooper had expected the Clankers to follow him, but he was surprised when Klarie padded alongside him, too.

"You can go with them," he said, more gently this time.

Klarie shook her head, and the split ends of her grown-out black bob brushed her shoulders. "I know. But I'm coming with you."

THE MOMENT she saw the wall of rubble, Vera broke into a run. Cooper tried to keep up with her, but every muscle in his body ached with crushing fatigue. He barely managed a jog. Klarie lagged behind even him.

"Do you know how much running I did today?" she panted. "My legs are on fire, Coop."

Vera collapsed to her knees at the edge of the rubble and

immediately began digging. Cooper slid in beside her and caught her wrist. "What are you doing? You're going to tear your hands to shreds."

"He's under there!" Vera said. "I heard it, Cooper. He stayed to protect me, and if there's any chance he's still alive, I have to get to him. I *have* to!"

Klarie knelt down on the far side and began to work. Cooper watched in dismay as they both pawed fruitlessly at the heap of stones. At this rate, it would take them a hundred years, and they'd only move the stones a few inches at most. What they needed was—

He stopped short and turned back to where the Clankers hovered behind him.

What they needed was a system, and Cooper might very well have one. He made a big show of picking up one of the larger chunks of rubble, hoisted it onto his shoulder, and marched back past the row of Clankers. When he was fifty or so feet away from the avalanche of debris, he set the rock down, and went back for another.

"What are you *doing*, Cooper?" Vera demanded.

"Trying something. Bear with me." He picked up the second chunk and did the same. On his third trip, one of the Clankers followed him. He couldn't say with any certainty, but it looked like the same one that had brought him the royal jelly back in Parkton. When Cooper lifted his rock, the Clanker did the same with another much larger fragment. It rattled sounds to the others, and they followed suit, forming neat lines of workers who easily lifted pieces that all three humans would have struggled to move. Vera and Klarie stepped aside, and the

Clankers took over. They were calmer now that they had a task, and not one of them stopped to ask about Pammy.

Pammy. The simple fact of her name crossing his mind was enough to make him choke up. How was he supposed to know what to do now? He'd come to rely on her to call the shots. His job was to follow and do whatever he thought she needed.

Guess I'm not so different from the Clankers after all, he thought as he watched their busy labor. He could only hope that Guppie would be better off than Pammy was.

The Little Creek Four. It didn't have the same ring to it, but it was better than the Little Creek Three. He crossed his fingers and prayed that the old man could pull through one more time.

39

GUPPIE

WHEN GUPPIE OPENED HIS EYES, it was daylight, and he felt as though an elephant had been sitting on his chest all night. Holding his eyelids open soon proved to be too much effort, and he let them drift shut again, preferring to listen to the voices around him. That was easier, and even if he couldn't follow the words, it was comforting to know that he wasn't alone.

He must have slept again, because the next time he blinked, it was twilight. He was inside a building, in a room he didn't recognize. Vera sat next to him in a chair, with her legs pulled up to her chest and her eyes closed.

"Doesn't look comfortable," he murmured through lips so dry they felt like rice paper.

Vera's head snapped toward him. "Guppie?"

He tried to smile, although he could tell that he didn't quite get the movement right. "Hey," he grated. "Not dead, huh? That's a shocker."

She hurried over to sit on the edge of the bed and took his hand. "You probably shouldn't talk. You inhaled a lot of concrete dust, and your head..." She grimaced.

"Took a beating? You should see the other guy." He squeezed her hand and tried to sit a little more upright against the pillows. "If I can't talk, you should. What happened? How long was I out?"

Vera got up to retrieve a bottle of water and a paper cup. While she helped him drink, she said, "It's been almost three days. I didn't think you were going to... but here you are." She swallowed hard.

"Yeah." He wiped the back of one hand across his mouth. "And?"

She capped the bottle and set it aside. "And we won." The words were barely out of her mouth before she burst into tears.

"Aw, *Vera*." He wrapped one arm around her and pulled her sideways so that she settled next to him. Cold uncertainty settled in his belly, and he rested his chin on the top of her head. "Did she turn against us, or—?"

"No." Vera scrubbed at her eyes. "No, she... she finished it." She hiccupped. "Cooper's not taking it well. Len's been helping Lavelle run things, so we don't talk much, but she seems fine. Better than me, anyway."

She couldn't say the words aloud, and really, he didn't need to hear them. Guppie closed his eyes and lost himself in the memory of Pammy Mae charging into a wall of Clankers fists-first.

That's it, kiddo, he thought. *I bet you went down fighting right to the bitter end.*

"TRY AGAIN," Cooper said, standing up and tossing his wrench back into the toolkit.

"I've *been* trying," Guppie muttered. "Don't you dare imply that this is user error." He slid one booted foot forward and tried to maintain his balance. The exosuit he'd originally taken had been crushed, but it had been sturdy enough to keep him in one piece. The trouble was, he couldn't do much when he was wearing the whole suit. Punch a hole through a rock wall? No problem. Lift a truck over his head? Easy peasy. Do any damn thing with those damn turbo gloves that didn't involve breaking something or tossing it into orbit? Not so much.

According to Cooper, it wasn't as easy as sawing the suit in half and going about his day. Some of the guidance systems were contained in the upper half of the unit. The suit could still walk for him, more or less, but it required a little more input.

In other words, Guppie had been falling on his face all morning.

This time, he made it two whole steps before the left knee locked up. He instinctively pinwheeled his arms, which didn't help in the slightest, given how bottom-heavy the suit was. With a metallic clatter, he landed on his ass. *Again.*

Cooper applauded politely. "Smooth."

"Hey, *you* try learning to walk in a robo suit with one and a half legs." Guppie held out his hand to the younger man. "Now stop giving me lip and help me up."

Len poked his head through the workshop door. Phobos and Deimos bolted out from behind him and tackled Guppie, licking every inch of his face while he tried and failed to swat them away. Deimos managed to get most of his tongue in Guppie's mouth, and he spluttered in disgust.

"Are you still bitching about that leg?" Len asked. He pointed meaningfully to his eye. "Thought you'd have gotten over that by now."

Cooper hauled Guppie to his feet at last. Other than a blow to the back of his head, he'd made it out of the tunnel with little more than bruises from the collapse. His leg was another matter: between the damage to his soft tissue and the infection that had already set in, Peachey had been left with few options. Guppie didn't hold it against the man. He'd been a stubborn idiot, and now he was paying the price.

"Did you just come in here to torment me?" he asked.

"Actually, I came for Cooper. Estes is looking for you. There's something up with the Clankers, and the soundboard you made him isn't cutting it."

Guppie sympathized with Cooper, who had fallen into the role of translator to the Clankers. The human contingent was incredibly lucky to have him, though. The aliens were not, as he'd assumed, solely carnivores. They were omnivores of the highest order, and without the hivemind to drive them, they accepted Cooper's injunction to turn their attention to non-human prey.

"I'm on it. Hang tight, Guppie." Cooper trotted out the door and into the street.

They watched him go before Len whispered, "He seems better."

Guppie wobbled his head from side to side. "Better. Not great. Klarie checks in on him, too, you know. If you need details, you'll have to ask her. He doesn't talk to me about feelings."

Len nodded. "And Vera?"

Guppie scratched the back of his neck. "I'm trying. She's been really throwing herself into things at the hospital. Trying to get stuff up and running smoothly, so... She's busy."

Len smiled wryly. "But not great?"

Guppie shook his head.

Len let the subject drop and backed away from him, then held out his hands the way someone might if they were trying to coax a baby taking their first steps. "Show me what you've got."

Guppie groaned. "It's embarrassing."

Len waved to Phobos. "Hey, if little Tripod here can do it, so can you." The German shepherd wagged his tail. He'd taken a hit from a Clanker while defending Vera's parents, and his rear right leg had been so badly injured that he could barely put weight on it these days. It had slowed him down a little, but it didn't seem to bother him much. If anything, he'd become more affectionate lately.

"He's got spares," Guppie complained.

"And you've got an exosuit, so I figure that makes you even." Len waggled his fingers. "Come on, give me what you've got."

It wasn't pretty, and he had to stop and get his balance more than once, but by the time Cooper returned from his chat with the Clankers, Guppie had made it to the far end of the workshop. It wasn't anything to write home about, but it still felt like a victory. Small steps could still get him places, after all.

THERE'D BEEN a time not so long ago when Guppie Martin kicked up a fuss about walking from his house in Little Creek to town and back. He'd complained about it endlessly, and wished that there was something more he could do to fill the time. These days, he fought for every step, which made each mile he *did* cross all the more satisfying.

The survivors had begun to look forward rather than back. They settled into the least damaged portion of the neighborhoods surrounding the MedStar hospital and started organizing, planning for the next weeks, the next months, the next years. Guppie still felt like a drag-along most of the time, but he found ways to help, even if they weren't as useful as what some folks were doing.

Vera came home from the hospital one afternoon to find Guppie standing under one of the trees in front of the house she shared with her parents.

"Hey, Vera." Guppie stepped back from his project and held his hands out proudly. "What do you think?"

She tilted her head to one side and examined his handiwork. "It's a bird feeder," she said. "Did you make that?"

"I would have gone to the garden center, but funny enough, we don't have one local just yet." He placed his hands on his lower back and stretched until his spine popped. There were downsides to the modified exosuit for sure, but it was better than the alternative.

"I wonder why," she observed drily.

"I'm putting 'em up all over the neighborhood. I wouldn't mind seeing more birds around."

She shook her head and tried to hide her smile. It was a rare enough sight anymore, and he was proud to be the cause of it, even if her happiness was only temporary.

He shuffled backward toward the road. "Well, I don't want to keep you."

"You could, um." She tugged on the hem of her scrubs. "Come in, if you want. For dinner. Mummy would be happy to have you."

"I don't want to impose."

Vera clicked her tongue and glared at him. "Don't be silly." She took his arm. "Come up. You're not a bother, Guppie."

This time, he obliged.

40
LEN

LEN HURRIED through the streets of Le Droit Park, moving fast to keep himself warm. The dogs bounded behind him. Phobos hated the feeling of snow on his paws, while Deimos stopped every few feet to bury his face in the thick white powder and snuff happily.

When he thought of winter in Washington, Len mostly remembered brown slush that clogged the roads and stained his snow pants. Now, there were so few vehicles on the road that the streets, for the most part, stayed nearly pristine outside of the sidewalks.

"Almost there," he said, clutching the straps of his pack to keep it from bouncing too painfully against his spine. Their rations had come mostly in the form of canned goods this week. Their neighbors liked to wax poetic about the joys of fresh produce, and their plans to set out for the country come spring. Len understood where they were coming from, but he didn't mind the glut of nonperishables. For years he had assumed that, this far into the invasion, he'd be holed up in the bunker with just his dogs, his MREs, and his memories. Reality was upside down, but it still exceeded his expectations on every front. Endless meals of cream-of-mushroom were a small price to pay.

The door of their rowhouse was unlocked, and Len kicked the snow off his boots against the top step before following the boys inside.

He had barely made it through the door when Carla tackled him.

"Guess what happened today, baby!" she crowed.

He kissed her before squirming out of her grip. "You got a stable satellite connection?"

"Even better." Carla was practically bouncing on her toes with all the enthusiasm of a little girl on Christmas morning. She waited impatiently for him to remove his coat, then steered him through to the next room, where her computer screen showed a strange image.

Not everyone in the city had power, but Dr. Sharma and Carla had managed to convince Greg to help them build a generator that would allow them to run their equipment. At first, Vera had pushed back on the notion that computers should get priority when there were still residents who couldn't run heaters and lightbulbs, but Sharma had made an impassioned and compelling argument that relied heavily on the events surrounding the original Steward Message. In the end, Vera had relented, and the computers had been up and running since late September.

Carla dropped into her chair and pulled Len close. "Look at

this," she breathed, pointing at the pixelated image on the screen.

"I'm looking," Len said patiently. "It looks like something Guppie would draw in MS Paint. What am I supposed to make of it?"

"It's another message." Carla waved her finger a hair's-breadth from the screen. "From space. We sent out a transmission in the same format we got before, and this just came in."

"From who?"

He pictured the stars falling out of the sky and the screams of his neighbors echoing across the mountains as the world burned.

"From whoever sent us the first warning. From our *allies*, Len!" Carla wriggled with excitement. "We don't have to do this alone. They're going to help us rebuild. Can you believe it? We've made repeated contact with a friendly, sentient alien species. Oh, just wait, Stew is going to lose his *mind* when he sees this. I think I'm going to call it the Bonaparte Reply."

Len shook his head and slumped against her while the dogs curled up on their blankets in the corner of the room. "And then what?"

"Who knows? There's no precedent for anything like this. But it's going to be amazing, Len." She wrapped her arms around him and sighed with utter contentment. "They're on our side this time. They even thanked us for neutralizing the hive-mind!" She pointed at a cluster of pixels on the screen, which didn't look like much of anything to Len, but he decided to take her word for it.

It was a *hopeful* transmission, then. He honestly wasn't sure he believed it.

I wish Pammy Mae were here to see this. Len held Carla close and listened as she explained the meaning of every pixelated object on the screen. *I wish there was a way to tell her that she made all this possible.*

The hivemind took away our future.

And she took it back.

EPILOGUE

PAMMY MAE TURNED to examine her profile in the long mirror. She hardly recognized the girl in the reflection. The dress was made of peach silk and rose-gold tulle that lapped like scales down the front of her mermaid-style dress. She ran her hands over her hips.

"I love this one!" she called out of the dressing room.

"Well, let me see you, honey!" Emma Jean called from the hall.

Pammy opened the door and stepped out. "What do you think?" she asked, spinning one way and then the other.

"Oh, Pammy, just *look* at you!" Emma Jean clasped her hands under her chin and sighed dreamily. "You look *magnificent*."

"You don't think the open back is too much?"

Emma Jean's smile vanished in an instant, and her eyes blazed with a sudden ferocity. "Too much?" she repeated.

"Who's been telling you that? You just said you liked this dress."

"I do, but isn't it a little, you know..." Pammy wrinkled her nose and ran her hands over the ruffles. "My talent show piece and my interview answers and the rest are all kind of focused on me being, you know, *one of the guys*." She made air quotes with her fingers. "Is anyone going to take me seriously when I talk about ATVing and hunting and then turn around and dress myself like a princess? Maybe I should go for something more *country*. For the theme, I mean."

"Pammy Mae Johnson." Emma Jean crossed her arms and donned her *tough-love* expression. "Do you or do you not like how you feel right now?"

"I do," Pammy admitted.

"Then it's not too much. People are complicated. You don't have to be all one thing. You've got rough parts and smooth parts, and the sooner you embrace that, the happier you'll be. Either the judges will see it, or they won't, but that's their problem. Just be yourself, Button." Emma Jean tapped one finger against the tip of Pammy's nose. "As long as you know you're good enough, everybody else will stand back and get out of your way. I believe in you." She held Pammy out at arm's length and admired her. "Tomboy or princess, I believe you're going to change the world someday."

THE THRONG WAS NOT ENTIRELY ERADICATED. It lacked the power to control, but it lingered on, a passive observer with no unifying spark. Instead of one sun-bright consciousness, it was fragmented like shattered glass or scattered stars.

Pieces of Pammy Mae were spread out between them, so thin that she no longer knew herself. She was no wiser or stronger than she had ever been, but she was present, and she was happy. Her memories blended with the throng until they were indistinguishable from any other. She wasn't as she had been, but as she now forever would be.

The particles of Pammy dreamed of summer days and safe havens and the heady rush of making the impossible leap on her ATV only to land, safe and sound, on the other side.

The past and the future blended into one.

Pammy Mae was at peace.

The End

GET FREE BOOKS!

Building a relationship with readers is my favorite thing about writing.

My regular newsletter, *The Reader Crew,* is the best way to stay up-to-date on new releases, special offers, and all kinds of cool stuff about science fiction past and present.

Just for joining the fun, I'll send you 3 free books.

Join The Reader Crew (it's free) today!

—Joshua James

ALSO BY JOSHUA JAMES

Saturn's Legacy Series (4 books)

Gunn & Salvo Series (7 books so far)

Box sets

Lucky's Marines (Books 1-9)

Lucky's Mercs (Books 1-4)

The Lost Starship (Books 1-3)

With Scott Bartlett:

Relentless Box Set: The Complete Fleet Ops Trilogy

With Daniel Young:

Oblivion (Books 1-9)

Outcast Starship (Books 1-9)

Legacy of War (Books 1-3)

Heritage of War (ongoing)

Stars Dark (Books 1-8)

Printed in Great Britain
by Amazon